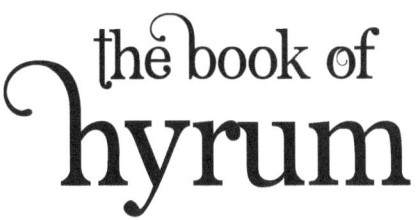

the book of
hyrum

MAX THOMPSON
WITH K.A. THOMPSON

Also by Max Thompson

The Emperor of San Francisco: The Wick Chronicles, Book One
Ozoo: The Wick Chronicles, Book Two
Forked: The Wick Chronicles, Book Three
The Space Between Whens: Wick After Dark, Book One
The Blessings of Saint Wick: Wick After Dark, Book Two
The Whens of Wick: Return of the Wick Chronicles, Book One
The Psychokitty Speaks Out: Diary of a Mad Housecat
The Psychokitty Speaks Out: Something of Yours Will Meet A Toothy Death
The Rules: A Guide For People Owned By Cats
Bite Me: A Memoir (Of Sorts)
Epistle: A Love Letter
There Once Was a Cat From Nantucket

Visit Max online at his blog, The Psychokitty Speaks Out
http://psychokitty.blogspot.com
or on Facebook
http://facebook.com/thepsychokittyspeaksout

Books one of his people (K.A. Thompson) wrote

The Charybdis Novels:
Charybdis
As Simple As That
Finding Father Rabbit

The King and Queen of Perfect Normal
The Flipside of Here

It's Not About the Cookies
Rock the Pink

Visit K.A. Thompson online at her blog,
Thumper Thinks Out Loud
http://kathompson.blogspot.com

the book of
hyrum

return of
the wick chronicles
book two

1

Will was almost to the lab's elevator on Union Square when his newest guard stepped out from the shadows, planted herself in front of the portal with her hands on her hips, and said, "No."

He took three more steps, the time it took for his brain to engage. He hadn't been headed for the portal but to the elevator, and hadn't expected anyone to stop him, much less a guard who had been assigned to him for only a month. He reached up to his shoulder to touch my front paw, a warning he was about to move, and he shifted his gym bag to change its balance, all while trying to figure out what she wanted.

The fact that he still had guards annoyed him. Aisha had insisted on it when the Cult of the Emperor was lurking around, trying to grab onto anything that would yield a small bit of his DNA— and then ultimately his clone—but he'd expected that when their activities were thwarted he would no longer have guards. He'd demanded T'Neeka Soto, head of the family's personal guards, to have them stand down, but she shrugged and told him that when the order came from the King, she would oblige.

Instead of reassigning the guards, Jax ordered them to consult with Aisha about Will's allowed activities, and portal travel was something he had promised her he wouldn't do until their baby was born. To make it worse, he added a fifth guard to the compliment, one whose only task was to enforce the portal ban, and she took her job seriously.

"Vicat." He was irritated. "That's not necessary, you know."

"Just making sure." She looked to me. "Same goes for you, Mister Wick."

What? I'm not allowed to use a portal?

"There are no such restrictions on Wick."

"The two of you tend to follow each other, Emperor."

It's not like she can stop me. What's she going to do if I decide to bolt right between her legs? Tell my mommy?

"Worse," she said after he relayed the question. "I'll tell the Queen."

I had things to say about that and would have if her gaze hadn't shifted, and if Will hadn't turned to see what she was looking at. Drew was jogging across the Square, carrying a metal box that was bigger than I was—which, to be honest, isn't saying much because I'm six pounds if I'm soaking wet and have just eaten half a cow. He hurried to catch up to Will, and when he did, he gave the guard a short nod and greeted her. "Mean lady."

The corners of her mouth tugged up.

"Is she withholding access to the portals to you as well?" Will asked him when we were in the elevator. "I was under the impression her only reason for living was to get in my way."

"She's just a killjoy," Drew said.

Will's inner total dad popped out. "What'd you do?"

"Nothing. Fine. She confiscated a bottle of Rage. Which I paid for and is legal for me to have."

"That's it? She took away your dirt-cheap bottle of bottom-of-the-barrel cinnamon whiskey?"

"*And* she threatened to tell the Queen we had it."

"Ah. We." The doors slid open, and we stepped into the lab. "I presume you aren't using the royal 'we.' Oz is not yet of legal age to consume alcohol in public, Andrew. Not without a parent."

"I'm her *husband*."

Will dropped his gym bag onto the table in the little kitchen. "All right, I'll give you that. Who else was with you? And where were you?"

"Fine. It was more than just the two of us, but she's still not one of our guards." He'd been at the corner bakery on Union Square with Oz, Zed, Jay, Sophia, and Zara. The bottle was on the table, unopened, when she swooped past, uttering a too-cheery "Nope" as she grabbed it and then threatened to tell the Queen if he balked. "I hadn't even cracked the seal. She had no proof that I was going to share it with any of them."

"Were you?"

"That's not the point!"

To make matters worse, when he got up to chase after her, one of his own guards caught Drew's eye as he shook his head no, warning Drew to let it go.

"I thought the guards were supposed to be hands-off," Drew grumbled.

"They suspected you were about to offer alcohol to my eighteen-year-old son and Oz's eighteen-year-old brother," Will said. "In public. A clear violation of more than one law. No sympathy on this one."

With a sigh, Drew set his box down on the center island. "Fine. But you agree, she's mean, right?"

"She's mean."

"Then why?"

"Jax thinks he's funny," Will said.

That was all Drew needed to hear. He tapped on the metal box in a look-at-this gesture and grinned. "Box of snot."

"I suppose there are worse things you could be saving in a box. None that I want to see, in any case."

"My snot runneth clear." Drew twisted the latch and pulled the lid back. From where I sat on Will's shoulder it looked like water, but when he tipped it an inch or two, the contents slowly oozed to the lip. "Finn's helping me run tests on it, but I'm, like, ninety-nine percent sure it'll carry a current and still insulate."

He'd been working all summer on this. The day after his last exam of the semester, he jumped into the project that he'd been itching to get to for months. The idea of how to cool down the computers he used to create holograms had been poking at his brain, and along with that was, he hoped, the answer to keeping robots and computer clusters at optimal operating temperatures for Elysium.

"Have you given it the finger test?" Will asked, chuckling.

"I did that *once*."

"You molested your dessert in front of the Queen," Will reminded him. "She had to throw a dinner roll at you to get you to stop."

The gelatinous abuse had been worth it. Repeatedly sticking his finger in his Jell-O (until Aubrey whipped a dinner roll upside his head) spurred the idea that brought him to this place: his gut told him there was something he could insulate the computer cases with that would help keep temperatures even without damaging the components, and as he got deeper into his research he also realized he could run nanobots through it. The nanobots multiplied the processing capabilities of the system's motherboards, which meant he could increase the resolution in his holograms.

The contents of the box had been his focus all summer, and he'd spent hundreds of hours working with Finn and one of his chemists on it.

"It hinges on how well it conducts," he told Will. "The last batch ran a degree and a half higher than I wanted. This did well in a quick check back in the shop, but I wanted to use Finn's toys for a better test."

"He certainly has all the cool toys," Will allowed.

"Is that why you're here? For the test?"

"I came to ask him a favor."

Will had forgotten his promise to bring George Denton, Jay's former stepfather, back from their birth When for a short visit with James. He'd made the promise before Aisha exacted another from him—that he wouldn't use another portal until after their baby was born. Jay had not forgotten, though he let it slide until his eighteenth birthday, when a slightly tipsy James admitted he felt a deep need to see his ex-husband and pressed Jay about where he was.

"I won't violate Aisha's wishes, but it matters to Jay that his father sees George," Will said. "I imagine he feels a need to catch up with George, as well."

Drew offered to take him. "We'd just be using the hospital portal, right? Jay can have lunch in the cafeteria with him, and then we'll come right back."

"Thank you. And take Oz," Will suggested. "Just in case."

Take me. He's afraid of me.

"We should take the mean lady," Drew grumbled. "No, wait, they might like each other."

George doesn't date women.

"He can have female friends, Wick. Something tells me those two would hit it off."

"Aside from that," Will said, "he's about to become a father. I don't think he'll have time for a social life for a while."

"He got custody?"

"Dallas wants nothing to do with the child," Will said, referring to the woman who had tackled her way into to this When and then sued him for paternity. "George offered her a considerable amount of money to continue the pregnancy and to sign off her parental rights. The remainder of the cult doesn't dare contest the agreement."

Even though Will and George hated each other, there was a truce. It was largely for Jay's sake; regardless of George's efforts to prevent him from having the surgery he needed, Jay would always love his former stepfather. He thought he understood George, the fear that surged through his veins with every beat of his heart, and that was enough for him to find forgiveness. Will had lived through a childhood filled with enough George-inspired misery that reaching the same point was more difficult, but for Jay, he tried.

Almost as difficult as reaching a modicum of forgiveness was getting past how disturbing it had been to learn that George offered up Will's DNA but handed over his own instead. He'd done it believing he was protecting Jay and that was something Will understood. Because of that, Will decided he could help. George wanted the fetal clone growing inside Dallas Engle and she did not; he gave Finn a small amount of money to open an investment account in this When, with riders that allowed the money to carry through several generations of Blackshears. After Finn opened the account, he visited the bank in several different decades to make sure the investment was still growing, and then went home to withdraw it all. He handed it over to George with an explanation: use it however he saw fit to gain custody, absent harming the mother.

Will hated George, and he hated the way he'd stood in Jay's way for so many years, but couldn't ignore that George did love Jay, fiercely, and he'd acknowledged that he'd screwed up. Will was certain he'd be a better father to that baby than he was to Jay, and Jay was quick to admit that if you removed the surgical hump between them, George was a good parent.

Drew wanted to know what happened if James and George saw each other and realized that ending their marriage was a mistake. "They were both seriously pissed off when they split, but Jay thinks his dad wants George back. What if George feels the same way?"

"Doesn't matter. Jax will not bend on this. George's order of exile is permanent."

Take James to George.

I knew he and Aisha had talked about it. If James decided his life could not go on without George, the only option was to take him forward. Taking him forward meant explaining everything. Aisha wasn't sure James could handle it, and if he could, he might not be willing to leave Jay behind.

It meant giving Jay a transponder, something

they both resisted. It wasn't that they didn't trust him; they didn't trust George enough to be sure that he wouldn't use Jay to get back to this When. If George forced his way through a portal, he was a dead man. He'd taken a swing at the King, he'd threatened members of the royal family, and he'd tried to abduct Jay. There was no coming back from that. His exile was a kindness to Jay, but if he came back without permission, the penalty was death.

"If James moved to be with George, there's, like, no chance George would ever use Jay to come back. Why would he? He'd have his husband and his kid, and Jay would be able to visit whenever he wanted."

Theoretically, Will agreed. "You try explaining that to Aisha right now. Last night she cried because Jay left her a dozen cookies out of a batch he'd made for Zara. An hour later she growled at her belly and ordered the baby to stop kicking for just ten minutes, and then cried because that seemed mean. This morning she was fascinated by her stretch marks and fifteen minutes later was upset because I clearly must think her body is ruined. And that's just scratching the surface of her moods lately. If I tell her I want Jay to get a transponder and for James to move two centuries into the future, she'll throw sharp things at me."

"But she's okay with Jay going for a visit?"

He nodded. "Supervised. And yes, we are aware that he's technically an adult. You'd be there mainly as his conduit through the portal, and to serve George a visible reminder that Jay is protected."

"No problem. We'll take him." He glanced at the clock above Finn's office door. "He's late."

"He's Finn. What did you expect?" Will peeked into the window on the closed office door, then into the window of the next office. He checked the restroom, then the room behind the cabinet that would one day lead down into the portal tunnel, mumbling that Finn was probably lost in work downstairs. He crossed the room to check the lounge near the kitchen, where people sometimes slept when they were working extra-long days, and then abruptly turned around. "I know how to operate the equipment. Let's start without him."

"Why?" Drew turned in the direction of the lounge, but Will nudged him toward the door leading down to Finn's workspace. "Is he in there?"

"He is, he's not alone, and I believe I have been scarred for life."

Drew's howling laughter echoed in the stairwell.

"On one hand," Will said as he pointed to the table Drew needed to set his box of snot on, "I should be happy they still have that. On the other?"

"Old people sex," Drew snorted.

"I could have gone the rest of my life without seeing that."

Think about how I feel.

"You're free to leave at any time," he said as he booted up the computer that ran the program Drew needed. "Anything you witness is purely by choice."

"And your commentary isn't necessary," Drew grumbled. He scooped out half the gel and dropped it into a clear container that had cables sticking out from each side, and then clipped wires from the computer to it. When that was done, he fished a small box out of his back pocket and poured its contents into the gel, then said to Will, "Program six-b. It'll activate the nanobots and then take them through a range of temps."

"Tasks?"

"Mostly grouping together, forming chains. I only need to see how well they maintain the ability to follow rudimentary commands and swap data while working in the gel. We don't even need to stand here and watch closely. Finn has a camera on this table." He pointed to a tiny, bright light overhead. "It'll catch everything."

"How wide a range of temperatures have you been using?"

"I'm accounting for the temperatures outside the containers," Drew answered. "Once I have a gel that will operate within about a quarter of a degree of normal room temps with a hell of a lot of electricity going through it, I'll lower the outside temps."

"And for that, we need the deep freezer you requested earlier in the year."

Drew nodded. "If this works, we'll need somewhere to test from sub-freezing temps all the way up to boiling hot. I'd like to find a place outside the city to do the bulk of the work, just in case."

His primary concern was that wherever they relocated to do the majority of testing on the gel and the nanobots would meet a fiery death. There was merit to his worry; when the military ran tests on their holographic training systems, the overheating was bad enough that everything went up in flames. They also lost dozens of mainframes meant for Elysium. Drew was confident that he could create the system that would work without blowing up, but it wasn't something he wanted to risk in the heart of downtown San Francisco.

"Someplace in mind?" Will asked.

"Wastelands. There are still several warehouse-sized buildings on the periphery, and we could draw power from the old solar farm."

Two panels from the old solar farm—a project abandoned nearly two centuries earlier because it had changed the migratory patterns of the birds and pushed out other wildlife—had been activated when Will built the gate on the Bay Bridge that sent thirty-year-old Finn home. The cables that ran hundreds of miles from the farm to the bridge had been buried to assure the power could be drawn on in an emergency and had been used a handful of times for military exercises, but never as a backup to the power grid. Drew wanted to activate a few more of the panels and to take over at least one of the warehouses.

It was land that could be used, regardless of how dead it appeared.

"Oz has ideas for other parts of the Wastelands," he told Will. We moved from the box of snot that he was electrifying to Jo's desk in the corner, close enough to keep an eye on things but far enough that if it exploded, no one would be hurt. "She wants to turn it into a tourist attraction."

"We've discussed it a bit," Will said. "Once she has a concrete proposal, I want her to present it to the King."

"What, like a formal presentation? In front of the council?"

Will nodded. "She's learning the ropes, so to speak. This is one of them. There are fine lines between telling her father an idea at the dinner table, telling him in his office, and presenting it to him at city hall."

"Yeah, I remember."

Drew had shown Jax his table-top hologram in his office, with General Myers present. He was surprised when Will ordered him to turn it off; he hadn't realized that showing it to Jax in his office was akin to offering it to the King. If Oz presented her idea to Jax at city hall, with the council present, she wouldn't be offering him an idea. She would be making a formal request and opening the idea up for discussion.

"They'll tear it apart," Will said. "If she stands her ground and can defend her position, they'll listen."

"Will they treat her like they would anyone else?" Drew asked.

"They won't hold back because she's the King's daughter. They certainly don't hold back for me."

"Do they ever shoot your ideas down?"

"Indeed. Most recently, a request I made to recreate the parklets that used to dot the city was eviscerated."

Before he could say anything more, the door popped open and Finn rushed in, brightening when he saw us.

"There you are! Sorry I'm late. I was tied up for a bit, Jo had things to discuss."

"Tied up," Will snorted. "Nice. We started without you. It's already running the third cycle."

"Any alarms?"

"Other than the sound of the electrical pulses, no sounds at all," Drew said. "If we get any, I expect them in the fifth cycle, when the nanobots begin more complex exercises."

Finn went over to peek inside. "Nano-gymnastics. That's rather elegant, don't you think?"

"It's oddly mesmerizing," Will said. "I'd liken it more to ballet than gym class."

"That would be a killer toy," Drew said. "A sealed container filled with the gel and a ton of nanobots, programmed to move like they're dancing? It wouldn't even take much, just some rudimentary programming, maybe a light source at the bottom to make them sparkle more. Or changing lights, assorted colors. It would be awesome."

Not amazing?

Will reached for a tablet on the desk and asked Finn if it would be all right to use it. He handed it to Drew and said, "Write it down and sketch it out."

"It could all be mounted on a base with a built-in audio streaming device," Drew said as he sketched. "User choice. The nanobots dance to the music, or you run it silent and just watch. That could be soothing as hell. Is this new, you think? Someone else hasn't done it?"

"Lava lamps come and go," Will said. "They have for centuries. The basic idea, one substance moving in another, is similar, but I believe what you propose is unique. The image in my mind is of a fully electronic and programmable...snow globe."

Drew didn't look up. "Yeah, but I think this needs to be a little bigger than a snow globe. Like...a head. Otherwise, it's just a shiny glass round thing. But maybe, you know, have different shapes. Boxes or globes or even long narrow rectangles for setting on desks. Kind of a workday distraction, something to focus on when the boss is being a jerk."

They fell silent, letting Drew get the things in his head out onto the tablet. Will watched as Drew scribbled furiously, and Finn kept an eye on the nanogel test. I stretched out on the desk because Drew's tongue was jutting out, which meant he was deep into his brain and that always meant it would be a while.

When the test cycle finished and beeped, Drew twitched but he didn't look up. Finn made notations for him and downloaded all the data, then unhooked the container from the wire mounts while Will grabbed another container to seal everything in. When they were done, and Will had closed the lid on the box of snot and put it into another container with the one they'd tested, Drew finally looked up.

He held the table out to Will. "Take a look."

Will read quietly for a few minutes, swiping back and forth between sketches, and then handed it to Finn.

"Doable?" Drew asked.

Finn nodded as he read. When he looked up, he looked at Will. "Jaden Parker. You should call him and get it rolling."

"Who's he?" Drew asked.

Will took the tablet back. "Patent attorney. I'll have him do a search and make sure no one else has done this."

"You'll need a manufacturer," Finn said.

"As well as distribution and sales. I have a few ideas already."

"So this is possible?" Drew asked.

Will turned the tablet off. "This is not only possible, I highly expect that by Christmas you'll see the first of your efforts for sale to the public. Congratulations, Andrew, you just created our first product, and essentially launched Ozoo."

2

Vicat was still guarding the portal when we left the lab, though she had moved to a nearby bench and wasn't standing right in front of it.

"Still no," she said as we passed.

Drew grunted at her, but his arms were full and he didn't want to stand there with expensive equipment weighing him down while he tried to convince her to give him back his bottle of embarrassment. He just kept walking, and when Will turned for the corner bakery Drew said he'd see him later and went home.

Aisha was at their usual table, but this time she didn't have coffee waiting for him and she didn't have a donut or scone sitting on a napkin in front of her. She had Eli; he stood near the table and they were laughing, probably at Will. When we were close enough, Will expressed surprise at Eli's presence because he'd been expected to stay in New York until the upcoming vote to admit Florida into the Consortium was over.

"New information I need to pass along to the King," Eli said. "Our stance is likely to change."

"Really now."

"They may wish they hadn't asked for an extension. If we'd voted six months ago, they'd be in. Now?" He exhaled sharply. "Florida's up to something, William. It has the stench of Levi Munson all over it."

Will didn't ask him the details because he knew Eli couldn't say much more about it. They chatted for a few minutes, then Eli kissed Aisha on the cheek before heading home.

Before Will pulled out a chair to sit, she said, "I couldn't bring myself to go in there and smell coffee, Bilbo. Your kid has been swinging from my ribs for the last two hours, and when I got here I decided that I didn't want to make an effort to move any more than it took to sit my ass down."

I jumped to the table when he bent over to kiss her. "I'm sorry. What would you like? I'll get it."

"Food. Real food." She held her hand out and asked him to help her up. "Mommy wants pizza. I called Jay and he's meeting us there."

"Mommy gets what she wants, then." He grimaced. "Oh. No. That sounds wrong. Unless there's an infant or toddler nearby, I am never calling you that again."

She calls you Daddy sometimes.

"It doesn't sound creepy coming from her," Will said as he scooped me off the table. They held hands as they walked across the Square and I wobbled a bit on his shoulder because Aisha no longer walked in a straight line and he had to keep moving to avoid stepping on her feet.

I think your kid is unbalanced.

"I think our kid is a gymnast," Aisha grumbled after he translated. "And doesn't nap. I swear, Will, this has been going on all day, and I'm not so sure I'm not hearing a tiny, evil laugh every now and then."

"Would you prefer we order in? There's no need to walk there if you're uncomfortable."

"I'm just whining," she said, leaning into him. "I need to move. I sat in front of my class all morning. By the end of it I was afraid someone would need to get a crowbar to peel me off the chair. And I felt lazy enough to call for a car. I didn't even want to walk the eighth of a mile to the bus stop."

There was only one more class before the final. Drew planned on being there, because she couldn't fathom walking around the lecture theater to keep an eye out for cheaters and the one or two students who looked like they were about to have a meltdown. With him there, she could sit in a comfortable chair up front and get up every now and then, and she'd be able to answer questions.

"The department head has already approved him as my T.A. for the fall semester," she said. "Two classes. I'll be on hand until the baby comes and then he's on his own."

"If he can stay focused, he'll be an excellent teacher," Will mused. "It's the focus you need to worry about. You may return to find your classes are filled with students who understand everything about Asimov's Laws of Robotics and Heinlein's concept of 'grok,' but very little about calculus."

"I'll have four or five weeks to teach him to teach. He knows the subject. He'll be fine."

Maybe Will should go snoopervise.

"Will is taking time off to immerse himself in fatherhood," he said. "But Andrew might need some reminders about staying on subject." He told her about the nanogel test and how easily he was distracted by the shininess of a new idea. "He left the lab without even asking what the results were. He had a solid idea and quickly drew up an incredible concept sketch, but he lost focus on what he was there for."

"Sounds like he focused on the new idea quite well. Why didn't you refocus him?"

It would have been easy to get Drew to set the tablet down and go back to the test, but the results would not have changed, and he knew it would make Drew mentally itchy if he had to suddenly stop. "It was interesting. Watching Drew switch gears was a glimpse into my father. He's so easily distracted, and I'm amused to see where he gets it from."

"I hear a 'but' in there."

"Perhaps not quite a 'but.' There is a difference between them. The other Drew's distractions, at least historically, led him to bigger things and he always completed his projects. My father is prone to mistakes that had he not been distracted, he would have seen early on."

Like the gates for the meteor. Drew had to fix that.

"Indeed, Wick. My father used my plans to build the gates, but he failed to account for failure. In the same situation, I believe Drew would have seen what needed to be done."

Drew would get that he already figured out transporters, too.

That made Will sigh. Finn had the answers, he'd just shoved them aside somehow and wasn't connecting all the dots. "He's stuck on the idea of transporting without using transponders. Give it time."

What, time for him to figure out you've beaten him to it? I know what you're working on when you're not helping Drew in the workshop.

When we were at the pizza place and seated—Will and Aisha sat together in a booth and I was on the other side, trying to see them over the edge of the table—she leaned against him. "How'd Drew's tests go? You never said."

"As close to perfect as one can get without worrying that there's a flaw in the equipment. He's nearly got it, and he has no idea."

Is the General going to take Drew's toys now?

"I don't think so, Wick. I'm confident that Anthony was truthful when he claimed his interest was personal. Once Drew has the patents secured, we'll let the General see a bit more and perhaps even let him play with something."

General Myers was itching to see what Drew was going to do. He was aware of the work with holograms and the possibilities for the life support systems on Elysium, but he had no specifics. All he wanted was to see Elysium become a reality in his lifetime. He wanted to set foot on it, breathe its air, and view Earth through its windows.

He's old. Drew better get cracking.

"He has enough to start the patent process," Will said. "The nanogel works. It needs to be tweaked, but it works."

"What's next?" Aisha set her head on his shoulder and yawned. "Buy that deep freezer?"

"We need to look into leasing a building in the Wastelands. We'll work with the freezer there and—"

Dude, she went out like a light.

"She's exhausted," he whispered. "We can be quiet until the pizza is ready."

You did this to her, you know. And you're making her work while she's growing a whole person inside.

"I am not—"

And she waddles. Like a duck. That's your fault, too.

He wasn't looking at me, and not because he knew it was his fault. Jay arrived, and Will held a finger to his lips to ask him to be quiet.

"Is she okay?" he whispered as he slid onto the booth seat with me.

"Just tired. Wick is blaming me."

"Well, yeah," Jay snickered. "Did you get a chance to ask Finn about taking me to see George?"

"Drew volunteered, if that's all right."

"You trust us to not wander around? Because we'll want to."

"I trust you. And I'll take you back in a few months so you can play all you want."

I thought you didn't want him and Zed to see the castle.

"I trust them."

"What happens after George comes back to see my dad?" Jay asked, still whispering. "I have a feeling Dad wants him to come home. I haven't worked up the nerve to tell him that's not even close to being possible. I mean, he knows it, but I think he figures I can charm Uncle Jax into it."

"Cross that bridge when you get to it."

"Easier said than done. He doesn't believe that I don't know where George is, and he's hinted at wanting an address. He really doesn't get why George was banned from Pacifica. I mean, he thinks the penalty should have been a few months in jail, not something that lasts forever."

"He took a swing at the King," Will reminded him. "He tried to kidnap you. He pulled a gun on me."

"I know. And I know that technically he could have been executed for just trying to hit Uncle Jax. All Dad sees is how screwed up everything between them was, and now he can't fix it."

"They haven't seen each other in a year," Will reminded him. "George has a life now. He's expecting a child soon. They have more to discuss than why he can't come home."

James didn't know about George's clone, the baby that was about to be born. It wasn't something easily explained, and there was no reasonable way to tell James that it was all taking place two hundred years in the future.

"I know they have a lot to work through," Jay said. "But what if they do?"

Will took a moment. "I imagine that will take several visits and many hours of discussion. If it comes to that, we'll have to tell your father the truth, and he'll have a decision to make. Stay here and count on you to take him to visit George or move."

"To the future."

"He'd only be a portal away."

"That would get so damned complicated," Jay said. "How long would it be before it's a pain to get someone to take me through? Because I know if he goes, he's not coming back, not if he and George really connect again. At some point, my asking is going to sound like nagging."

Will tilted his head to look at Aisha. "We need to discuss it. But you're eighteen now. If your father moves, mine will give you a transponder, and you'd be able to visit whenever you choose."

"I'd see a lot less of him," Jay guessed.

"Possibly. But the time you spend together might be of improved quality."

"There's that. The odds of him whoring his way around Pacifica there will significantly shift."

Aisha took a deep breath and then blinked rapidly. "Who's a whore?"

"I am, Mom," Jay said. "I skipped the summer semester to work the streets."

"I hope it pays well." She gave Will a kiss on his cheek. "Sorry about that. How long was I asleep?"

"Hours. You missed dinner. We ate without you. Jay is about to leave for a triple shift working in Dogpatch tonight."

I don't think she believed either one of them, mostly because the pizza guy picked right then to bring it to the table.

Don't you have to have sex to be a whore?

"I believe it's part of the job, yes," Will answered.

Are you having sex, Jay?

"I am not passing that question along, Wick. It's none of our business."

Jay picked a few pieces of sausage from his pizza and put them on the table in front of me. "I can guess. And no, Wick, not yet."

Good thing he gets an allowance, then.

How come I don't get an allowance? What if I find a girlfriend? I might need money.

"If you get a girlfriend, I'll give you an allowance."

What about a boyfriend?

"Same."

Good. Because Lux is coming to visit, and we might want to go down to the Ferry Building and buy some shrimp.

"Lux is not your boyfriend," Will said. "If anything, he's your brother. Your dating Lux would be like me dating Jax."

"Gross," Jay muttered. "Besides, they're both

neutered. At least you and Uncle Jax could, you know, do stuff."

Mass said he could de-neuter me.

"Is that what you really want, Wick? To spend two days in surgical gel, and then suffer through the bath after?"

"I had a bath after my surgery?" Jay asked. "Like, Mass *bathed* me?"

"Mass is not the one who bathed you, but yes."

Jay grimaced.

Tell him you weren't there for that part. I was, but you weren't.

"I suppose it really doesn't matter," Jay said. "I mean, I did say I was okay with you both seeing me bare ass naked afterward. It's just the idea. That had to be seriously *thorough*."

All the nooks and crannies. Does he want to know about the pipe they shoved up his asterisk to get all the nanobots out?

"Wick, you realize you would essentially go through everything Jay did if you choose this?"

I don't really want to. I want the option to.

"You always have the option. That's not something I would deny you, but I don't see a point unless you have a burning desire to procreate."

I don't.

"Then why ask about it?"

All I wanted was an allowance. The idea of a girlfriend or a boyfriend was to justify it.

Will leaned back and folded his arms. "All right. An allowance is a reasonable request. You should have the ability to save for things you want and not worry about whether or not we feel it's necessary."

Seriously?

"Seriously. I'll start an account for you and deposit funds weekly. You can use it for toys that you want and gifts you wish to give others."

Do I have to use it to buy shrimp treats?

"No. Your food is the responsibility of the family. That includes special treats when we're out."

"And how much does a cat need each week?" Aisha asked. "Enough for an ounce of fresh catnip? Two?"

"Enough that he can save for special occasions," Will said. "Consider how long he waited for that hover cart. And how much he borrowed from Drew for last Christmas."

Oh. I have to pay him back for that, don't I?

"It was taken care of. But this coming Christmas, if you choose to buy gifts, it comes out of your savings. Does that sound fair?"

It sounds fair, but it also sounds like you're already turning into a total dad.

Granted, that had been my goal during a good chunk of last year, to make sure he knew he was ready for parenthood.

I didn't think it would be turned on me.

Two hours after being granted an allowance, I risked the first week of it. As Will got ready to take a shower Aisha said she was going to the kitchen to make them a snack, so he shouldn't take long.

She's gonna make hot chocolate.

"It's summertime, Wick. Not exactly hot chocolate weather."

Wanna bet?

"All right. I'll bet. What's the wager?"

Half my allowance this week. I lose you don't have to open the account yet. I win, and I get extra.

"Fine. You have a bet."

How much is my allowance, anyway?

"It will be enough, I promise."

Can I save up for a car?

"You can. You can save for anything you choose, Wick. But saving for something isn't the same as being able to get it."

I just want choices, that's all.

My current choice was to not watch him shower, so I went into the kitchen to keep Aisha company. She didn't notice when I jumped onto the island, and I decided to stay quiet so I could watch her. She moved around with her hand held to her back and exhaled hard a few times, but she seemed content; when she turned toward me, I saw her belly twitch, a hand or a foot poking at her from the inside.

She stopped and looked down, smoothing her shirt so that it was pressed tight against her skin, and she smiled softly.

"Hey there," she whispered. "Thanks for not stomping on my bladder this time."

I felt my ear twitch; it heard Jay approaching before my brain did.

"I want to say I've never stomped on your bladder, but I'm pretty sure I probably did about eighteen and a half years ago."

"I talk to the baby a lot. Might as well get used to it."

He took a half step back when a tiny elbow jutted out. "Whoa. Can I?"

She took his hand and set it on her belly right where the baby was moving the most. "Pretty active tonight. I have high hopes that this means she's wearing herself out and I can sleep tonight."

"We all keep saying 'she.' Are you guys ever going to find out for sure?"

They'll figure it out when the baby pops out.

"Will it matter?" she asked as she turned back to what she'd been doing: making hot chocolate. "We just don't want to refer to the baby as 'it.'"

Jay thought they were setting up expectations but finding out for sure would shift those and build excitement instead. While he made the argument for finding out the baby's gender, Will came out. His hair was still wet and uncombed, but he'd put pants on, which was an improvement from walking around in his underwear. He leaned against the island near me and listened, and his hand went to my head for a few behind-the-ear rubs.

"I'm not sure we want to know beforehand, Jay," Aisha finally said.

When Will didn't say anything, they both turned toward him.

"Bilbo?"

The petting stopped. "Truth? I'd like to know."

"You know what I think," Jay said. "And I know, whatever gender this kid is assigned doesn't mean it'll stick. Someday you might be dealing with another me. But still."

Before she could respond, Will said to Jay, "It's her call. Whether I learn now or two months from now won't change the outcome. No more pressure, all right? This isn't a democracy. Your mother is fully in charge of this pregnancy, and we bend to her will."

"Well, make me sound like a dictator," she grumbled, even though she didn't seem at all upset. "Sweetheart, I just thought you wanted to wait and be surprised. I'd like to know, too."

You people need to talk more.

"When can you find out?" Jay asked.

"I have an appointment next week—" Her eyebrows knotted when Will pushed away from the island and went into the bedroom. "What the hell, Will?" she called out.

He came back with his phone and was punching numbers before he was all the way back. It was almost nine o'clock, but he didn't think it was too late to call Mass and ask if he knew off the top of his head. Aisha and Jay waited quietly, stiffly, as Will spoke to Mass, and she twitched when Will set the phone down and touched the little picture that turned the speaker on.

"All right, Mass," he said. "We're all here."

Mass's voice sounded like it was erupting from the countertop. "Aisha? You're sure you want to know?"

"I'm sure."

"Jay?"

"Hell, yeah."

There was the sound of tapping and a distant grunt when he said to give him a second. "All right," he finally said. "I wanted to pull it up to make sure I had it right. How do you feel about traditional gender colors?"

"What?" Will was confused. "I don't care for gender stereotypes, Mass, you know—"

"Get your shorts out of your ass, Will. Just… paint the nursery blue, all right?"

The sudden burst of quiet slapped against the kitchen island and exploded like a water balloon. I heard Mass snicker, but Will and Aisha stared at each other, until Jay uttered, "I'm a big brother."

"That is how it works," Mass said.

"We're still having a freaking tea party," Jay said to Will and Aisha.

"It's a boy," Aisha finally said, her voice soft.

"Hang up for them, Jay," Mass said. "And tell your Mom to call tomorrow. I'll set her up with a new scan so she can meet her newest little boy face to face."

I pushed the phone closer to Jay because Will was making his way around the island to hug her. After a long moment of holding her, he reached an arm out to Jay and pulled him close, too, planting a kiss at his temple.

This is too sweet. I'm gonna hurl.

No, really. Stop it.

When they pulled apart, Will's eyes were red and wet, like he was trying not to cry.

"Are you okay?" Jay asked.

Aisha's hands went to Will's face, thumbs brushing over his cheeks. "I think he would be this way no matter what Mass said."

He nodded and set his hands on her gigantic belly. "I think my soul just exhaled," he said. "I didn't realize how badly I wanted to know. A boy."

"Not disappointed?"

"Not in the least."

Jay wanted to know if it was a secret. Because if not, he wanted to call Zara and tell her.

Aisha leaned into Will and against his lips said, "Let him tell her."

"Wick will tell Drew."

"Then let's see how long it takes for the phone to ring."

I took that as permission and ran alongside Jay until we reached the front door. He went to his room to call Zara, and I headed through the cat flap, zooming down the stairs as fast as I could, yelling Drew's name before I had jumped off the last step. I ran through the living room and kitchen looking for him, and when he wasn't there, I darted into his and Oz's room.

Drew, Drew, Drew, Drew, Drew, Drew, Drew.

He was at his desk, working. Oz was on the sofa watching a video, and she startled when I bolted through the cat flap yelling for him. I launched onto the coffee table and told him to stop working; he sighed and set his stylus down because experience had taught him that I would not give up when I had something major to tell him.

"All right," he sighed as he dropped next to Oz. "What's so important?"

It's a boy.

He looked confused.

Will and Aisha called Mass and asked him what she's got growing inside and it's a boy.

"I'll be damned. Do they know you're telling me?"

It's not a secret and they said Jay could call Zara and tell her and I could tell you and you can tell Oz and—

"Take a breath, Wick."

"World coming to an end again?" Oz asked.

"Aisha's having a boy. I guess they found out tonight."

Their happiness was a lot more subdued than I expected, but they still got up to find Jax and Aubrey, who did exactly what Will expected and called to order them downstairs, because Jax wanted to have a celebratory drink with Will and Aubrey wanted to hug Aisha until she nearly peed herself.

That last thing might not take long.

We wound up on the balcony with Jax and Drew, and they stared down at the Square while Will called Finn to tell them to stop what he and Jo were doing and come over, because he had news, and drinking was about to commence.

Finn wouldn't commit until Will assured him it was good news, and then from behind him Will heard his mother ask, "Is Aisha having my grandson or granddaughter?"

"How the hell?" Will sputtered.

"You're drinking. What other news would it be?" Finn said.

They watched as Finn and Jo left the lab and jogged across the Square, as excited to get here as they were happy. Eli drifted upstairs and Jay came downstairs, Zed came out of his bedroom, and before I knew it, we were back on the balcony with a bottle of scotch.

"The girls are inside, and the boys are outside," Jay observed. "This seems wrong."

Jax poured a splash into a glass for each of them, even for Jay and Zed. "It's only wrong if someone is where they don't want to be."

Jay looked to Will for permission before he took the glass Jax offered.

"To fathers and sons and brothers," Jax said.

"And to Will," Eli said. "Who's about to become all three."

"He already is," Jay said, sniffing at the scotch. "He's had a year and didn't break the stepson. So he's good."

Will got up long enough to plant a kiss on Jay's head. "Thank you. And yes, the scotch will bite back."

"You get used to it." Drew peeked over the edge of the balcony. "Mean lady is down there. I bet she still has my whiskey."

"Is that her new name?" Will asked. "Mean lady?"

"Only because we all made a pact to try to not abuse Aubrey's list so much."

"I didn't realize how much I swear until I tried to stop." Jay took a cautious sip, grimaced, and then poured what was left into Eli's glass. "I get buzzed easy, and I have an exam in the morning."

"Same," Drew said, though he slugged back the rest of his before he got up. "Will, major, major congrats. I can't wait to meet the little guy."

I thought everyone was going to be more enthusiastic. This is the most exciting thing to happen since I caught the fly at their reception. Why aren't they happier?

"Everyone is excited," Will said. "But the real celebrating happens when he's born. And truly, they need to be able to get up in the morning and be awake enough for their exams."

Jax was looking over the balcony now, too. "So, how's the new guard, Emperor?"

"You're an ass. You know damn well I'm not using the portals."

"Just doing my bit to make sure you keep your promise."

It wasn't a promise, Will argued. Aisha asked, and he agreed; that's all it was, an understanding that she was uncomfortable with him popping off to other Whens unless it was an emergency. If there were a need to use one of the portals, he would consult with her first.

"Yeah, but this is *way* funnier."

"My grandparents are on the other side of that portal," Will reminded him. "I might like to see them, you know."

"I'll bring them for a visit," Finn said.

There was no point in arguing. "Why her?" Will asked Jax. "She's a middle-aged guard stuck perpetually at a sergeant-grade rank. She hasn't been promoted in two decades and should have been released the second time she was passed over."

"She wasn't passed over. She's turned down every promotion offered, and she remains in service at the whim of the King."

"What is it the kids say these days?" Eli mused. "She has 'mad skills.' She's always wanted to fly under the radar. I honored that, and Jax honors that."

Will knew she was a skilled fighter; he'd read her file and watched videos of her earliest days in training along with more recent ones during her stint as a combat instructor. It didn't explain her lack of rank progression, and it especially didn't explain why she was given such a subdued, boring assignment.

"When I explained to Soto what I wanted, she howled and called Vicat over to discuss who was best suited for the task," Jax sat. "Vicat volunteered on the spot. I think everyone in the guard wants to see what happens if you try to push your way past her."

"I have a good idea of what might happen."

Eli snorted. "Son, that woman—" he gestured in the direction of the portal "—might be the only member of the guard that can knock you onto your backside."

"If she's that good, and she's a much-needed combat instructor, why did she take the assignment?"

"Because," Jax said, "she thought it was funny, too."

◆◆◆

"You need to sleep," Will whispered in the dark. "One more day, then the semester is over and you can do whatever the hell you want."

"Until the start of the next one." The bed shifted as she rolled onto her back. "At least he's sleeping now, thank god."

I was curled up on the foot of the bed between their legs. Will reached over and set his hand on her, very carefully, making sure the movement didn't cause the baby to begin a late-night round of amniotic gymnastics.

"I'm sorry if this is hard," he said. "Blame me."

"Oh, I blame you, mister. Every day I mutter a string of expletives aimed right at you for doing this to me. I conveniently ignore the fact that not only was I present and willing for his beginning, it was half my idea."

"And I'm all right with that." He kissed her arm, the part of her closest to him. "He needs a name."

"I was planning on calling him You Devil Spawn for the rest of his life. Or Demon Child. I have a feeling it might fit." She sighed and lifted her head. "Navel Destroyer would work, too. Look at that thing. I had an innie...now I swear Wick could use it to scale, just for the exercise."

I'm not climbing you. That's creepy.

"What's a good mountain climber name? Sir Edmund? No...too close to Redmond. I mean, I like Red, but I don't want to—"

"Rhys," Will whispered.

She sat up, and when she spoke her voice was tangled in tears. "Will."

"I know you miss your parents. I thought that if we named him after your father—" He sat up with her. "I admit, I was far less certain about your mother's name if we had a daughter."

"Oh my god, she would haunt us if we had," Aisha sniffed, chuckling. "Ismildra. She *hated* it. Dad called her Izzy instead."

Izzy, he was all right with.

"I barely remember them, Will. I miss the hell out of them, but I can barely remember what they looked like, and their voices are gone. But I have a feeling my father would be so honored. What about Finn? He won't be hurt, will he?"

He nudged her to lie back down so they could cuddle. "My dad will understand."

"If he doesn't, we'll just have to have another one."

"Don't tempt me."

"You know we'll be tempted," she said.

"Unless Oz and Drew start their family earlier than you expect, we're going to be tempted, just so there are little ones running around here."

"I'll have another if you want. I also reserve the right to change my mind if he's like Oz was when she was three."

There was a long stretch of quiet until she whispered, "Did we just name our son, Bilbo?"

"We just named our son, Enzo."

"Middle name? My dad's was Davonte. We can go with something else."

"Rhys Davonte," Will muttered. "Not the name I would expect with a surname of Salazar."

"Because Salazar is my mother's name. His family name is Simmons. Very British."

"I just assumed—"

"They weren't married, Will. My aunt said he asked her every Sunday like clockwork, but she didn't see a point. They were together, they were happy. She didn't want to rock the boat."

"And here you are locked into a decree," he said, amused by the idea. "You can rock the boat until it capsizes, and you're still stuck with me."

"That's fine." She gave him a quick kiss and then settled against him, ready to fall asleep. "You're stuck with me, too, and I'm pretty sure I can out-bitch you with my eyes closed."

Wise man that he is, he did not agree with her.

3

Vicat was already standing in front of the hospital portal when we got there. Will had with him a small cadre of the guard, including T'Neeka Soto, but when we rounded the hallway corner Vicat didn't snap to attention and she didn't seem at all impressed by the number of guards on this assignment. She wasn't in uniform; she chose to block Will's way wearing faded jeans and a t-shirt, and she'd dropped a sweatshirt onto a waiting-area chair a few feet away.

"You can back off," Will sighed. "I have no intention of using it."

"And yet you brought backup. That won't help, Emperor."

She knew why we were there: Drew and Oz were taking Jay through, so he could visit with George and then bring him back to see James. The guards accompanying Will were there to make sure George didn't leave the hospital. James was around the corner in Mass's private lounge, just off his office, which was just a small room with a refrigerator and a sofa and a few decorative tables. It was comfortable enough for a long visit, but not private enough that George could slip away. Even if he could sneak past the guards in the hallway, others were waiting along the way, and every exit was covered.

Will thought it was overkill and said so. Head Guard Soto admitted that it was, but George had been exiled, and she wasn't letting him sneak out of the building, not on her watch.

Vicat couldn't have cared less about George. She was there to block Will's way.

"I'll wait here," Will told Jay. "Take your time. I know you have a lot to discuss with him."

"I'll make sure he knows there's no chance he can stay," Jay said. "No matter what Dad says to him."

"Remove the temptation before it happens?" T'Neeka asked Will.

There was no temptation, and Will knew it. If George came through that portal with any intentions, it would be to convince James to go home with him. George had fatherhood waiting for him in his birth When, and no matter what Will thought about him personally, he was sure that meant more to George than anything else.

Finn kept in touch with him so that he could keep Jay up to date with the things going on in his former stepfather's life. Those were things Jay could discuss with Will, but not James because James had no clue that the man he'd left yet still loved was nearly two centuries from existing.

Oz and Jay were the first to return. Before they were completely through the portal, Vicat stepped aside and quietly moved to the rear of the guards who waited to escort George to Mass's office. If Will wanted to, it was his chance to dart through the portal, just to be able to prove that he could.

Five seconds later, George and Drew stepped out. George was carrying a bottle, and before he said anything else, he held it out to Will. "A small token of thanks. Not just for this, but...everything."

"Chambrizi." Will grinned. "Thank you. This is genuinely one of my favorites."

I jumped from Will's shoulder to Drew's, and we trailed behind them on the way to Mass's office. They made small talk; Will asked about his child, George asked about Will's, and none of it felt like two people who hated each other.

Are they like best friends now?

"They're just playing nice," Drew whispered.

Jay stepped up next to Drew and said, "George is nervous as hell. And Dad literally threw up this morning because he's so jittery. What if they can't talk?"

I can run ahead and jump on James's lap and purr for him. That might help.

"Well?" Drew asked Jay. "Would it? Your dad likes Wick."

"Maybe just give him to me, and I'll go in with George for a few minutes. Wick can crawl all over Dad and calm him down a little."

Drew set me on Jay's shoulder—which was awkward because he wasn't used to carrying me like that—and we went in just ahead of George. James jumped up when the door opened, and he sighed audibly, grateful that Jay had come first. We stood near him as George came in, and when he did, I stepped over to James. He was shaking, and his heart was beating hard and fast; George looked just as nervous and was completely tongue-tied.

"Come on," Jay finally said. "You've seen each other naked."

That made James laugh. I rubbed against the side of his head, and he reached up to pet me, but he looked at George and barely blinked.

"I've missed you," George said. "And I'm sorry."

James sucked in a deep breath. "I've read your letter a hundred times. I've tried to read between the lines, wondering if you were saying more, if there was something I didn't see."

Jay reached for me. "I know Will told you that you have until five or so, but Mass said he doesn't need his office or lounge until tomorrow. Just...there are guards right outside the door, and the room isn't soundproof, okay? Text me if you need anything."

He reminded George that he wasn't allowed to tell James where he lived, and we left.

"I figured you'd stick around for a while," Drew said.

"Get in the middle of that? Not a chance. They'll either wind up having a scream-fest, or these poor guards are getting an earful of...fun."

♦♦♦

While we waited for James to either text Jay or for a guard to call Will, we went to the workshop. Drew had insulated two of the computer casings with the new gel and was eager to test it beyond the few times he'd booted it up to make sure it would still run. Will went into his office to call Aisha, leaving Oz and Jay to help Drew set up.

"I wrote a new program," Drew told them. "It's intensive enough to draw more power than usual and hopefully won't blow up the computer."

The floor panels began to hum and the projectors lit up. He tapped a few keys at the control panel and then stepped back to watch. The image formed from the ground up, layering upon itself until we were standing in front of a tall baby dragon, its shiny black scales reflecting light that wasn't there.

"Jeff!" Oz squealed.

"I did it from memory," he said. "How about it, Wick? Did I get it right?"

I miss Jeff and Fluffy.

"So do I. Maybe we can visit them soon and see what they're up to."

I'm guessing about forty feet. Jeff, anyway. Fluffy is probably the same.

"Funny. Oz, stroke his chest."

She stepped onto the deck and reached out carefully. When her hand connected, she grinned. "This feels like he did, Drew. The same velvety smoothness. And it's like his flesh under the scales gives just a tiny bit when I lean in."

"No personality, though. This is basically just a moving picture."

At that, the dragon's wings twitched, and he let out a smoky breath. Jay took several steps back, not trusting that what he saw wasn't going to stretch out and bite down on him. Drew assured him that wasn't possible, not yet. Once he was sure he had the level of insulation in the casings that he wanted, he would gradually hook up the rest of the array. When that happened, the pretend Jeff would be able to bite.

The office door creaked open. "Impressive," Will said. "How's the temperature?"

Drew glanced over his shoulder at the monitor. "Steady. Quarter of a degree higher than I'd like."

He had Oz step off the deck and then moved the dragon around. It took wobbly baby-steps across the floor, wings twitching but never fully extending, and its mouth opened and closed as tiny puffs shot out the nostrils.

"Can it fly?" Jay asked.

"Eventually," Drew answered. "There aren't enough display panels here, but once we expand into a larger space? Totally possible."

Will had his eye on the temperature. "No increased load, even with movement. What we need is to lower the room temperature and bring that quarter degree down. Do that, and you can start adding computer clusters."

"And after that?" Oz asked.

"Once he has every cluster running and if the temperature holds, then we can progress to a larger display floor." He reached over and turned the display off. "It's time to look into getting space in the Wastelands."

"Sweet," Drew uttered.

"If we do that, you have one more thing to get done before we begin operations there," Will said. "It's not an option."

"Sure. What?"

"Learn to drive, get your license, and get a car."

"Come on, Will."

"If you don't do this now, you'll be thirty before you do. Get your license, Andrew. No license, no Wastelands."

I waited in Mass's lounge with James while Drew took George home. James sat on the sofa with his hands on his knees, staring at me as I sat on the little table but not seeing me, and he kept sniffing. When he gripped his knees so hard that his fingers went red, I reached over with a paw and tapped the back of his hand.

If you sit back, I'll jump on your lap and purr for you. It might make you feel better.

When that didn't work, I jumped over anyway and leaned against his stomach. After a moment he started to relax and then sat back in the chair. His hands automatically went to my back, and he started petting me. It wasn't my favorite way to be touched—he stroked my back and not my head—but he was upset, so I forgave that.

"He's moved on, and yet he hasn't." He spoke in a whisper, to himself, though I was sure Jay and Will could hear him from where they waited outside the door. "He's got this whole life wherever the hell he's living. He's having a kid. A *kid*. And I can't believe I'm not part of it."

He wants you to be, though, right?

"So many times we talked about having one of our own. I knew he wanted that. He was always adamant that Jay was enough, and he didn't want him to feel like he was being pushed out of the way. But I know he wanted one."

What about what you wanted?

"He wants forgiveness. I don't know that I can give him that."

The door creaked and Jay stepped in, lingering just inside. "I forgave him, Dad. He's ten kinds of screwed up, but he loves me. He knows the mistakes he made, and he's sorry for them."

James wasn't sure it was genuine sorrow or frustration because he'd been exiled from home.

Jay dropped onto the sofa next to us. "Did Mom ever talk to you about George's trust fund? The one he set up for me?"

"I know she's aware of it, but we never discussed its terms. You'll get it when you're twenty-five."

"Did you know about the rider attached to it? He set up a surgical fund for me. If I hadn't had surgery by my twenty-fifth birthday and still wanted it, it was paid for. He didn't understand it, but he covered the bases for me."

James gave a slight nod. He'd known but didn't think it was enough. "He should have signed the damned paperwork when you were four years old."

"He was protecting his daughter."

"You believe that?"

"Yeah, I do." Jay slid closer, reaching over to scratch behind my ears. "Did he ever tell you about his sister?"

"He had a brother, Jay. Do you remember him?"

"Kind of. But he also had a sister who died when he was three years old. It's a screwed-up story, but the gist of it? She's why he balked at my surgery. She's also why he's hated Will all these years. You know they went to pre-school together, right?"

He gave James the abbreviated version: George's sister slipped in the tub when he was three and she was two, and their parents blamed him for her death. He had teased her; she stood up in the bathtub because of him, slipped, and hit her head. Until the day George left home, they blamed him.

He hated Will because Will had asked him about it when they were four and running around the school playground. Jay didn't tell him that Will asked because they had bumped into each other and he'd seen the image in George's head. He only told him Will had asked, and it terrified George that he knew about it at all and was sure Will would tell everyone else.

He didn't want to be marked as a baby-killer. Even at four years old, he knew it would stick.

"George has been running scared his whole life. And yeah, he fought against my surgery. He couldn't wrap his brain around the idea that no matter what my body said, I was actually male. He really did think he was protecting his little girl. *Your* little girl. But damn, Dad, he loves me no matter what. He's proud of me. Not of Jaime Okuda. He's proud of James Junior. He calls me Jay, and even Mom admits he makes a serious effort to not screw up his pronouns and the couple of times they've had contact, he's only referred to me as Jaime once."

"He still got in our way, Jay. He manipulated the Third Parent Act and used it against us. I'm not sure I can get past that."

Jay turned on the seat to look at James. "Gonna be blunt. How many times did you cheat on him? How many times did you basically shove that in his face? Because he got past that. He still loves you, and I'm betting if he could come home, he would."

"That's really none of your business."

"Kinda is. Because I saw it happening, I knew it was happening, and I knew how hard it was for him. That's my shining example of commitment, Dad. You screwing anyone who came along, and Mom trying to hide everything. I still don't have a sense of what normal is."

"You have a nice, normal life now, Jay."

"Now. But that doesn't change the first seventeen years of my life. And yeah, it's messed me up. You met Zara, you like her, right?"

James nodded.

"I'm not sleeping with her, you know. And it's not because we both don't want to. Like, really want to. I keep telling her I'm not ready to go that far, but the truth is that I'm terrified of who I'll turn into if I do. It's what I saw my whole life. You had George, you had someone who loved you, but you were always looking for the next person. And what if I'm like that? What if I finally have sex with her, and it's mind-blowing, but my brain shifts gears and starts telling me that yeah, that was fun, but maybe the next girl will be even better? So I string Zara along and test that theory out. Over and over and over. I don't want to be with her, looking over her shoulder to see who else is out there."

"Jay. Don't blame—"

"George wants forgiveness, Dad. He's already granted that much to you. You still love him, right?"

"I will always love him."

"Then fucking get over it."

I moved back to the little table, because I wasn't sure if James was mad or not and I didn't want angry fingers digging into my back.

The stretch of quiet almost hurt.

James's voice cracked when he said, "He can't come home. He can't tell me where he is. What's the point?"

"Did he tell you he wants you back?"

James nodded.

"Then start there. Write him a letter, I'll find a way to get it to him. And no, I don't know exactly where he is, either, but Will knows the people who know. It might be long and clunky, but you two can figure out a way to talk."

There was a soft knock at the door, and then Will stepped in.

"George's life is complicated right now," Will said. "But I will certainly forward a letter to him, and with the King's permission I can bring him back for another visit."

"And if I want to leave with him?"

"Would Dad be exiled, too?" Jay asked Will.

"No, he would not. Worry about it when it becomes an issue," Will said to James. "But by all means, feel free to write to him."

"And be prepared for him to not answer," James said to himself. He sighed and looked up at Will. "Why are you doing this? He wanted to kill you."

"I now understand why. And truly, if he still wanted to kill me, I'd be dead."

At nine o'clock, Will headed for the roof with two tiny glasses and the bottle of Chambrizi George had given him. Aisha was stretched out on the bed, reading, and didn't need me, so I followed him up the stairs. He knew where he would find Jay: the same place he'd found Drew two years earlier, flat on his back on the grass, staring up at the sky.

Like he had with Drew, he laid next to Jay and propped his head up on folded arms and watched quietly for a time. Unlike Drew, Jay inched closer and rested his head in the crook of Will's arm. I thought the silence was going to go on long enough that it felt weird, but Jay surprised me.

"Did I really screw it up today with my dad, or did I just sort of screw it up?"

Will chuckled, a soft snort through his nose. "You didn't screw anything up. The things you said to your father were truths and were perhaps things he needed to hear."

"Yeah, but I blamed him for my own hang-ups and that probably wasn't fair."

"Fair or not, it was the truth."

Jay wanted to know how much of the conversation Will had heard. He didn't mind that he'd heard all of it; he didn't want to repeat it. All he wanted was Will's opinion: did he go too far, and did his dad take any of it to heart?

"If you're worried he'll hold anything you said against you, I promise, he won't. If he truly wants to repair his relationship with George, the things you said were things he needed to hear."

"He's gonna want to move, you know. And I don't know how he'll take the whole thing. If he doesn't believe it, he might walk away without giving any of us a chance to prove it."

"Trust him," Will said simply.

"Yeah. I know." Jay sat up and turned to see Will. "You heard everything about Zara, then, didn't you?"

"I did." He sat up, too, and gestured to the seats near the fire pit. He fired it up, opened the bottle and poured them each a drink, and took his time before he went any further. He told Jay how to enjoy the Chambrizi—just a tiny sip that stays on the tongue, and breath in a bit through your lips—and propped his feet on the rim of the fire pit. "You are not your father, Jay."

"Yeah, but—"

"You understand I respect him? I have a deep appreciation for how good a father he's been to you and how hard he fought for what you needed. I equally appreciate the relationship he maintained with your mother, and how much it matters to them both that they parented you together. He's a good man, Jay. As are you. But you are not him."

"I bet he didn't think he would be the way he is when he was my age, either."

"Probably not. But the things about him that you find troubling are largely matters of choice. As are the things you worry over."

"Will, I'm worried I'll seriously hurt Zara."

"Let me ask you something. When you're working on a drawing, each stroke is a choice, isn't it? Perhaps subconsciously, but still a choice."

"I suppose."

"Do you ever sit back and wish you'd done something different?"

"Yeah. Most of the time. I always see little mistakes."

"But do you erase part of your work and try to fix it, or accept that your drawing makes sense as it is, and in spite of flaws only you can see, it should stand as it is and be appreciated in part because it has flaws?"

"Nothing's perfect. Sometimes I erase mistakes that will really ruin something, but I leave a lot of things because someday I'll be able to look back and see how I progressed."

Will nodded. "Someone less mature would either erase and ruin what they created or tear it up and start over."

"You're gonna have to spell this out for me, Will."

"Your father is a good man, Jay. But he lacks maturity. You, on the other hand, have displayed quite a bit in the last year."

"Yeah, no. I'm still the little bitch who threw a temper tantrum when I thought you'd cheated on Mom."

"Hurt feelings to which you were entitled, given the examples you grew up with. I have no doubt that you learned from those examples and will endeavor to not repeat them."

"Endeavor," Jay snorted.

"Do you love Zara?"

"Yeah, which is why I don't want to blow it, even though I'm totally blowing it."

"You're not blowing it. Do you want to be with her?"

"I *am* with her. If you mean, do I want to have sex with her? Hell, yes. But I need to be sure I won't—"

"You won't. That's not who you are."

Jay took another sip of his drink, imitating the way Will drew in air through barely parted lips. "You know you're basically telling me to go sleep with her."

"I am aware."

"You're probably also aware that we don't really have a place to go. Her dad hovers like a freak when we're over there, even if we're in Sophia's apartment. Which she would let us use, otherwise. I'm sure as hell not doing it in a car. Or on the beach. Or any other of the hundred places horny teenagers around here go."

"You want it to be special."

"Yeah, I kinda do. Didn't you?"

"Truly, I just wanted it to be with your mother." Will got up, taking the glass from Jay. As he did, he bent over and kissed the top of his head and said, "You're eighteen, old enough to rent a decent hotel room. Talk to her, find out where her head is at, but don't push her away because you're afraid of turning into your father. You won't."

At ten o'clock, Aisha was in the kitchen scooping chocolate ice cream into a bowl, and Will watched, trying to not grimace, as she topped it with sliced grapes, vanilla pudding, and whipped cream. She offered to make a bowl for him, baffled when he said he wasn't hormonal enough for even a bite of that.

She kissed him before she sat down with it. "Hm. Whatever you had to drink, I think I like it."

"George's peace offering. I shared a bit with Jay."

"So now Jay is in his art room, buzzed, trying to paint tiny flying penises all over an expensive piece of canvas, isn't he?"

"I believe he's calling Zara, and I promise, he's not drunk. Literally, he took three very small sips, just enough to be able to say he'd had a drink with me. I think he and Zed are on the same page with alcohol. They like the idea but, but not the taste."

"Good thing Drew likes a couple of drinks. So you still have a drinking buddy other than Jax."

You haven't gone out and had any lately.

"I know, Wick. I find staying home to be more satisfying right now."

"You can have a boys' night out, Will. I'm perfectly safe at home without you. Aubrey and I can grab Oz and sit here and watch some sappy movie while they drink wine and I inhale popcorn."

"Popcorn with what? Hot chili peppers and chocolate sauce?"

She jabbed her spoon in his direction. "Hey. I will fling a grape at you."

"That would require sharing and I don't think where your ice cream is concerned, you're the sharing type."

She set one on the spoon and cocked it back. The only thing that saved him was Jay coming out of his room, phone in hand, wanting to ask Will a question he clearly didn't want Aisha to overhear.

"What are they up to, Mister Wick?"

A little over six feet. Jay is taller now, though.

"You know, don't you? This is one of those times I am so jealous that I can't understand you."

I jumped over to the kitchen island where her tablet was and patted it with my paw.

"That's sweet, Wick, but I know how difficult that is for you. I'd only ask you to do that if it was an emergency."

It wasn't, so I jumped back to the table.

That looks really gross, you know. But if you can get Will to eat a bite, I'll give you my allowance this week.

"You will not," Will said as he came back to the kitchen. "I'd try a bite absent the pudding and grapes, otherwise, no."

"Killjoy," Aisha snickered. "Do I get to know what Jay needed?"

"A credit card. He wants to take Zara out for dinner, but the restaurant requires a card to hold a table."

"Uh huh." She scooped up another spoonful. "Just dinner?"

"I assume dessert is involved, as well."

"Dessert. Is that what we're going to refer to it as? Come on, Bilbo. Are those two *finally* going to hook up? He needed it for a hotel, didn't he?"

"Their plans are none of my business."

"Yet you gave him the card."

"Because I know you would not disapprove, yes, I gave him my credit card. He'll reimburse me."

"Like you care if he pays you back."

"I care if I was wrong and you do disapprove."

"You know better. And I'm sorry, but chances are, for the next few months, he's going to have a better sex life than you will." She stuck the spoon into the middle of the ice cream. "You were right, this was gross. I should have gone with my first impulse."

"A little bit of everything in the fridge?"

"Be nice."

Hot chocolate. It's hot chocolate.

Will got up and took the bowl to the sink. "What would you prefer? I'll make it."

"I would prefer wild, hot, screaming sex. I'll settle for hot chocolate."

"I'll make hot chocolate. And sex is not off the table, Enzo. Just not...wild, perhaps."

Her hands went to her belly as he turned to get a pan out of the cabinet.

Dude, she's crying.

He set the pan down and came back around the island, and when he reached for her hand, she stood up and buried her face against his shoulder. "It doesn't have to be hot chocolate. I really will make anything you want."

"This isn't fair to you, Will. I'm huge, and I'm afraid of hurting him, and I know I'm hurting you—"

"You're not hurting me. I swear."

"I wasn't like this with Jay. But dammit, I'm terrified of doing anything to hurt him. I jogged six steps to get to the elevator at school and started crying because what if he bounced off my ribs and bruised? And it's not reasonable, I know it's not."

"Anything you feel is reasonable," he whispered against her hair. "And I understand your restraint. I imagine that at this point an orgasm would feel like an earthquake to him." He pulled back, jerking his hands back and forth, making explosion sounds. "It might be a little disturbing."

She was still crying, but that made her laugh.

"You're tired, and it was a long summer semester. I'm fine, and I will continue to be fine. The only thing that matters to me is you, Jay, and Rhys."

"Rhys," she sighed. "You're already calling him by name."

Jay came out of his room again, this time with a reading tablet in hand. "You okay?" he asked as he dropped it onto the table on his way to get a snack.

"Her ice cream was gross," Will said, to which Jay nodded as if he understood. "I'm making hot chocolate if you'd like some."

Jay saw the pan and snorted, "You're making air."

"And damned fine air it is. Do you want some, or not?"

He said he wanted some, and while Will made that he was making toast because he knew that Aisha liked to dip toast that was dripping with butter into her hot chocolate, which made her start crying all over again.

4

Drew bought a car. He grumbled about it, but he took Will's advice and chose one he could use for years, with space for kids and their assorted junk, and then he reluctantly let Will teach him to drive. Oz had tried, in fits and starts, but his disinterest in doing more than circling the garage drove her nuts, and she gave up. Even with Will, he kept grumbling, until his third lesson, when Will forced him out onto the Great Highway and made him speed up to ride with the flow of traffic.

"I can hire a car to get to work, you know," he said, once he'd maneuvered into the medium-speed lane. "Oz drives, Zed drives, Jay drives. I can convince someone to give me a ride. Taxis exist."

Oz, Will argued, would be spending a considerable amount of time with her father over the next year. Zed and Jay had social lives and school. Drew needed to be able to get himself to the Wastelands and back, but more importantly, Will needed him to be able to drive well enough to handle an emergency.

"Aisha does not drive," Will reminded him. "I don't think I'll ever get her to the point where she's not terrified of the idea."

"And I'm not?"

"Your parents didn't die in a horrific crash. Subconsciously, she's determined to not have a wreck be the reason her children don't have a mother. I know her, Drew, she's also going to worry endlessly when she returns to work, and the baby is with me. Once we open a testing facility in the Wastelands and I have him with me, her days will be nothing but agony over the idea that if something happens, I'll be too distracted to get us home."

"You need me to prove to her I'm a safe enough driver to haul your ass if there's an emergency at home."

Will nodded.

"You're blowing smoke up mine, but all right."

"Truly, I am not. The further she progresses with this pregnancy, the more anxious she is. Knowing you can drive reasonably well is one more assurance, Andrew. Intellectually, she knows that we'll have hired a hundred other people, and someone will be on hand, but she needs to have someone she trusts. Someone who grasps that the baby comes first."

"Before you."

"Indeed. I need that as well. If there's ever a choice to be made, he comes first. And I know you'll honor that."

Baby Rhys comes before me, too. Got it?

"Rhys?" Drew grinned. "Is that his name?"

"After her father. And yes, Wick, we got it. But please don't feel like this is a demotion of sorts."

It's not. It's my baby, too. He comes first.

"Your baby," Drew repeated.

I was there. I kept frogs and bugs and a bunny from jumping on them. So he's mine, too.

"He also believes he's married to Aisha as much as I."

I am.

"Can't argue with the logic, then," Drew said. "All right. I'll take this seriously. Were you serious before? That if I didn't learn now, I wouldn't until I was thirty?"

"Other Drew did not drive until he was thirty. And yes, I have mocked him for it."

"Good. Any chance Oz and I can meet up with them again? I know they can't tell us about our kids or anything, but we really want to know more about why she's dead set on us not giving up the monarchy when the time comes. And, you know, warn us if one of us is going to screw up bad enough that we have issues."

He thought it could be arranged but didn't think there were any marital roadblocks in their way.

"Is it hard?" Drew asked. "Like, knowing us, and knowing them, and knowing that we love you like crazy but we'll be gone before you're born?"

"What makes you think you will be?"

It's a good thing Drew's new car came with the best and newest passive controls available because otherwise, he would have had his first accident.

◆◆◆

Oz would present her idea to the King with the council present, no matter how good or bad an idea it was. Jax wanted her to have the experience. He'd been given several chances to present ideas to the King when he was young, often with Will by his side, and he learned to argue and bargain with them, when to push and when to back off. They'd convinced the council to maintain the woods of the Presidio and around Land's End, and Golden Gate Park was brought into the agreement at the last minute when Will discovered a member of the council had plans to raze part of it over for a housing development that was not needed.

Still, Jax didn't want her to present an idea he was wholly unfamiliar with. If it were reasonable, he would tell her. If he knew it would fall flat, he would be honest but would still require her to present it.

We were in the living room, digesting Sunday dinner—real live fresh dead roast beef with potatoes and enough vegetables to make Will happy—and I was on Jax's lap because he hadn't had enough lap time lately and I felt guilty about that.

"I'll be with her," Will said. Aisha was curled up on the sofa next to him, barely awake. "If you're worried about her nerves—"

"I'm not, and you won't be there. Oz doesn't need a babysitter."

"Yes, I do," she said meekly.

"Just refrain from swearing at them, and you'll be fine. But tell me what you're thinking about, here, while you're just a daughter talking to her father. Once you're in the council hall, it won't be that. I won't treat you like my daughter. You have no standing as the crown princess there."

"Well, make it sound like fun, why don't you?"

She reminded him of the little boy he'd once been, and his dreams of running away to the Wastelands, where there was surely an old western style town, complete with dirt roads and horses tethered to posts outside the saloon. There was enough space in the Wastelands to build that: a centuries-old town, everything built to fit the style of the old west, with hotels hidden behind wooden walls, restaurants serving cowboy-worthy dishes, and employees dressing and acting the part.

"Immerse people in the experience," she said. "Have a town sheriff, a blacksmith, cowboys riding into town and wrap a subtle educational layer around it. Make it dusty and dirty, with everything, down to the music and food served, true to what people perceive of the era."

"You'd need more than that to draw visitors in. That's a one and done vacation. For it to be profitable, you need repeat customers."

"There would have to be a lot to explore," she agreed. "It's more about location. Put in in the middle, where there are massive chunks of undeveloped land surrounding it. The state builds and owns the town, but private developers could buy up the land around it, with use restrictions. It *has* to be a vacation hotspot. A mix of high-end and affordable hotels. Amusement parks. All within an hours' drive to either Las Vegas or Disneyland. That could become the trifecta of vacations—a couple days here, a couple there, then move on to the third. With the right offerings, it could pull a worldwide audience."

He could see it. As she listed the possibilities and all the potential activities within the town itself, his inner six-year-old bubbled to the surface, and by the time she was finished, he was genuinely excited.

"You've researched the property titles and local ordinances to assure it's a viable idea?" he asked.

"Pacifica owns the land. It all comes attached to the old solar farm, which we could use for power. But I think that, too, needs to be renovated. Tear down the old panels and install new. We'd be able to garner ten times as much power without the massive heat buildup."

"Tearing it down has been bandied about for years," Will said. "It's nearly useless as it is, with all but two of the clusters covered."

"It's impractical to go through the expense to replace something that's not being used on land likely to sit idle," Jax said. "Every newly constructed building has its own solar built in. That essentially has made the farm moot."

"It might be necessary, depending on how big this becomes," Oz said. "Renovating the farm will cost billions up front, but over twenty to thirty years will generate a profit. Anything not used in development can be stored and shifted into the power grid and then to other areas in Pacifica and Midlam. It's a job initiative, too. Not just in the building of everything, but running it, staffing it, and maintaining it. New roads and sky lanes will be needed and with that the jobs for laying down the magnets and overlays."

"Bring every shred of research you have," Jax told her. "Present it as if it were a done deal. I suspect the King will be very interested, and where the King shows decided interest, the council listens."

The warehouse buildings dotting the edge of the Wastelands were old, and I was pretty sure that one of them had a slight lean to the left, which didn't seem to bother Will or Drew. Finn was less than certain; he got out of the car and stood in the dirt-covered parking lot and stared at it with his hands on his hips and tilted his head to match the degree of lean.

Will hadn't wanted to come, not on this day. He wanted to be at city hall, standing by Oz as she gave her presentation, but Jax made it clear that not only would he be barred from the council hall, he would be denied entry into the building.

"Give her this, Will," Jax said on his way out the door. "If she convinces them, it's her victory. If she doesn't, she's tough enough to stand the disappointment and it's a lesson learned."

That didn't keep Will from wanting to be there to stare down the council for her. He got into Drew's car reluctantly and grumbled under his breath.

"Isn't this what you wanted when Jax was in her shoes?" Drew asked as he started the car. "To be slowly eased into the job instead of dropped into it?"

It didn't matter. He felt like he should be there with her.

"I let you leave to be on your own when you were three years younger than she is," Finn reminded Will. "She's twenty now. That's approximately thirty-two in Will years."

"Ah, bite me." He pointed straight ahead and told Drew to head toward the Bay Bridge, engage the lifters in five seconds, and then bring the car to speed as quickly as possible. We were taking the sky lane to the left of the bridge, far enough away that plowing into it wasn't a worry. Still, Drew looked a little green when the lifters powered up, but he didn't hesitate when it was time to accelerate, and once we were at speed, he relaxed and grinned.

He stayed relaxed until we were a few miles out, and only tensed up a little bit when it was time to slow down and re-enter the flow of traffic. There were few cars on the road approaching the Wastelands, but this was the first time he'd gone above the flow, and he worried he would land on top of a car carrying kids or elderly nuns.

"Passive controls are engaged," Will reminded him. "An attempt to enter the traffic flow too close to another vehicle will result in your car maintaining height until it's safe to descend."

Once on the ground, his brain shifted gears quickly. He noted the same thing that seemed to trouble Finn—the leaning warehouse of the Wastelands—but wasn't bothered by it. They were leasing the one three spaces over because it was nearly ready for use and was already hooked into a power supply.

"Three weeks, and the other building will be upright and safe," Will told Finn. "It's also deep enough to lay out a track. If you're interested."

"For?"

"First step in cargo transporting. Give up the bowling balls, Dad. There's space here for a tracked gate."

"That would require transponders."

"Then do that. But be the first to use a transporter, regardless of how."

He argued that it was cheating; he wanted a point-to-point transporter that worked on its own. The objective was to eventually be able to send anything to any other location in the world, not piggyback off portal technology.

"It's a step," Drew said. "Do it that way and then maybe your way will flesh itself out."

Finn had more to argue about but was cut off by the whine of a car overhead. It shifted and landed ten feet away, and when the door opened, Will groaned.

"There's no portal here," he told Vicat. "Go home."

"No portal *yet*," she said. "Where Dr. Blackshear goes, new portals tend to follow. And I admit, I'd like to see that happen. I can hear them, but I'd like to see one."

"You can hear them."

"I hear bacon sizzling. I assume it's the portal I'm standing in front of and not that I imagine it."

She must have cat ears.

"The portals have sound for a reason," he reminded me. "It's subtle, but anyone paying attention can hear."

"Sounds like hair in a candle flame to me," Drew said.

"And unimportant. We're not opening a portal here today. We're here to inspect a new workspace for Ozoo Enterprises. Nothing more."

"Without any of your guards," she said.

Drew glanced over his shoulder. "Um, yeah, I didn't tell anyone we were coming out here. Why didn't anyone follow?"

Will assured him that if he signaled, his guards would appear. "And she knows that."

"You're exposed with no visible means of protection," she said. "Regulations—"

"Regulations were crafted to allow the royal offspring a modicum of normal life, without the perception of constant supervision. Only the King and Queen are required to have visible security when outside their home. You should be aware of this."

"I have a different understanding of the written rules," she said. "I can quote—"

"And you will not." He gestured to the warehouse and began walking. "However, you're here, you might as well take the tour and see for yourself that there's nothing to see."

There was nothing for her to see, but plenty to get Drew excited. The building was ancient, yet everything he hoped for. The front half was multi-leveled with large offices and a lobby, and the back half was open space with a ceiling that peaked and made him crane his neck all the way back to take it all in. Everything echoed in here; footsteps, breathing, and my meow sounded like Fluffy on steroids. Will set me down but told me to stay close because he didn't know if there were vermin inside, and two minutes later told me that I had tested the echoing out enough and to please be quiet.

"In the front left is where the deep freeze unit will be," he told Drew, using his hands to draw a picture in the air. "You'll have three times the floor space that you currently occupy, which will give you enough square footage to expand the number of computer clusters in the array as you increase capacity."

"Amazing," Drew breathed.

"To the right, a lab for work with nanobot development and technology expansion. And to the back, your space for the chemists who will consult in development of the gel. When construction is done and everything in place, we'll need to have a minimum of fifty employees ready to go."

"How many once it's fully running?"

"At least a hundred," Finn said. "But at some point, you're going to have a thousand or more. Getting the systems for Elysium on point will require a number of people high enough to make you want to wet yourself."

"Experience?" Drew asked, chuckling.

"When construction started on the portal tunnel, I had no idea what I was in for, and I wasn't starting from scratch. It became overwhelming quickly. That's partly why I kept the lab and the few people allowed in. It made the endeavor feel less intimidating. You might want to keep space close to home and limit access to it. Just for yourself."

They'd already planned on leaving the workshop. Arrangements had been made to move Oz's dojo equipment from the second story to the multi-purpose room on the eighth floor at home. Most of Drew's equipment had been boxed and taken to storage, leaving him with only rudimentary things to tinker with.

"We only have the building until the end of the year," Will said. "The space has been leased."

Finn took a few steps, turning to take in the enormity of the space. "Are the other buildings as big?"

"The one that leans is bigger," Will said. "It runs deeper."

Finn turned to Drew. "I like the idea of more space to test the transporters. If I take it, I'll have an entire lab level there for you to use. It's secure space and as private as you'd like it to be. All my technicians are vetted and will leave your work alone."

Unless you merge your stuff with Drew's, and then you can share everything.

"What was that, Wick?" Drew asked.

Merge. You're going to consult a lot, anyway.

"I have a number of government contracts," Finn said. "I'm not sure how well privatizing will work."

"Dad, we'll have the government poking into everything we do. We've applied for the patents, and once those are secure, Anthony Myers wants an official look. Ozoo Enterprises will provide a considerable amount of tech to the government. I don't think it will be a problem. But don't feel pressured. We can work together without being part of each other's companies."

Finn laughed. "I don't have a company here, I have a few licenses. Just enough to allow me to apply for grants."

"Will seems to have access to a lot of cool stuff," Drew said.

Will nodded. "To be fair, so does he."

At the same time I heard a loud popping noise behind us, Will's head turned and Vicat's hand went to her sidearm. They stepped between the noise and Finn and Drew, with Vicat taking a few cautious steps forward. When a creak echoed around us, followed by distinct footsteps, she let out a sound that hurt my ears and made my furs stand on end, and within seconds Drew's and Will's guards ran in.

"Get Wick," Will ordered Drew.

He scooped me up and shoved me inside his sweatshirt, which wasn't one that Aubrey had made for him to carry me in. He zipped it up part way and held me close as Will directed them toward the front door, and he didn't ease up until we were standing in the middle of the parking lot where Will warned him from going too close to the car.

Vicat stood between us and the warehouse, gun in hand.

"You knew the guards were truly with us, then," Will surmised.

"I was not informed," she said, not taking her eyes off the building. "I took you at your word."

"What the hell was that noise you made?" Drew asked.

"An alert to search," she said. "Might be nothing."

"Might be a giant rat," Finn mused.

"Rats, coyotes, mountain lion, fox, armed intruder," she said. "Take your pick. I'll be happy if it's just a hungry little bobcat."

It was not a bobcat.

A few minutes later, a guard from inside made a noise not unlike the one Vicat had nearly destroyed my eardrums with, and she stepped back, her arms held out from her sides as if to protect us. There was nothing she could do if someone were about to fire a rifle at any one of us, but she was ready to take the first shot.

"They found someone," Will said for Finn and Drew's benefit.

"Still could be nothing. Vagrants use outbuildings for shelter all the time." Her stance stiffened as the door popped open and one of the guards came out. Behind him, escorted by another guard, arms pinned painfully to his own back, was a short, thin, dirt-encrusted man with a matted beard and choppy haircut. His clothes were dirtier than his flesh, worn at the knees and sticking to his skin in places, and when they were close, he dropped to his knees.

"Don't force him down like that," Will said to the guard. "Help him up."

A guard on either side grabbed him by the arms and lifted. Will took a step closer, his eyes narrowing. "You look familiar. I know you."

"Nuh," the man grunted.

"He kinda looks like Red," Drew said.

At that, the man jerked his head up. "You know Red?"

"More importantly," Will said, "do you? Who are you?"

"Hyrum. Is Red okay?"

Drew started to say something, but Will held his hand up to stop him. "Why are you here?"

"Sleeping." He answered as if it were obvious. "Do you have any water? I'm really thirsty."

"I can arrange that," Will said. "I need a better explanation first. Why are you here, specifically? Where are you from, and where are you going?"

"Pacifica," he answered, confused. "To see the Queen. To warn her about Daddy."

"What?" Drew sputtered.

"Daddy. He wants to kill the prince. Then he's going to kill Red." His voice wavered. "He's going to kill them all."

Will turned to Drew. "Hyrum Munson, Levi's middle son."

"I'm Hyrum!" he agreed enthusiastically. "I need to get to Pacifica. Can you get me there? I need to see the Queen."

5

With assurances that he was, in fact, in Pacifica, and a promised that once he was seated in the guard's air van Will would have cold water and a snack for him, Hyrum Munson climbed into the back seat and sighed loud enough that I heard him from fifteen feet away. It sounded like relief wrapped around exhaustion, with tinges of excitement that he was going to see the Queen. Will stood at the car door, and after he'd handed two bottles of water and a snack pack filled with cheese and crackers to Hyrum, he outlined what Hyrum could expect: he was not going to see the Queen immediately, but would be taken somewhere to get cleaned up, where he would be provided with clean clothing and a shower, and where he would be fed a full meal. While he was doing that, Will said he would call the Queen and she would be available once he was done.

"You know the Queen?" Hyrum asked.

"I know her well."

"Is she your friend?" he asked, hopeful.

"We're close friends. She'll be pleased to see you, Hyrum."

He asked Vicat to ride with him and directed another guard to bring her car back, then climbed into Drew's car.

Finn took the controls on the way home. Drew was too distracted, and Will needed to contact Jax before the guard did. He sat in the back seat with me and made several calls, one to warn Jax what was happening, and then to Mass because he wanted Hyrum to be seen by a doctor before he was exposed to anyone else.

Jax asked him to not call Aubrey; he was done at city hall and would go home to get her, but he didn't want her to hear about her brother on the phone.

Mass didn't flinch at the sight of Hyrum, and he didn't react to the smell that slapped at him the moment he entered the room. He greeted him like he'd been a patient of his for years, and when Hyrum asked if Will could stay while he was examined, Mass pulled a chair out of the corner and told him to get comfortable. Guards remained in the room, near the door; their presence upset Hyrum, until he was promised that the only people in the room would be men and they would respect his privacy. Vicat waited in the hall, without objecting to her gender being an issue for him.

The exam took half an hour, and Hyrum was quiet and still through the whole thing. He was keenly interested in all the equipment and flinched once or twice when Mass touched him with something cold, but he didn't say another word until Mass told him they were done.

"Was I good?" he asked Mass.

"Very good, thank you. I'm sorry if the cold instruments bothered you."

Hyrum grinned and bobbed his head enthusiastically when Mass asked him to stay on the exam table for a few more minutes.

"He's malnourished," Mass told Will. "There are several spots of skin cancer on his arms and his neck, but we'll take care of that before he's released. He mostly needs good food and rest. A significant amount of each."

And a shower.

"Can I see the Queen now?" He sounded like a child asking for mommy; he sat up and dangled his legs over the side of the table, rocking his feet back and forth. "It's important."

Before Will could answer, the door slammed open and she was there. Aubrey bolted across the room, her brother's name strangled in tears, and she reached for him. The grime, the matted hair and beard, and the smell didn't register with her; she scooped him into a tight hug and held onto him, crying.

Jax was a few steps behind her. He waited at the door for a moment, whispering to her personal guards to stick close but to give them space.

"How much has he told you?" Jax quietly asked Will. "I called Red. Hyrum's been missing for two years. Two damned years and no one said a thing. Every time she asked about him she was told he was out or he was busy."

"He's made repeated requests to see Aubrey.

He says that he needs to warn her about Levi and his plans to kill the prince, and his intention to then kill Red."

"That was two years ago, Will."

"I know. He is not aware that his father is gone, and I didn't feel it would be appropriate to tell him."

Jax nodded, and then went to them. He gently pulled Aubrey away from Hyrum and asked for an introduction, tolerating with amusement when Hyrum twitched back a few steps and then bowed to him. Will picked me up and we left the room because he thought this was private and not for our entertainment.

He groaned a little when he spotted Vicat. "You don't need to be here," he said.

She gave a light shrug. "There's a portal nearby. Maybe I do."

With a heavy sigh, he gestured to the waiting area chairs and sat down. "You know better," he told her. "I will not access a portal until after the birth of my son. I realize that the King is amused by having you stand in my way, but unless there's an emergency, I will not use one."

"Yeah, I know."

"Then why?"

"Just doing my job, Emperor. I don't get to decide if my orders are serious or not. Until the King orders me to leave you alone, I'll keep doing what I was told."

"Fine. You owe the prince a bottle of Rage, and I expect it will be returned or replaced. It's not your job to monitor the activities of the royal children."

"Of course, it is. If they're about to do something stupid and I can stop it, I will. I'm sworn to protect the family, Emperor. That's you, your wife and kids, the crown princess and her brother, *and* Prince Andrew. My actual assignment is irrelevant."

"He's old enough to possess a bottle of alcohol, Vicat."

She leaned away from him a touch. "Rage. You know that crap is loaded with ethylene and propylene glycol, right? It's popular with kids because it's cheap, but half of them wind up in the ER and some of those kids wind up dead. It's pure shit and is *not* legal to possess. You should know that."

"I've seen it for sale in—"

"You've seen its big brother, Liquid Rage. Not the same stuff. I don't care if I pissed off the prince, Emperor. He's not getting that bottle back. Ten minutes after I took it, the contents went down the drain, and the bottle went to recycling."

Dude, she's got you.

Will nodded. "Indeed. Then, please, accept my thanks. I'll have a discussion with Andrew."

"Don't make me sound nice. He calls me 'mean lady.' I like that." She got out of the chair. "Am I dismissed? I'd really like to get some food."

"I'm not your superior. Do what you want."

"Good. Stay away from the portal. I need a couple hours to myself."

She's pushy.

"Indeed."

Kinda reminds me of you.

"Stop it."

You used to take Drew's things, too. Just saying.

"Will." Jax was at the doorway, beckoning him in. "He keeps asking where you are. Aubrey thinks he'll be happier if you're in here."

Hyrum was sitting on the exam table again, swinging his legs back and forth, and when he saw Will he smiled. Aubrey stood next to him, holding his hand, trying to soothe herself as much as she was trying to keep him calm. As soon as Will walked in, they both visibly relaxed.

"Water man!" Hyrum beamed. "I was hungry, and he got me food. I was thirsty, and he got me water. I was a stranger, and he took me in."

"Book of Matthew," Aubrey said gently, impressed.

"Did I say it right?"

"You said it perfectly. It's not the exact words that matter, Hyrum. It's how you mean them."

A cloud of confusion brushed across his face. "Daddy hates it when I say it different, you know that. Daddy said, 'Don't be *stupid*, Hyrum! Say it the *right* way!' I can't remember all the words, Aubrey. I try but they don't stick."

"Sweetie, you said it exactly the way I wanted to hear it. I'm proud of you for remembering that quote."

"Red gave me a bible with pictures!" He lowered his voice, whispering, "But we can't tell

Daddy. I know that's a sin, but I remember things better when I have a picture. I can't read good, but a picture helps me."

Mass stepped up to Jax's side and whispered to him. "Look at the screen over his shoulder. There are poorly healed bone breaks all over his body. And the brain scan shows a hell of a lot of damage. He didn't get any of that playing sports."

Jax was not surprised. "Hyrum did not meet his father's expectations. He was only six or seven when Aubrey left home. God only knows what happened to him after that."

"God and me," Mass said. "We're looking at four decades of abuse on those scans, minimum. Prenatal injury to his brain. That was done to him, Jax, it wasn't a naturally occurring matter of his birth."

"We need to get him cleaned up," Jax said. "Without letting him look in a mirror. I imagine he has no idea how rough he looks, and not knowing his frame of mind?"

"I'll make a call. We'll take care of it." He hesitated. "He's an adult, but I'll feel better if you take official responsibility for him. He'll need an analgesic patch before you stick him in a bathtub. Without it? His skin is raw. It'll hurt. But I won't medicate him without permission."

Jax nodded. "Aubrey and I will act as his guardians."

They led him down to the pediatric floor, where there was a large bathroom with a deep, wide bathtub. The mirrors had been covered with sheets and medical tape, and when he asked why, Aubrey told Hyrum that the room was too bright with lights reflecting off the mirrors, and the sheets would come off when everyone had adjusted to the light. She shooed everyone out, including the guard, and only relented to someone else being there when Hyrum asked if Will could stay.

"He's a boy, too," he whispered loudly. "Mom would say it's okay. He's the Water Man."

"What would Mom say about me staying while you took a bath?"

"You're my sister. That's like being a girl but different."

Will sat in a small plastic chair near the door. It was meant for someone half his size, and his knees came up to his chest, but he didn't mind and kept me perched on his shoulder.

While Aubrey filled the tub, Hyrum tugged at his clothes, wincing when he had to tear fabric away from places where it stuck to flesh, and when he was down to his underwear he started to cry.

"Do you need me to leave, sweetie?" she asked.

"No." He showed her the palm of his hand and rubbed at a streak of dirt that cut across it. "Am I in trouble? If Daddy sees how dirty I am, I'm getting a spanking. He hits *hard* now, Aubrey. I don't want a spanking."

"Daddy's not here," she said gently. "No one is spanking you, I promise. Do you remember the man who was with me, Jax? He's the King of Pacifica. He won't let anyone hurt you."

"You're the Queen."

"I am. He's my husband. Did someone tell you that?" When it was clear he wasn't going to, she pulled his underwear off the rest of the way and guided him into the tub. "You were just a little boy when I left. I don't know how much you know about me."

"Mom told me. She said 'Hyrum, I've got a secret for you.' And I promised I wouldn't tell anyone, but I think Red knows because he's smart and knows important people. And then she showed me pictures of you because you're a grown up now and I wouldn't know you, and said she needed me to go find you because no one else would be able to get as close to you as I could." He giggled when she poured warm water over his shoulders, and then leaned into her hands. "Did I do a good job? It took days and days, but I found you."

"You did the best job, sweetie. Mom was right. No one else could have gotten this close. Not even Red."

"Is Red okay? Daddy wants to kill him. Mom said so."

"Red is fine," she said. "I promise. I talked to him just a little while ago. Did Mom tell you why Daddy wants Red dead?"

Hyrum slapped at the water with his open hand. "Because he's weak! He never should have been anointed, and he has to die so Daddy can ask Jesus to pick a new second minister." His breath shuttered, and I felt Will stiffen, ready to spring if Hyrum looked like he was going to hit Aubrey next. "Daddy's a bad man. He's *wrong*. Red isn't weak. He's just nice."

"I know, sweetheart. Red saved my life when I was a girl, did you know that?"

He nodded. "I'm not supposed to tell anyone. Red got lots of money from Mom that she saved without telling Daddy about it, and he gave it to Aubrey so that she could run away where Daddy could never touch her again. Did you do that?"

"I did. Red made sure I got all the way to San Francisco, and Daddy never touched me again."

"Then you became a princess and now you're the Queen!"

"Just like that!" she said, laughing with him. "But you know what? I met Will before I met Jax."

"Water Man?"

"We just call him Will. We met in a coffee shop, and he told me he had a friend I would love. And he was right."

"His friend was Jack?"

"Jax. It's short for Jackson."

"Is he going to like me? I don't think he likes me."

She sat on the edge of the tub. "What makes you think that?"

"Because the first thing he wanted was to make me take a bath. Just like Mom. 'Oh, you stink, Hyrum! Get in that bathtub right now! We could grow potatoes on you!'"

"That sounds just like her," Aubrey snickered. "I promise, Jax only wanted you to have a bath because he thought you would feel better after.

When he gets sweaty and dirty, he always feels better after he's had a bath or a shower."

Hyrum looked down at the water. "I don't think I'm clean yet. I made some dirt soup." He giggled and scooped water in his hand and held it out to her. "Hungry?"

"I think I'll wait for dinner, sweetie." She drained and refilled the tub, and they were quiet for the rest of his bath. She scrubbed him until his pink showed, and then helped him wash his hair and beard, and when that was done she asked him if he wanted to keep it, or if he wanted to shave it off.

"Men have beards," he said. "Except Red. His wife doesn't like beards, and he likes her, so he shaves his off."

"You can keep it. Maybe we'll just trim it a bit?"

He shook his head. "I'm not a man. I'm still a boy. Mom said so. I'll always be her boy."

"All right. Then we'll shave it off." She tucked a towel under his chin and started to trim it until he flinched.

"Beards are for men. You're a girl."

She didn't know what to do, but she wasn't handing him the scissors. Will set me down and got up, and asked Hyrum if he would be more comfortable if he helped instead. Hyrum nodded enthusiastically, which made Aubrey chuckle as she handed the scissors to Will.

"I can soap that boy up and wash every inch of him, but the horror of me cutting his beard."

"You're not a boy!" Hyrum insisted. "You're a girl!"

"She's a woman," Will corrected as he knelt next to the tub. "She's also a wife and a mother and is only trying to help you. She loves you. She's not trying to upset you."

"Aubrey is a mother?" His voice was a loud whisper, something I suspected he did a lot of. "That means she—" he giggled "—you know."

"I heard that, Hyrum," she said from across the room.

He was still giggling and didn't care.

Once Will had trimmed his beard enough to shave, he held the razor out for Hyrum to see. "This is probably different than what you usually use. There's not a blade in it, so nothing can cut you. It's just a bright light—" he flicked it on and set a hand on Hyrum's shoulder when he flinched "—and it will feel warm but not hot. It can't hurt you, all right?"

"You do it to you first."

"All right." Will held his arm out, and ran the razor over his forearm, neatly shaving a wide line from elbow to wrist. "See? It's fine."

Hyrum rubbed a finger over Will's arm and then nodded. "If I say ouch you have to stop, okay?"

"I promise."

Hyrum barely breathed as Will shaved him. He closed his eyes once and whimpered when Will had the razor on his neck, but he held still until Will turned it off and then asked if he wanted the shower for a minute to get all the little hairs that bite off.

"That's what they do! They bite! No one else believes me!" He stood up and nodded, allowing Will to rinse him off with the shower hose. Aubrey brought a giant towel over and told him to dry himself off, and then patted a stack of hospital clothes that he could wear.

Hyrum looked at them suspiciously. "I don't want someone else's underwear. That's gross."

"They're new, I promise," she said. When he scowled, she added, "I wouldn't lie to you, Hyrum."

"Okay. Can I see myself?" He pointed to the sheets covering the mirrors. "I can see okay now. The light doesn't hurt."

Once he was dressed, Will pulled the sheets off and shoved them into a hamper. Hyrum rooted in front of the mirror, touching his face, frowning.

"That's not me. He's skinny."

Aubrey stepped next to him, slipping her arm around his shoulders. "You lost some weight on your trip, Hy. You walked a very long way. Over two thousand miles."

"I look old, Aubrey."

"You look handsome. You know, the last time I saw you, you were a little boy with cherry popsicle all over your face, and you were arguing with Ruth over her doll. I've missed you so much."

He wound the front of his shirt through his fingers and stared down at them. "Why'd you leave? You didn't say goodbye. Mom said Red was saving your life, but you didn't say goodbye."

"Goodbye sounds like forever," she said. "I didn't want it to be forever, sweetheart. If I didn't say goodbye, that meant I would see you again. And here you are. My perfect, wonderful baby brother."

"Don't let Daddy kill anyone," he whispered. "If Daddy kills someone then he's going to Hell."

"Red is fine," she reminded him. "The Prince is fine. Mom is fine, too. In fact, I think she's coming here to see you because she misses you. You've been gone from home for a long time."

"I need a cheeseburger, Aubrey," he said, still whispering. "I'm too skinny. I don't want her to see me skinny. She'll cry."

"Oh, angel, she's going to cry no matter what. That's what moms do when they see their boys after a long time. It doesn't mean she's sad, it only means that she loves you."

"Okay. Can I still have a cheeseburger?"

"Anything you want."

"I don't want peanut butter."

"Then no peanut butter."

"Fries?"

She nodded.

"Beer?" He giggled and pulled away from her.

"Now you're pushing it. How about a soft drink?"

"Root beer?"

"Root beer."

He looked at Will. "I like you a lot, but I like root beer more."

"As one would."

I rode on Will's shoulder to the cafeteria, where Hyrum sat at a round table with Jax and Aubrey, oblivious to the armed guards surrounding them, oblivious to the idea that if he made one wrong move toward Aubrey, the Water Man would slam him to the floor without so much as a second thought.

6

Lacking high-speed transportation and not wanting to take the time to drive a car requiring gasoline, Red and his mother waited for Jax to send a shuttle from Pacifica. Hyrum was kept on the pediatric floor of the hospital because there were things for him to do that wouldn't overwhelm him, and he was allowed to watch cartoons in the playroom. While Jax helped him find one he liked, Aubrey quietly picked up all the crayons and markers and handed them to a guard, asking him to take them to the nurse's station.

"He eats crayons," she whispered to Will. "Give him the markers, and we'll be scrubbing ink off him for the next week."

"Perhaps he's outgrown that," Will suggested.

"Will, he hasn't outgrown anything. He'll be eight years old forever, with tendencies towards four and five. You have no idea—" Her hand went to her mouth for a moment. "He's so much more verbal than I would have ever hoped. Yet he's still so much himself that I have no idea how he survived walking all this way."

"He may have had help."

"We asked him. He says the only time he interacted with others was when he ventured into convenience stores, and a few random encounters at rest stops. I think he was avoiding people."

Sounds familiar.

When I spoke, Hyrum spun around on the sofa to look. "Water Will, can I pet your cat?"

Will nodded, but Aubrey held him back. "Hy, you have to be very gentle with Wick, all right? He's tiny and could be easily hurt."

"I want to pet him not eat him."

It's okay.

Jax got up and gave his spot to Will. He tapped his leg on the side away from Hyrum, which meant he wanted me to stay on his lap. Hyrum reached over and carefully set his fingers on my head, and carefully stroked my fur.

"He's soft like Lazybones."

"Who's that?" Will asked.

"My cat. I had a cat when I was little until I was twenty-three. Mom said he was a lazy bag of bones."

Aubrey leaned over the back of the sofa. "Did Daddy like him?"

Hyrum nodded. "Lazybones hunted mice and snakes and that made him a good boy." He bent toward me, his breath moist on my ears. "Don't eat mice. They taste bad."

"You didn't," Aubrey chortled.

"I wanted to be a good boy, too. Daddy just looked and said, 'Well, I bet you won't make that mistake again.' And I didn't." He leaned back, resting his head on the back of the sofa, where he could see Aubrey, and yawned. "What time is it? I lost my watch. Don't tell Daddy."

"I won't tell anyone," she said. "It's eight o'clock. Are you sleepy?"

"Bedtime is nine."

"But are you sleepy?"

He nodded. "Can I sleep in a real bed? I'm tired of sleeping on the ground. There are bitey bugs on the ground."

She assured him there was a comfortable bed waiting for him just down the hall, with its own bathroom and an entertainment monitor. He looked confused and crinkled his nose.

"A TV, Hyrum. You can watch cartoons in bed if you want."

"Oh no," he said as he got up. "That's not allowed, Daddy said so. Who do I have to sleep with? Do we get our own beds?"

She led him to the room and opened the door, expecting him to be happy with his private room. Instead, he stepped in and whimpered, trying not to cry. "I don't want to be alone again. I miss sleeping with Spencer. He always told me stories and he took the bed under the window so I didn't have to anymore. I was sad when he moved away. Then Joseph moved, too."

"Jax?" She looked at him helplessly. "Can we get another bed in here?"

Before he could answer, Hyrum asked if Will could stay. She started to argue against it— Will needed to get home to his wife, and I needed food—but Will thought Aisha would be fine if he stayed the night with Hyrum, and surely someone would go get food for me. No one suggested that I go home with them; they knew better.

"Litter box?" Jax asked.

"Toilet. He knows how to use one. It's awkward, but he manages."

A bed was rolled in and placed near Hyrum's, though Will told Jax he would stay awake in case Hyrum needed something. While Hyrum played with the remote to the monitor, trying to decide if he wanted to be naughty and turn it on or not, they stayed in the doorway, speaking in near whispers, hoping he would stay focused on the TV and not them.

Jax looked over Will's shoulder and then at Aubrey. "I hate even thinking about this, Will, but it you get the chance..."

Will nodded.

"Without being intrusive," Aubrey said. "Please. I only want to know what he's feeling and what happened to him over the last two years."

"The hell with that," Jax said. "I want to know what Levi did to him. I also want to know how much we can tell him. How much can he take?"

"I'll use my judgment," Will said.

She didn't want to leave. This wasn't just family visiting on a whim; he had crossed over two thousand miles to get to her and leaving felt like abandonment.

You're not sleeping anyway, dude. Give her the bed, and you can keep watch in a chair.

Jax knew better than to argue. Aubrey gave him a kiss and then went into Hyrum's room, and he watched her, sighing. "Dig deep if you have to, Will. Make sure there's not another reason for him to be here."

An hour after Jax left, after Hyrum and Aubrey had time to cuddle and share bedtime stories, Will set his pointy finger on Hyrum's forehead and put him to sleep. Aubrey's mouth slacked open, and she started to protest, but laughed instead when Will said, "Like you wouldn't have done several illegal things to have that skill Oz was a toddler."

"As long as he's just sleeping."

"Sleep only. And if he wakes during the night, I can repeat it."

"Does that work on adults?"

"Do you want it to?"

She curled up on the bed and watched her younger brother sleep, so focused on each breath he took that within twenty minutes, she drifted off, too. Will waited over an hour, making sure they were both deeply asleep before he moved to the other side of Hyrum's bed and placed his hand on his forehead.

I watched from the foot of Aubrey's bed, not daring to move, not even when Will's shoulders slumped, and tears rolled down his cheeks.

◆◆◆

Aubrey stirred before dawn; she stayed in bed and watched Hyrum sleep, until Will shifted in his chair and she remembered that she wasn't alone with her younger brother. After she pulled the blanket up to Hyrum's chest and kissed his forehead, she nodded toward the door, silently asking Will to go with her.

At five in the morning, Aubrey was decidedly un-regal and didn't give a damn. She leaned against the wall by the door and sighed, pulling her arms tight to her stomach. "Did you sleep at all?"

"No, and before you get upset, I am fine with no sleep for a night or two."

"Did he wake up?"

Will nodded. "Once. He needed to use the restroom and was asleep again within seconds."

"With help?"

"He's exhausted, Aubrey. Help or not, he needs the sleep. I made a judgment call—"

"I don't mind, Will, I was only curious. And thank you for taking care of him. If it had been any other of my siblings, I'd be less stressed about how calm they were...how calm he is. Hyrum is special. He's my biggest regret about leaving home. The thing I feel the most guilt over."

"He seems happy," Will said.

"Even when the worst was happening, he was happy. He just wants to be sure he's being good. If you tell him he is, he'll be the happiest person you've ever met." She ran fingers through her hair, trying to tame it. "Did you listen to him at all last night? Any idea where he's been?"

Hyrum left home just before the war started. He set out with a detailed map and, he was told, plenty of cash to get him across Midlam into Pacifica, and he had several pictures of things that his mother had told him were safe to eat. She sent him with plastic cutlery and instructions to only drink bottled water or water from a fountain, and if he wasn't sure what to eat, he could buy bread and peanut butter along the way.

He was supposed to follow the old Interstate route that ran in a nearly straight line from the Tennessee border with Florida to California, but along the way the numbers jumbled in his mind, and he couldn't remember that the road he wanted was I-40. All he was sure about was the letter 'I,' so he picked the next one and followed that until he hit cold and snow and decided that was the devil's work, and the Queen would not be where the devil was.

Eventually, he made his way south again to I-80 and then I-15, which sounded more correct to him, so he followed it a short distance until he lost sight of the road and had run out of food and water and couldn't find a store. He found the solar farm and then the warehouse buildings north of it, and stayed there for three days, licking water from plants he found outside and praying that he would find bread or peanut butter.

Will didn't tell her about his terror. He'd been constantly afraid from the moment he left home and felt overwhelming shame and guilt for things he'd had to do along the way. Taking care of basic biological needs had confounded him until he realized he had no choice, but relieving himself outdoors was something his father would have beaten him over, and he was embarrassed.

There were a hundred things Will didn't tell her; it wouldn't do any good for her to know the abuse he endured after she left, and how ashamed he was of it.

"He doesn't know about the war, and certainly nothing about your father's death. He's been consumed with finding the Queen—and you should know that in his head, Aubrey and the Queen are separate things, even though he understands that you are both his sister and the Queen. I can't explain it."

"Our mother must have stressed that it was the Queen he needed to find. That's something he would latch onto."

"His internal dialog is quite a bit more mature than I expected. His memory is nearly eidetic, at least in terms of who said what. I sensed quite a bit of mimicry in him."

Aubrey nodded. "'Daddy said,'" she sighed. "Of all the places he could have stopped. I know you don't believe in God, Will, but I can't help but think Hyrum was led there because it was where you would find him."

"I won't dismiss the possibility."

They turned at the sound of footsteps down the hallway. Two of Jax's guards were heading toward us, with Jax and Red Munson trailing, along with Red's youngest daughter, Bree. When she saw Aubrey, she began to run, and the only thing that kept her from squealing Aubrey's name was Will's stern look and the finger he put to his lips.

Aubrey picked her up in a tight hug and gave her a kiss.

"Is Uncle Hyrum in there?" Bree whispered. "I miss him."

"He's here, sweetie." She leaned forward to give Red a kiss, and then Jax. "He's asleep right now."

"Can I sit with him? I'll be quiet. Daddy said he might be calmer if I was here."

Red nodded. "He and Bree are friends as much as they are relatives. If he wakes up, he'll be happy to see her."

Aubrey reminded her to be quiet, and let her in the room, watching as Bree settled into the chair Will spent the night in.

"I had no idea," Red said, before Aubrey could get a word out. "He'd been gone for at least two weeks before I was told he was missing. David had people out looking for him—"

"Our mother sent him," Aubrey said. "Surely she told you *something*."

He shook his head. "She was the properly distraught mother whose child wandered away. I never even suspected."

"Where is she?"

"She balked at the last minute and refused to get on the shuttle. She said she couldn't see him like this, but the truth? I think she's afraid of what you'll do to her."

Icily, "She should be."

"Not now," Jax urged. "We can pick apart the reasons he's here later."

If there was anything left to discuss, it was shoved aside when Hyrum said loudly, "You can't come in. You're a *girl*," and Bree shot back, "I wasn't going to *watch*, doofus."

Red started to go in, until Aubrey put her hand on his chest. "He doesn't know Levi is dead. Don't tell him, not yet."

They left Jax and Will in the hallway, and Will pulled the door closed to give them privacy. He nodded toward the waiting room three doors down and when the guards started to follow, Will told one of them to stay outside Hyrum's room.

"I have no idea what ultimately caused Hyrum to be the way he is," Will said when Jax was seated, "but he is remarkable. Aubrey was correct when she said he was virtually stuck at eight years old, but his vocabulary far exceeds that, and his thought processes are quite mature. He has a sense of logic I did not expect, and he knows more than he thinks he does."

"Levi beat the hell out of that kid on a regular basis." Jax's jaw twitched. "From the time he was able to speak, Levi hit and kicked him."

Will nodded. The abuse went far beyond that, clouding Hyrum's earliest memories. Will caught glimpses of him being pushed down the stairs when he was a toddler, beatings he endured for not being able to recite bible passages correctly, and for leaving a single pea on his plate. Levi punched him in the head repeatedly when he had difficulty with potty training, and once threw him out a window for the crime of being fourteen and utterly normal.

"He'd been asleep." Will's voice was thick. "Levi stormed into the bedroom, realized Hyrum was dreaming and aroused, and shoved him out the bedroom window. The only thing that saved him from significant injury was a fabric patio covering."

None of it surprised Jax. He'd known, from a few days into knowing Aubrey, that the Munson children were beaten for the hell of it.

Will sighed hard, leaning his head back against the wall behind him. "That's not the worst of it, Jax. When Aubrey left—"

"Oh, Jesus, no."

"Swirling around those memories is the same thing: 'Daddy said not to tell.' I saw nothing to indicate that anyone else knows what Levi really did to him. They knew he was beaten, perhaps a bit more than they were, but no one else knows... that."

Jax buried his face in his hands. His voice was muffled when he said, "We can't even kill the bastard for this. He got off too damned easy."

"Blame Russia," Will said.

"Yeah, maybe not." With another sigh, Jax looked up. "Dad's been getting a lot of backchannel chatter. Florida might not have wanted him for trial, but they sure as hell wanted him for execution."

That made Will sit up straight. "*Red* ordered it?"

"It was most likely the Quorum. Red's own apostles."

"What's the end game in that? Execute Levi for crimes against his church? Or did they want him out all along?"

Jax wasn't sure, but Eli was paying attention to the Quorum's activities in soliciting votes that would gain Florida admission to the Consortium. While he trusted Red, Eli didn't trust the apostles or their representatives, save one; he said it felt amiss, a thread of frigid wind snaking through a hot room, and unless he was off by a mile, the Church of Florida was looking to expand.

7

If he was disappointed that his mother did not come with Red and Bree, Hyrum hid it well. He bubbled with joy that Bree was there, and when Aubrey told him that they would all stay and visit for a few days, he squealed and then solemnly promised that he would be good.

Their visit came with promises to Jax: she would not, initially, be alone with him, and if they left the house, Will would act as their escort. He would have preferred an extra guard or two but agreed that more armed men might agitate Hyrum, and he trusted Will. He pushed back at her argument that Hyrum would never hurt her. She'd last spent time with him when he was a small boy, and he was now fully grown physically and might not know his own strength, and she couldn't know his current temperament.

"It's also for his protection," he pointed out. "Will can handle Hyrum without hurting him. Your guards would protect you above all, which might mean *fully* subduing him. It's been years, angel. The truth is that we don't know what he'll do."

She'd agreed, but it rapidly became a moot point. Once they were sure that he wouldn't be overwhelmed by everyone, he met Oz and Drew, then Zed and Jay, and when Will introduced him to Aisha he inhaled sharply and squealed, "Ohhhh! It's a baby!" and then shoved his hands into his pockets.

"He learned the hard way that women don't always like it when someone touches their baby belly," Bree explained. "But he loves babies."

Aisha sat on the sofa and patted it, inviting him to sit next to her, and then took his hand to set it on her stomach. His mouth hung open, awestruck, and when the baby kicked he giggled and leaned close, his nose grazing her belly.

"'For this child I prayed, and the Lord gave me what I asked for,'" he whispered. "That's from Samuel. I'll pray for you, okay?" He sat up and looked to Aubrey. "Did I get that one right?"

"That was perfect, Hyrum."

He needed clothing. The things he'd arrived in were too dirty and worn to be saved, and the hospital scrubs he'd been given were too big, and he only had one set. Will gave Aisha a kiss and promised he would be home for dinner, and we headed out with Oz and Bree in tow to outfit Hyrum. The guards made themselves scarce, though never out of Will's line of sight, and he knew a dozen more were set up in Rack's department store a quarter mile away. Aubrey was determined that Hyrum be allowed to pick out the things he liked, though ten minutes in she realized he'd never been given choices before and was afraid to tell her what he wanted.

"Pretend it's your birthday," Bree told him. "If you had a wish list, what kind of clothes would be on it?"

"Oh." He bent over to whisper to her. "Underwear. Mom said next birthday I could get new underwear because mine are old and saggy."

"Underwear," Bree repeated. "All right. Grandma is kinda weird for thinking that's birthday clothes, but all right."

We started in the underwear department. Bree could only tell Aubrey two things: he probably preferred briefs because he'd been taught those were holy, and he'd never had anything other than white. "Church stuff. You know."

Aubrey did know.

"How are briefs holy?" Oz whispered to Bree.

She waved her hand back and forth. "Keeps stuff from flopping around and tempting boys to grab on."

Hyrum looked at the rack with bright white briefs displayed in convenient three and six packs, but he kept twitching toward the display next to it, his head hung as if he were ashamed to be there. He was clearly looking at all the colors.

Will grabbed two packs off the rack Hyrum most wanted to choose from. "Any color you want. It doesn't have to be white."

"Isn't that a sin?" Hyrum asked Aubrey.

"No, sweetheart. Will is right, you can have any color you want."

"Are you sure?"

"My dad has *black* underwear," Bree said.

"She's right, you can have any color. No one else is going to see them, anyway."

He giggled again, and asked, "Pink?"

Will put back the packs he'd grabbed and found one with bright pink and even brighter blue, which made Hyrum gasp. "Boys can wear pink," Will said. "Do remember Drew? Drew wears pinks sometimes."

I'd never seen him in it, but I made a mental note to tell him he did, in case Hyrum asked.

"Does Red really wear black underwear?" Oz asked Bree when Hyrum wasn't next to her.

With a laugh, Bree shrugged. "I don't know. I just think he should be able to do what he wants for once. No one ever asks him."

He let Oz and Bree help him pick out jeans— something he'd never owned—and, after being promised they weren't considered underwear, a few t-shirts. He balked at shopping for shoes, but he listened when Bree reminded him that Aubrey was the grown up and she made the rules.

"She's the Queen. You don't get to tell the Queen no when she wants to buy you some shoes. That's worse than telling your mom no, I think."

When everything was paid for and bagged, he hugged Aubrey and thanked her. "This was fun except for the socks and shoes."

"Hy," Bree hissed.

"You're welcome, sweetheart." She kissed him on the cheek. "I'm sorry I made you get shoes, but you have to have them."

"Cuts on your feet, never feels sweet," he chanted.

"My mother," Aubrey said to Will as we headed outside. "That sounds like something she'd tell him just to keep him from taking his shoes off the second he was outside."

"Go to the left," Will called out to Hyrum and Bree, even though Oz was right there and would have made sure they went in the right direction. She stuck to Hyrum's side, even when he and Bree started skipping, and when he came to a dead stop, she only went half a step beyond him.

He turned to stare into a store window, so close that his breath fogged the glass.

"We can go inside," Aubrey told him.

Hyrum shook his head, hard. "I'm not a little kid."

She looked up at the sign. *Foster's Toys and Things.* "Well, hon, Bree is a kid, and she might like to go in."

"I'm not a kid, and *I* want to go in," Will said.

That was all Hyrum needed. He rushed to the door but held it open for Bree and Oz, and the moment he was inside he shoved his hands into his pockets.

"Pockets, Bree," he said. "No touching, only looking."

Bree did not shove her hands into her pockets. "I'm not gonna slap stuff off shelves, doofus."

"You can touch," Oz told him. "Just don't break anything. Look." She plucked a toy car from the closest display and showed it to him. "It's just a toy."

"But Daddy said—"

"Daddy's not here, Hy," Aubrey reminded him. "You won't get in trouble if you touch things. And you won't get in trouble even if you accidentally break something, I promise."

"You can get away with a lot without that old fart around," Bree grumbled, which made Hyrum bark out a laugh and then clap his hands over his mouth to stop. She pinched up a fold on her jeans and told him to look. "Jeans, Hyrum. I'm wearing *pants*. People do things different here. And *my* daddy says it's okay."

"Red *lets* you wear pants? But you're a girl."

"And you're a boy who just bought pink underwear. Live it up." She looked at Aubrey. "He doesn't have toys of his own anymore. Grandpa threw them all away. All he gets to do is play with stuff his nephews bring over, and when there are no grownups around, I let him play with my dolls."

"Bree don't say that! I'll get in trouble!"

"No, you won't," she told him. "Aunt Aubrey doesn't care if you like dolls. Do you?"

"No, sweetie, I don't. Hy, did Daddy really throw your toys away? Why?"

"I'm too old to play with toys. Daddy said so." He lowered his voice as he imitated Levi. "'Hyrum, you're over thirty now. You don't need blocks, you need common sense. Now go clean the kitchen.' And dolls are for girls."

Will slid his arm around Hyrum's shoulders, fingers lingering on his neck. "I'm not too old for toys. I'd like to get something today, Hyrum, but I don't know what."

"You want toys?"

Will nodded. "It's been a long time since I've had any, too. You know, Aisha and I are having a little boy, and I think I need to practice so I can play with him when he's a little older."

"I can help you pick things."

"Good. What do you think? Stuffed animals? Building blocks? Maybe a train?"

"I like those," Hyrum said reverently. "The blocks that stick together are fun. You can build lots of things. Like a castle!"

Oz started for the aisle with the toy blocks. "Oh, man, Zed is gonna love you."

The living room looked like the toy store had thrown up in it. Jax dropped into his comfy chair and stared at the toys scattered all around, and then asked Aubrey if he simply didn't remember their kids making such a mess, or if he'd blocked it out.

"The nanny picked up their toys," Will said.

"The nanny made them pick up after themselves," Aubrey reminded him. "And I thank you for that. But yes, Jax, sometimes it looked like this and I didn't mind. I don't mind. They've been having so much fun."

That included Oz, Drew, Zed, and Jay. They happily sat on the floor and built things out of blocks, then had car races which Bree always won because Hyrum insisted she get to go first.

When it was time for them to calm down because bedtime was approaching, Jay brought out a stack of paper and colored pencils, and the floor was covered with giant kids on their stomachs, drawing pictures and coloring outside the lines.

Red watched intently as Hyrum outlined a house with faces looking out the window. "He drew a face for each of his brothers and sisters, and one for Mom. There was a girl's face for you, Aubrey, yet he left our father out of it."

"You draw your heart's desire," she said. "Or your nightmare. Everyone was inside the house. Maybe he felt like we were all trapped."

"We were, to an extent. He surely was, more than the rest of us."

His life would be different, Red was sure of that. The home he'd return to would be free of Levi's tyranny; he would have everything that comforted him, and none of the things that terrified him. He could curl up on the sofa and memorize bible passages with their mother and not worry about what would happen if he forgot a word. Playing outside would not invite pain. "He can learn to ride a bike, finally. If Mom will let go a bit, he can explore the neighborhood and just be himself."

"He explored the country," Will reminded him. "He survived. When he returns home, don't be surprised if he rebels against expectations a bit. At some point, he's going to realize he did what only a man could do."

"Mom sent him," Aubrey reminded Red. "She let go a long time ago."

"Will you be able to forgive her for sending him?"

"If she comes here and faces it, perhaps. There's a part of me that wants to revoke his travel rights until she does. I'll keep him here if that's what it takes, Red. He may be forty-three, but he's still a little boy. I couldn't protect him before, but I damn well can now."

"And that's why she's afraid of you." With a tired sigh, he got up. "I promised I would call her, no matter how late. I'll stress that she needs to come."

He went into the guest room, which he was sharing with Bree. Hyrum was in Zed's room on a mattress that he and Jay pulled down from the guest suite upstairs; they were supposed to go to sleep, but light bled from under the door, and Aubrey knew Zed and Jay were sitting on the floor with him, reading bedtime stories and watching forbidden videos.

Once Red's door clicked shut, Jax said, "I'm sending guards with a shuttle to pick up your mother tomorrow. Red is also asking your brothers and sisters to be prepared to leave Florida on the pretense of a reunion. We'll provide transport when it's needed."

"Red confirmed Eli's suspicions?" Will asked.

Jax nodded. "The Quorum laid fairly low after Levi's capture and waited to see what Red would do. He feels them pushing back at the changes he wants to make and thinks a shift is imminent."

"Red is head of the church," Aubrey said.

"Its prophet. His decisions are supposed to be the result of a direct line from God."

"Church hierarchy," Will said. "It's politics cloaked in choir robes. The ambitions are the same. Bring wealth and power to those who sit in control and convince the masses that everything is being done for their own good."

Jax reminded her that while Red was the sanctioned head of the church, the apostles with whom he served had been appointed by Levi. While some possibly sided with Red, it was likely that most of the Quorum still held tight to Levi's agenda and would undo every step of progress he'd made.

"Why now?" Aubrey asked Jax.

"Because the Consortium vote is looming, and now we have Hyrum. We know that Levi discussed church business at home—your mother testified to it at his trial. Where your mother was, Hyrum was always close by. They know he overheard much of it. They presume he'll talk. And to keep the scope of Levi's plans from getting in their way, they'll destroy Red and everyone around him."

Will didn't think Hyrum was a lynchpin. He thought they would go after Red regardless; he didn't share Levi's vision of how the government and church should be run and that made him a heretic. The members of the Quorum probably hadn't known Hyrum was anything other than missing. In their eyes, he was defective—Aubrey started to protest that notion, until he shook his head, he didn't agree—and wouldn't make it fifty miles from home before something happened. "What we need is Eli digging a little deeper. He may have access to better intelligence than anyone else right now."

"Gossip," Jax said. "He's getting the better gossip."

"Indeed. Perhaps that's what we need most right now. Pure, backstabbing, bitchy gossip."

I woke Will at three in the morning. Aisha was awake and sitting on the sofa in the dark, rubbing her belly, sniffling. I didn't bother slipping into his dream where I could gently pull him out of sleep; I jumped up to the headboard, then launched and landed on his stomach.

I'm small. I was reasonably sure it wouldn't hurt him or fracture his steel six pack.

He woke with a "what the hell?" on his lips and slid out of bed when I told him Aisha was in the living room, crying.

"Can't sleep?" He sat next to her, gently, and slid his arm around her shoulders. "You could have woken me."

"You didn't sleep at all last night," she said.

"Is he kicking?" He set a hand on hers. "I'll give him a stern talking to, if you like."

She didn't smile. "Will you be honest with me? Like, brutally honest?"

"Not if you're going to ask me if that baby bump makes you look fat. What's wrong?"

"Are we heading into war? Could Florida blow up that badly?"

He wanted to be able to tell her that war was not a possibility. Red was not made of the same brittle plaster as his father; he was far more considerate and willing to look at all sides of an issue. But the truth was that while Red held the First Minister's seat, he had a Quorum to answer to, and many of them were chafing at the changes he'd made, and they wanted him gone.

"Florida is very much a patriarchal society, and Red has no sons to inherit his position. If the Quorum doesn't get what they want, they'll remove him."

"And that means?"

"They'll find a way to kill him and then elevate someone of their own political bent to lead their country and church. Right now, Red is the voice of reason as far as the rest of the world is concerned. If he's gone, Florida reverts to a government made in Levi Munson's image, and he wanted war. He wanted to push beyond Florida's borders, and he had Russia's backing."

"So, war." She blinked, sending tears over her eyelashes. "Just as we're about to have this baby. And if conscription is enacted, Jay is old enough to be drafted."

"War is not a given, Enzo. Right now, we're stuck in a phase of speculation. But even if they attack, Rhys is protected. He'll always be protected."

"And Jay?"

"Jay is not subject to the draft. While he's not in line for the throne, he is, officially, Prince James of the House of Blackshear. We can't stop him from enlisting, but he can't be drafted."

You can drag him through a portal if he tries to join the army.

"Indeed," Will chuckled. "We have options. Send him to live with George for the duration."

"Don't think I wouldn't," Aisha said. "George might be a stain on the face of the earth, but he would take Jay in. I hate admitting it, but he wouldn't turn his back on Jay and I would send him in a heartbeat. George would make room in his life for Jay, no matter how long he needed to stay."

Will didn't want to put the cart before the horse, even though we didn't have a horse and I thought it would be fun to get one. All they knew for sure was that Hyrum was here, Red's position was not as firm as it should be, and he disagreed with his Quorum. It might mean nothing, and until they had proof that there was anything amiss, it wasn't worth more than a bit of mild concern.

"I won't tell you not to worry, but I honestly am not, not yet."

"You'll tell me when you are?"

He promised he would.

It's a good thing Oz wasn't there to see his lie color flare all around him.

8

Aubrey's irritation with her mother evaporated in the time it took for Valerie Munson to walk from the door to where the Queen waited in the center of the living room. After a hug that went on so long I was pretty sure we missed both lunch and dinner, Valerie pulled back and said, "I sent him away to save his life, Aubrey."

"Mom—"

"Levi was about to unleash hell. I was afraid that Midlam and Pacifica together, they would destroy Florida. I wanted him to run. I wanted him out."

So why didn't you say anything when the war was over? At the trial? Or for the two years after?

Neither Will nor Drew were there to ask my questions. Oz wasn't there to tell if she was lying. But I wanted to know.

Aubrey did, too, but didn't get the chance to say anything.

Hyrum heard Valerie's voice from Zed's room, and sprinted down the hall calling out, "Mom! Mom! Mom! Mom! Mom!" and he leaped at her when he was close enough. "I did it! I found the Queen!"

Still, while Aubrey let go of the irritation, when jockeying people around, she didn't offer Valerie the guest room. Valerie was placed in Drew's old, newly renovated apartment with Red and Bree; Hyrum didn't want to give up his spot in Zed's room, and half the time he convinced Jay to stay the night as well.

The expected few days turned into an extended visit, which no one minded except, perhaps, for Valerie. She had planned on staying just long enough to be polite and then wanted to take Hyrum home, but Red wasn't in a hurry to go anywhere, and until he said it was time, she wasn't going to ask to leave.

There was a new rhythm to life in the royal house. Eli came and went, and each time he returned he had new information for Jax and General Myers. Aubrey submitted a request to take the semester off—which was not really a request but more a notification that she would not start the year with her newest fifth graders— because things were happening, and she was determined to see to Hyrum's needs. Aisha and Drew spent time each evening going over the curriculum he would teach once her baby was born, and each night ended with a promise: it's only for four weeks, I promise, I'm only taking four weeks off. Jax quietly ordered a safe house in Nevada prepared and stocked for over two dozen people because he suspected that it would soon house most of the Munson family.

Mostly, though, there was a happy current of wonder and play. The kids who were not really kids spent their afternoons stretched out on the floor playing with Hyrum, and they introduced him to their favorite books and family-friendly entertainment videos. The laughter that vibrated from the walls wasn't laced with adult innuendo; it was pure, childlike joy, and when the school semester started Hyrum was not the only one who was sad that they each had to leave every morning.

He had his own routine by then; every morning began with prayer and bible study, led mostly by his mother but subtly guided by Aubrey. She used the time to figure out how well rounded his education had been; Valerie admitted that after his second attempt at kindergarten he'd been made to stay home because he couldn't keep up and there was no such thing as individual education in Florida schools. She'd taught him to read well enough to sound out words he didn't know, and he soaked up church history through the stories she read to him. Levi refused to allow him to learn anything to do with the world outside Florida, though he couldn't keep Hyrum from hearing the news when he wasn't home to command every movement the boy made. Hyrum grasped the basics of the things his mother taught him, but he couldn't connect information and couldn't make sense of complex ideas.

She settled for making sure he could care for himself—he was the only boy in the family allowed to cook and to clean because Levi recognized that he would never have a wife—and was satisfied that he could puzzle out words on a page and he could follow directions.

Where Valerie and Aubrey sharply parted ways about Hyrum was the medical treatment he'd been given. There was no point in taking him to a doctor for what Valerie thought were bumps and bruises; every little boy had those. There was no one she could take him to who would explain his limitations beyond a litany of tired religious excuses: Hyrum was a punishment for her sins, and if she repented well enough and God chose to reward those efforts, he would be healed.

She pushed back at the idea that he could see a therapist in Florida. There was nothing a 'mind-doctor' could do for him; he was a little boy, and always would be. What was the point? Yes, he'd been spanked, hard and unfairly, but all the boys had endured it and they were fine. This was something best left alone. She'd prayed about it, and that was the answer.

"I am his mother, Aubrey, and I will do for him what the Lord tells me."

That was, she presumed, the end of that. Aubrey wasn't ready to challenge her mother on a front of faith, but she listened and waited for the thing that would open Valerie's eyes.

She didn't think it would open hers, as well.

Days later, Zed crept into their bedroom before dawn to wake Jax. Hyrum was deep into a meltdown and Zed couldn't handle the issue at hand. Aubrey woke and started to get up because he was her little brother and would be calmed by her presence; she had the ability to soothe with touch, and that was probably all he needed.

"It has to be Dad, Mom," Zed insisted. "If you walk in there it'll break his heart."

Jax told Aubrey he'd be right back and headed for Zed's room.

"What's wrong?" she asked Zed before he could follow Jax.

He sat on the edge of the bed. "Delicately? Hm. Yeah. I woke up and heard him crying. When I got out of bed to see if he was okay, I figured, you know, he'd had a bad dream, and I could read a story to get him back to sleep. But he was curled in a ball crying his eyes out, blubbering, 'No, no, no, it's only for daddies,' and when he realized I was up, he started begging me to not tell Daddy, because Daddy would punish him again."

"Zed—"

"Morning wood, Mom, that's all. I tried to tell him it happened to everyone and he probably just needed to pee, but he wasn't hearing me."

She sighed. "Jax can handle that. I'm glad it's not worse."

"No, Mom, it's horrible. I asked him what he meant, that it's only for daddies, and he said it's for making babies and for punishing bad boys. And he didn't want to be punished again. It hurts too much."

She knew what he meant, but wouldn't let it sink in. "My father was heavy-handed—"

"Mom, no. Hyrum thinks getting a random boner is a sin so major that it justifies being... sodomized. I'm freaking glad I didn't tell him to just rub one out. He'd have probably killed himself over the idea."

Jax might have been able to handle it, but she flew out of the bed and down the hall to rescue Hyrum from the monster who had hurt them both.

She was right in that her touch soothed him; he stopped crying and agreed to let Zed read another bedtime story to him, and he nodded when she promised that no one in this house gets punished.

That morning, Aubrey stopped Valerie from beginning their morning prayers together. It no longer mattered what she thought; Hyrum was seeing a doctor, period. They argued in the kitchen until Aubrey practically had her mother pinned against the counter and jabbed her pointy finger toward Valerie's chest as she said, "He raped Ruth. He raped Elle. He probably raped Sarah. He raped me. All of us, Mom. Repeatedly."

"I know that. He was horrible—"

"He raped Hyrum." She stepped back, giving her mother breathing space. "He raped *Hyrum*."

Aubrey expected surprise. She thought Valerie would be broken by the idea, that it was news and she'd had no idea. Instead, Valerie sighed. "I'd have killed that man if I could have. Every day I prayed that the Lord would find a way to take him. And he did."

"Look at the cost," Aubrey seethed.

"The Lord works—"

"Don't. Don't place everything that happened to us at God's feet. Because if you do, you're blaming *Him* for the deaths of thousands of people. God didn't make us all suffer and then allow bombs to destroy an entire city until it was simply time to take Dad from this earth. All of it was his own work, his own evil."

"Then you blame me for not stopping it."

"I don't think you could have. He would have killed you. But don't invoke the name of the Lord when you don't think you have control. You *do* have it. And right now, all the control needs to be focused on Hyrum, because the little boy inside him is broken and terrified."

Valerie tried to wave it off. "It's over. He knows it will never happen again."

"But he *doesn't*. He doesn't know that his father is dead. Because the wonderful person he is will grieve the loss of the man as much as he fears the monster. No more wallowing, Mom. I'm taking him to see someone. End of discussion."

Aubrey braced for Valerie's anger. Instead, Valerie put her arms around her daughter and kissed her on the cheek. "I envy your strength. And before you say it, I know envy is a sin. But I do, Aubrey, I envy how strong you are. Take him to see your doctors. And when they say he's ready, we'll tell him about Levi. And God help me, I hope I don't cackle with joy."

◆◆◆

He saw the therapist every other morning at nine o'clock. The only way to get him out the door without tears was if Will walked with them;

at first, it was fear, and he'd decided that if Will were there, nothing bad would happen. Will was the Water Man; he was the one who gave Hyrum water and food when he needed it most, and he would make everything okay.

It also might have been that on the first day Will promised him that if he went and cooperated—he refrained from telling Hyrum to be good—then afterward they would stop at the bakery and have a donut. Aubrey laughed because she knew what Will did not: he'd just tied the donut to the therapy, and not for only the one day. She also knew that Will was not a fan of sweet things and would not be happy about it.

While Hyrum spoke to the doctor with Aubrey sitting quietly in the corner of his office, we waited in a colorfully bright room with comfy chairs and a monitor that always had children's programming running. Will muttered under his breath, but he couldn't change it because kids were coming and going, so he sat back and watched a giant anthropomorphized elephant named Mr. Happy teach kids about friendship and community, with the occasional lesson on letters and words.

Halfway into the second week, Mr. Happy was planning a vacation with his friend the goat, Mr. Grumble. They boarded a boat for a cruise to Hawaii, and halfway there Mr. Happy became decidedly upset. He had no clothing for dinner. "I forgot to pack my trunk," he told Mr. Grumble.

Aubrey and Hyrum came out of the doctor's office just in time to hear Will snap, "Dammit, Happy, get your shit together."

Hyrum's giggles were almost enough to cover Aubrey's shocked, "William!"

Will gestured to the monitor and said, "His trunk—"

Dude.

"Fine." He got up and settled me into the sweatshirt pouch, and then held the door open for Aubrey and Hyrum. From the first day, as soon as we were on the sidewalk, Hyrum reached for Will's hand and held it until we reached the bakery. It surprised Aubrey at first, until Will explained later that he thought the sessions with the therapist unsettled him, and for whatever reason, he found comfort in holding Will's hand.

"Please don't be offended. He probably doesn't stop to think that you notice. And if he takes your hand, he feels...less."

Other people noticed. Nearly everyone we passed—locals, they weren't at all surprised to see the Queen—smiled. Hyrum's presence had been noted in the news; most of Pacifica knew that the Queen's mother and brothers were visiting, and because he had been missing so long, it was deemed appropriate to keep him here long enough to rest and recoup his lost strength.

Holding hands with the Emperor was adorable, and they approved.

Every morning as we crossed Union Square, Vicat waited on a bench near the portal, daring

Will to make a run for it. As soon as she spotted Aubrey she stood, and when we were close, she nodded and said, "Ma'am," and then smiled at Hyrum, who had decided she was the Cat Lady, no matter how many times Will told him her name was Vicat.

"He's not far off," she told Will. "And I don't mind."

"So," Aubrey said to Will as they had coffee and donuts, "are we now fans of Mr. Happy?"

"We are not," he said. "Have you ever watched that? All the veiled—" he glanced at Hyrum, who was licking the chocolate frosting off the top of his donut "—Mr. Happy raises his trunk a bit too often to be appropriate."

"I guarantee you, one day Rhys will be a fan, and he'll have a stuffed Mr. Happy of his own."

"I am not buying a Mr. Happy."

She smiled at him over the lip of her coffee cup. "Oh, but Aunt Aubrey will."

"I like your baby's name," Hyrum said around a chunk of donut he'd tucked into his cheek. "Reeeeeeeese. Will I still be here when he's born? Mom says we might have to go home soon, but I want to meet him."

"You'll still be here, sweetie," Aubrey said. "Are you anxious to get home?"

He shook his head, hard. "I like it here. Everyone is nice, and I get to play with real toys, and no one gets mad when I..."

"What, Hy?"

He screwed his nose up while he considered what he wanted to say. "Dr. Cheshire says that I'm not a little boy and it's okay if man things happen to me, even if I'm not a daddy. And Jax didn't yell and me and Zed said, 'it happens to every guy, even me, but I'm not gonna prove it so don't ask.' And if I say the wrong words, no one makes me say them over until I say them right, and Dr. Cheshire says that's because I say words the way I'm supposed to, and it's okay. Mom says I'm still her little boy, but I'm not *really* a boy anymore. But I'm not a man. I know I'm not."

Aubrey opened her mouth to speak—it was certain she wanted to make him feel better, to say all the right things, all the things an older sister should—but Will leaned back in his chair and asked, "Do you want to be a man, Hyrum?"

Softly, "I don't know."

"There's no wrong answer," Will said. "You're wonderful whether you're a boy or a man, or if you're somewhere in between."

"In between like a young man?"

Will nodded.

"But I'm forty-three, Will. I'm almost your age."

"I know. But it's just a number. Don't be in a hurry to be something different, Hyrum. We all love you and want you to be here with us, whether you're a grown man, or a very tall, very hairy boy."

"Okay." Hyrum smiled and then leaned over to give Will a wet, chocolate-frosting kiss on his cheek. "I love you, too." He started laughing, covering his mouth with both hands, but Will sat there with the frosting on his face, pretending he had no idea what was so funny.

♦♦♦

After lunch was study time, though Aubrey never called it that and stressed to everyone that they not refer to it in any way as school work or that she functioned as his teacher. His experiences with school had left a stain on his psyche, and thirty-five years later he still balked at the notion that he was entitled to or belonged in an educational setting. As far as Hyrum was concerned, Aubrey enjoyed it when they read stories together and it made her happy when he could ask and answer questions about the books they used. She'd determined that he read at a second-grade level but could puzzle out stories in her fifth-grade reader texts, and she picked stories that gave him information about the world outside Florida.

His favorite stories revolved around Eli and Jax; he liked that he knew the people he was reading about, and he squealed in delight when she told him that the Emperor in the latest story they were reading was Will. "Did you know," she said in a stage whisper, "that for *years* Will wouldn't even tell us his name? We just called him 'Emperor.' I think he thought that was funny."

Hyrum thought so, too. "An Emperor is a king," he said. "Jax was a prince. He wanted to have a better rank!"

"And now they're the same."

Hyrum crinkled his nose. "Will is Jax's brother so why didn't he know his name? I know my brothers' names, even the pretend ones. Red is really Redmond and Joe is really Joseph. But David is a dick." His eyes went wide. "I'm sorry. Please don't tell Daddy!"

She explained about how close they were, the best of friends, and how King Eli had taken care of Will when he was a teenager—though Eli had made Will think he was taking care of himself—and they all loved each other so much that Eli adopted Will as his own son. "Do you remember meeting Finn and Jo? They're Will's real parents."

"Are they mad that Eli took their little boy?"

"No, sweetie. They love Eli and Jax, too. We've all kind of adopted each other and created a big, sloppy, happy family."

He wanted to know if that was like Will and Jay; he knew Will wasn't Jay's father, but he'd said that Jay was his son. "I don't understand it. Jay and Aisha have the mark, so why did Will—"

She stopped him before he could get his brain around that thought. "Hy, that's something the church is very wrong about. They don't have any kind of mark. They're just people."

"But Daddy said that people who have dark skin are being punished for the bad things they did in the pre-existence. It's the mark."

Daddy's a douche, Hyrum.

She took a deep breath. "Hon, do you think Jay and Aisha are bad people just because they aren't white?"

"No. I like them."

"Daddy always said that because he didn't know any better. He was repeating things that he was taught, because in a book that was written hundreds of years ago, a book that *wasn't* the Bible, someone said that."

"But the Bible says that. 'Then the Lord put a mark on Cain—'"

"The Bible doesn't say what that mark was, Hyrum. But plenty of people decided it was skin color and used it as an excuse to treat other people poorly." Another deep breath. "When you look at Will, do you see a white man or a man of color?"

"He's white."

He's pink.

She turned her tablet on and searched for photos of Jax's—and by extension—Will's ancestors. She pulled up pictures of Queen Wyatt, one of the early monarchs in Pacifica's history, and pictures of Blackshear cousins and spouses. "This is Will's great-great-great grandmother," she said, though there were a few more greats in the mix. "Her skin looks quite a bit like Aisha's doesn't it?"

"Nuh," he grunted. "She's darker than Aisha. And she's pretty like Aisha." He bent toward the screen, his nose nearly touching it. "She has really long eyelashes. And I like her earrings."

"All right." She flipped through a dozen other pictures. "These are some of his relatives, the people he descended from. Will isn't exactly white. And I think if we looked back at our own family, maybe a few hundred years, we'd find out that we're not, either."

Hyrum pointed at one of the pictures on the screen. "Who's that? He looks mad."

"That's Prince Louis. He was Queen Wyatt's third son."

"He never got to be King?"

"No. After his oldest brother had children, he was no longer in line to be King."

"That's probably why he was mad."

"I think it was just a bad picture." She searched for another picture of him. "Here. He's smiling in this one. And you see the collar on his shirt? He became a priest."

"Daddy's a priest. So is Red and David and Spencer and Joseph."

"That's right. Louis was a man of God. And he wasn't white."

"Okay." He twitched at the sound of footsteps on the stairs, and when he heard voices, he jumped up. "Zed's home!"

She'd lost his focus and knew it. "All right. Go play."

I jumped from the breakfast bar to the table and rubbed against her chin.

"He has a good heart, Wick. But I'd forgotten how much bigotry is woven in Florida's church culture. How can I let him go back to that?"

◆◆◆

For the first time, Aubrey made dinner in the staff kitchen, where there were enough tables and seats for the entire family. "Just one meal," she said. "It would be nice to actually see everyone during dinner and not shove the kids off to another table in the living room." She sent Oz and Drew to clean it—the only ones who used it were the kids, and she didn't want to deal with whatever was growing inside the refrigerator or the oven— and had Jay and Zed and Hyrum carry down food and supplies. I didn't like it; noise bounced off the ceiling and the windows here more than upstairs, but I got my own chair next to Will's so I couldn't complain out loud.

The chair was a message. Three times already Valerie had shooed me off the breakfast bar, and not very nicely, complaining that I was filthy and animals on the counter were disgusting. Aubrey warned her against it the first two times but didn't see the last time when she sent me flying off the edge with a not-so-gentle shove.

I'm petty sometimes. I told Will.

He set up the chair for me, with a box on the seat so I could see everyone better, and he chuckled to himself when Valerie took in a tight breath when he set a plate in front of me. Red heard her, too, and Red had no problem with me being there.

"Wick is family, Mom. He's even had a seat at my table and shared food with my family."

"That cat," she said, looking right at Aubrey, "is spoiled."

That made Bree giggle. "You always sneak food to the cats under the table, Grandma. Even when my cat Doof got old and lost his teeth, you gave him food."

"Bless the beasts and the children," Hyrum said, looking at Wick.

Aubrey wanted to know what that was from, because it wasn't a bible verse that she was familiar with, and he tended to quote verses she knew.

"It's a song." His eyes went wide, and he quickly covered his mouth with both hands. From behind them came a muffled, "I wasn't supposed to tell."

"I'm not familiar with it," she told him. "Where did you hear it?"

He shook his head vigorously.

"You're not in trouble," Red said, glancing at his mother. "There's nothing wrong with music. Even the bible says to make a joyful noise unto the Lord."

"Psalms," Hyrum said, still muffled.

Red reached across the table and tapped Hyrum's knuckles. "Put your hands down, Hy. Where'd you hear this song?"

"Joe," he whispered. "It's old, old, old. He played it for me on his music player, until Daddy took it away. That was forbidden."

"Ah. Old digital technology," Red explained. "Joseph got his hands on a storage and playback device. He had that thing for years before Dad found it. If you want to know about popular music from the second half of the twentieth century, he's your man."

Joseph was a brother Aubrey hadn't met yet. He was born after she left and had never come to visit after the war was over and Levi was dead. She'd spoken to her youngest sister, Sarah, on video chat several times, though they'd never met in person, but Joseph was elusive and she knew little about him. Red thought he struggled with mixed feelings; Aubrey was the sister no one was allowed to discuss, the one whose name invited anger and invectives. The little he knew about her came from Levi's twisted mind, and he had yet to come to terms with the idea that not only had Levi lied, but she was also Queen of Pacifica.

The family wounds, she thought, could take decades to heal, if ever.

Dinner was well under way when Eli came in, startling Valerie when his voice boomed from the entry, "There the hell you are. I've looked all over this damned house." Hyrum shot out of his seat, his hands over his head, and he squealed, "Eli!"

Eli pumped his fists over his head. "Hyrum!" Then, "Sit down and finish your dinner, son. You still have vegetables, I see."

Hyrum did as he was told, but under his breath, he muttered, "Peas mashed muck. Hyrum says yuck."

"Not a fan?" Eli asked as he took the lone empty chair across from Will. "I love peas."

Hyrum made a face that let everyone know what he thought about them.

"How about carrots?" When Hyrum nodded, Eli reached across the table and spooned out a liberal serving of cooked carrots. "Eat those instead. Leave the peas."

Oh, Valerie's gonna explode.

Will leaned forward to look at her. She was glaring at Eli. He noticed but didn't care, and turned to Jax. There were things to discuss after dinner, best talked about in Jax's office. He wanted Will and Red there and then further irritated Valerie when he suggested that after they'd done the dishes, all the kids should go out for ice cream—if they finished their carrots.

As Hyrum shoved as many carrots into his mouth as he could, Bree looked to Red for permission. He nodded and told her she could go, but only if she promised to listen to her cousins and to help keep an eye on Hyrum. Valerie's mouth opened—she was going to forbid Hyrum from leaving, probably because he didn't eat his peas—but Red's eyebrow went up, daring her.

"Whether she likes it or not," Red said later, "by our own traditions, I am now the head of the family. Even I think it's wrong, but I can put my foot down every now and then to make sure he has a bit of fun."

"If you ever tell me what to do, sweetie," Aubrey told him, "I'll order your head on a platter."

He was pretty sure she would have done that even if she wasn't the Queen.

I went with Will to Jax's office because I didn't want to listen to Valerie complain to Aubrey that she was already tired of people making decisions for Hyrum that were hers to make, and I really didn't want to hear Aubrey lecture her about the subvert racism Hyrum had been taught.

The only part of me that wanted to stay was

the part that wanted to see what Aisha would do if she were part of the conversation.

"Here's the long and short of it," Eli said as he dropped into the comfy chair in Jax's office. "Most of the western players will vote in line with Pacifica if we cast the first vote in favor of admitting Florida to the Consortium. A few would definitely flip if we vote no, others I'm not as sure about. Most of the middle eastern and smaller players will vote no, regardless. I've listened to their reasoning, and I don't disagree."

"Reasoning?" Jax asked.

"Your Quorum," Eli said to Red. "How many support the changes you've made to Florida's constitution?"

"It doesn't matter. Where amendments are struck, and others added, I have sole discretion."

"But do they *support* it? Recognizing your right as the head of the church and as its prophet doesn't equate supporting your position. Do they support that you're pushing them from the far right to the middle line?"

"No, I suppose not."

"Yet they want a seat at the Consortium, a decidedly moderate institution."

Red nodded.

"Levi was deep into Russia's pocket, we know that," Eli said. "His Quorum is, as well. They want the seat for no reason other than it gives Russia ears in the Consortium, something they've never had."

"If their application is overturned by the vote?" Jax asked.

"So beat the drums of war," Eli sighed. "Your elders still want Midlam, Red. They feel it's owed to them, though I cannot fathom why. If the vote doesn't go the way they wish, you're going to be ousted, a new First Minister installed, and we're back to where we were two years ago, fighting over land in Kansas."

When Red didn't say anything, Eli went on. "How many nukes do you have now? I know it's more than you had at the end of your father's reign."

Visibly uncomfortable, Red said, "We have the right to weapons of self-defense. Any build-up in armament is simply a stockpile for defense."

"And how do you propose to launch a defensive strike with a nuclear weapon?" Will said, not expecting an answer. "And understand, this is not news. We've been aware of the installations. Laser drilling is not easy to hide."

"Then you know how many we have."

"Your brother is far more forthcoming." Eli leaned forward, his arms resting on his legs, and he was not happy. "You've more than quadrupled your missile silos in under two years, all while negotiating fair trade agreements with Pacifica. You've entered into land lease agreements in Midlam—"

"All in good faith," Red argued.

"*Your* good faith, perhaps. But you're virtually a lone voice in your government. You have support from your brother, Spencer, who is little more than your lackey, but as far as I can tell, no one else. And we all know what they mean when they say they'll oust you from your position."

Jax wanted him to get to the end game.

"Pacifica's only choices lead to war. If we vote to admit Florida into the Consortium, we face a slow but firm affront in the U.N. *and* the Consortium. They'll have a place at the table and Russia's resources to buy public influence. They'll push back in elections, and they'll buy votes. They'll win. Deny them entry to the Consortium, and they'll attack. The truth is that Russia doesn't care which way it goes. They want war, and they want land in the North American continent."

"But which do they want more?" Red asked.

"Doesn't matter." Jax's chair creaked as he leaned into it. "Our choices are essentially war now or war later."

"Consider it carefully," Eli said to Jax. "I have thoughts, but I'd prefer to give you time to consider your own position."

"Duly noted." Jax got up, signaling an end to the meeting. He led the way out of his office, telling Red good night as he headed down the stairs. Eli hung behind, and when Red was down far enough, he followed Will and Jax upstairs.

The kids hadn't returned yet, so Jax grabbed a bottle of scotch and headed for the balcony. He stopped long enough to kiss Aubrey and tell Aisha where Will was and asked where Valerie had gone: downstairs, because her nose was out of joint and she might as well give up because they were all going to drag Hyrum into the pits of hedonistic despair.

"Over ice cream?"

"God forbid, they might let him get chocolate syrup on it. Or worse, a cherry on top."

"The horrors."

Out on the balcony, he poured scotch into Will's and Eli's glasses and then leaned against the ledge. It was quiet down on the Square, but I could hear pigeons nearby so I tucked under one of the chairs, sticking only my head out so I could see them.

"Tell me your thoughts, Dad," Jax said. "I already know my position."

"I've gone over it both ways in my mind a hundred times. The bomb will blow, the question is whether we want the fuse to burn slowly or to get it over with quickly. Admitting them allows us time to see what they're really up to and act on it. But that also gives Russia and her allies time to dig in and for that bomb to get so much bigger. I'm not in favor of giving them more time than they've already had. Force their hand, son. Order me to vote no and deny Florida the seat they want."

"You want war sooner rather than later."

"I don't want it at all. How much do you know about the last timeline?" He looked at Will. "Does he know how the war ended?"

"Will's filled me in," Jax said.

Eli nodded. "I've poured over documents in the Old Mint. My gut tells me that one way or the other, this leads to Finn finishing his work with the teleporter."

"And sending a MOAB into the heart of Florida," Will sighed.

"But this time we know it's coming, and Aubrey's family can be saved. Vote no and let the chips fall where they may but get those people out of Florida while you can."

"A majority of Munson's family may side with the Quorum," Will said.

That didn't matter. She would want them alive either way. Jax knew that. "The safe house is ready when we need it, but I can't force them to leave their homes, especially if they side with the Quorum. Did Spencer give you an idea how many of his brothers agree with Red?"

"He believes Joseph, the youngest does. The one he's most concerned about is David. He seems to be molded in Levi's image. One of Aubrey's sisters, Ruth, is married to the son of an apostle, but Spencer feels she'll take the first opportunity to leave."

Will found that odd. "I presumed that her sisters would all stand by their husbands. It's a cultural mandate."

"Personal hell overrides culture," Eli said. "Her husband is a proponent of polygamy and actively petitions the Quorum to restore it as its rightful place within the church. Likely because she has borne him no children."

"I wasn't aware the Church of Florida ever supported polygamy," Jax said.

"A pebble in the foundation of their religion," Will said. "It was short-term practice in the church from which they grew, in the eighteen-hundreds. Given that Florida has historically banned divorce and rarely grants annulments, I'm not surprised that some members would openly favor the idea."

I thought Valerie was the first divorcee. She said Levi wasn't her husband anymore, at his trial.

"He died before she could petition the church to allow it," Will said. "Red would have granted that to her, as his right as First Minister. He's painted a picture of progress in Florida. Education has been opened to women, and they've been given the vote."

"By law, yes," Jax said. "But women aren't rushing to return to school, and even if they'll vote, they'll vote the way their husbands and fathers order them. Red is looking through an optimistic lens. He's enacted laws and amended their constitution, but nothing has really changed."

The vote, Jax decided, would be a firm no. Eli would cast the first vote just after the opening of the Consortium assembly, with remaining members voting over the next several days. The spreading out of the vote gave Florida time to lobby for inclusion, but it also gave Pacifica time to spread the word to anyone unaware of the backroom politics being played.

◆◆◆

"When Jax and Aubrey shoved their kids into a shuttle and sent them off at the start of the war, they sent you with them. And every single one of those kids was capable of handling life on their own, in a reasonable situation. Valerie essentially shoved an eight-year-old out the door with a map and some peanut butter and told herself she was doing it to save his life and that he was capable."

Will listened to Aisha's voice in the dark. Stretched out in bed, hands touching but not holding, they tried to pick apart the knot of the day, which for Aisha had been mostly tied by Valerie Munson. He waited because he knew she was thinking out loud, and she hadn't asked for an opinion. She'd chewed on the fat that padded the conversations she'd listened to quietly all evening; Hyrum was expected to toe the line at the same time he was expected to be her little boy, and it had irritated her beyond reason to have Eli overrule her at the dinner table, and then to give Hyrum permission to go out. Aisha admitted that he should have asked, but it was harmless. Ice cream out with his nieces and nephew; he was safer with them than he was with her.

When she realized she was winding down, she reached over without looking and set her hand on his hip. "All right. Your turn. Tell me why I'm wrong."

"You're not wrong," he said, rolling to his side. "Her life experience has been vastly different than yours. I don't think it's a stretch to assume her emotional maturity is not as well formed as yours, and she's certainly far less educated. In her heart, she truly believed she was saving Hyrum's life. Her world view was Florida-inclusive, and she had no way of knowing how starkly different everything outside their borders could be."

"And the damned peas?"

"Control. Didn't you want Jay to eat his vegetables?"

"Eli offered him a reasonable option. Hyrum hates peas. Surely in forty-three years, she's come to realize that's a losing battle. And you backed him up."

Will backed him up because he knew why Hyrum hated peas. When he told her why, she sighed, "That is so messed up. All right, then why didn't she tell Eli to mind his own business?"

"For the same reason she won't tell Jax to back off, or me, or Drew. She believes she is less, Aisha. In her world, men make the rules and determine appropriate behavior. She didn't dare complain because it violates her religious beliefs. We are made in the image of God, and she's designed from a spare part."

"And Hyrum? He's an adult male."

"He's a little boy in her eyes. He was never anointed as a priest, the custom when boys reach age twelve in Florida. That's a clear-cut admission to manhood, and he was never allowed in. If he's a child, he's her responsibility and under her control."

She rolled over, pressing her belly against Will's. "I'm not sure how I'd handle it if this little guy had half of Hyrum's issues. I shouldn't judge."

"He's had every inch examined, Enzo. He's healthy."

"Little shit has given me stretch marks. Not just on my stomach, either. My poor boobs."

"As Wick would say, they're magnificent."

"They're a mess."

"Every one of those marks is part of the roadmap to the birth of our son. They're beautiful."

"We'll see how you feel six months from now when I still have a flabby belly and stretch marks all over."

"That wouldn't change a thing. In fact, if you don't want to be alone in this, I'll stop going to the gym and I'll gain twenty pounds."

"Don't you dare."

Fine. I'll gain twenty for him.

Now kiss. I know you want to.

"Indeed, Wick. I do."

They fell asleep still holding onto each other and barely moved all night. It was a good thing they got a long night's sleep because it was the last one they'd get for a while.

9

I woke at a little before five in the morning. The window seat in Will and Aisha's room was a good place to watch Jax run laps around Union Square, and it amused me because on the days Will did not run with him, he jogged slow enough that Eli could walk beside him and he looked like a man struggling to take his final steps. At least twice a week Will purposely did not run with Jax, for no reason other than he wanted that time for them. He thought they had talked more in a handful of those quiet mornings than they had in an entire calendar year while Eli lived in Scotland.

Sometimes Eli joined in when Will was out running, too, but his idea of participation was cutting across the Square and meeting them on the other side for a few seconds, mocking their speed.

They often ran too fast for him to get to the other side in time, but that didn't stop him. He sat down and waited, and the mocking began when they were within earshot.

Jax and Eli were out there, guards strolling ahead and guards strolling behind because running was not happening. Jax wasn't even pretending; he walked beside Eli, who was talking as much with his hands as his mouth, making Jax laugh, breath fogging in the early morning air. That was the picture I wished some intrusive paparazzo would plaster all over the Internet, instead of the serious and grim photos of the two that often appeared.

Vicat was already on the Square, waiting on her bench. Will had asked her why she bothered so early in the morning, and she shrugged, reminding him that if he was out running around the Square at stupid o'clock, he might be tempted to take a run at the portal. "I'm looking forward to the morning when I can tackle you away from it."

Without staring, she kept an eye on the King and his father, as well as their guards. From the bench, her view was probably not much more than heads bobbing up and down, but she watched from the moment they entered her field of vision until they disappeared around the corner. When Jax and Eli finally stopped in front of the stairs, she glanced away. There was nothing to see, really, just Jax giving his father a kiss on the cheek before he turned to go inside.

Eli wasn't done with his morning stroll. He headed up the stairs, one guard ahead and one trailing him, and when he was halfway across Vicat jumped up, her mouth open as she yelled. Eli froze for just a split second and then ducked as she leaped at him, taking him to the ground at the same time several flashes of light popped from a window nearby. She stayed on top of him as his guards crumpled to the ground, blood splattered across the cement.

I screamed. I wanted Will to wake up, so I screamed like someone had stepped on my tail, and I didn't stop until he was out of bed.

Three seconds later he was pulling on pants as he ran for the front door, yelling at me to find Drew and yelling at Aisha to stay away from the window and go downstairs to get Aubrey.

She did not stay away from the window.

Ten seconds after Will bolted out the apartment door, she was nearly dressed, and Jay stumbled out of his room, bleary-eyed, wanting to know what was going on. His first thought was of the baby—is it time? Is everything all right?—but Will was already gone and Aisha was upset, so he knew it was not time nor was everything all right.

"Something happened to Eli on the Square," she blurted as she headed out the door.

I didn't wait to see what he would do. I scrambled after her and we followed Aubrey to the front door, with everyone else behind us.

Guards made them wait on the sidewalk in front of the door. Even when Aubrey demanded one of them tell her what had happened or she was marching over there, he said firmly, "Ma'am, I can't allow that. Please go back inside."

No one went back inside.

Drew was the first to spot the anomaly to our left; there was a man hanging half out a window of a building on Stockton, the wall below him painted in blood. He nudged me with his foot and nodded toward the Square: they can't stop you. Go.

I went.

Two guards were on the ground, blood pooled around them. Will and Jax hovered over Eli, with more guards surrounding them; he was sitting upright, a scrape across his chin and he was holding his arm, but he was talking. Vicat sat nearby, the back of her shirt pockmarked with blood stains, though I didn't know if it was hers or if she'd been splattered by the dead guards.

I ran back to the steps and as loud as I could I said, *Eli is all right. He's not happy, but he's all right.*

Drew repeated it for everyone, and Aubrey sagged with relief.

"Anyone hurt?" he called out.

Two guards. Make them go inside. They don't want to see.

Jax's head guard was tugging on his arm, demanding he go inside. When Jax refused twice in a row, his guard nodded to another, and each took one of his arms, and he said, "Your Majesty, this isn't an option. You're going inside."

Will helped Eli up. "We're all going inside. Vicat, you, too. The medics can treat you there as well as here."

Eli looked helplessly at the dead guards. He balked at leaving, but there was nothing else that could be done for them. Before the city fully woke, when people walking to work and to school left their homes, the Square would already be cleared and cleaned up, the man hanging out the window would be gone, and there would be no sign that someone had just tried to kill the old King.

◆◆◆

Shirtless, shoeless, Will followed Vicat into the guard lounge. It was across the foyer from the guard desk and they left the door open, which I took as permission to enter and observe. The lounge was spacious and explained why none of them ever used the staff kitchen—they had everything in here. They had sofas and chairs and a giant wall monitor. There were two refrigerators which were stocked, I was sure, by the leftovers the Queen provided almost every night. There was an exercise area and beyond that a locker room. A guard could stay here for days or even weeks and not need anything other than clean clothes.

When the medic arrived, Vicat whipped off her shirt to allow him an examination of her injuries. She had several bloody streaks across her back, shallow burn marks that, had she not jumped on Eli, would have cut right through him. She shrugged when Will asked how bad it was. "I've had worse. I took a shot through Ethel and Gertrude while we were canvassing the perimeter around Base One in Kansas a couple years ago. That messed with my head. This? Eh."

"Ethel and Gertrude," Will repeated.

"Men name their junk, I name my boobs."

I jumped onto the table, where I could bonk her chin with my head.

She saved Eli.

"Indeed, Wick. What caught your attention, Vicat? Jax's guard reported that he heard you call out just before the shots were fired."

She'd noticed the window open a few seconds before, when Jax and Eli were saying goodbye. It bothered her; it was early morning and there was a damp nip in the air, far chillier than most people would prefer. An open window made no sense.

"I saw the glint from the tip of the rifle while it was still in the room. I moved. That's it."

That was not it.

While leaping for Eli, she pulled her sidearm, and after she landed on him, she fired. Two shots, one cleanly through the assailant's head.

"I wasn't fast enough," she said, though to my ears she was not making an excuse but rather stating a fact. "We're down two men that we shouldn't be."

"Not to minimize their loss, but you saved the life of the King's father."

She nodded. "I told you, the actual assignment doesn't matter. The royal family does. I technically abandoned my post, but I won't apologize for it. There wasn't enough time to adequately alert his guards."

He didn't think anyone would label her actions as having abandoned her post. He waited as the medic began sealing her wounds; she didn't flinch, but he knew it was painful and trying to speak would confirm that pain. He waited until she visibly relaxed; the medic was putting his things away, and she'd reached for her shirt.

"Who are you?" he asked. "Most of your records are sealed. You have no surname of record, and your given name has been struck from your file. You've never had an assignment close to the family and yet nothing we do surprises you. In fact, when Soto assigned you to the portals, you asked no questions. Everyone asks questions, even if they've heard whispering about the possibility of time travel."

She shrugged again.

"You've declined every promotion offered and yet remain in service. On Eli's orders. And prior to your date of enlistment, you don't seem to exist."

"Ah. Well, some of us were hatched in the royal guard armory. Experimental division. We were born eighteen and ready to serve."

"From which When are you?" he asked bluntly.

She got up. "I need a shower. I smell like burnt flesh and antiseptic."

"Don't think I won't follow you in there. It's a simple question, Vicat. When?"

She glanced around. There were three guards on the sofa, watching the news. Another was pulling something out of the fridge, and the medic was halfway out the door. Will watched her struggle with what she wanted to tell him, and how she looked at the other guards, then stood up and bellowed, "Clear the room."

They cleared the room.

When the door clicked shut, he sat back down and motioned for her to do the same.

"You know," she said as she sat, "you

technically don't have the authority to do that. Most of these kids don't grasp that. I do."

"They understand I have the King's ear," he said, reminding her. "Which When, Vicat?"

"Yours," she finally said. "By the years of our When, I'm a year younger than you are. By the years that passed here, I'm ten older. Time's a bitch."

He wanted to know how she got here—that was simple enough, Finn had arranged it and one of his techs had brought her here—and how she wound up in a protected position in the guard.

"I had skills," she said. "Those skills were offered to the King."

"Eli knows who you are."

"He did, at one time. I'm sure he's forgotten by now. But, there was a scuffle once, I pulled his guard out of some trouble...he knew my history, Emperor. He allowed me to stay put and not advance because he knew that I wanted to be close to anyone who might be able to get me home later."

"Why remain hidden? I would have kept the secret of your When."

She kept away from him for the same reasons everyone else Finn had deposited around Will did. It was the price Finn exacted for being saved. "And I didn't mind. I don't need the money that comes with rank and I certainly don't want to take a promotion someone else could benefit from. I've done what I've loved, I've taught these kids to save themselves. God knows I wish I'd had the skills when I was young."

"Hard life at home?"

"I don't remember the worst of it, to be honest. My parents gave me up when I was a toddler. I got lucky and landed with a great foster mother, but so did ten other kids and there was a lot of scrapping going on. I learned to fight just to keep the little assholes off my back." She snorted. "I love those little assholes, don't get me wrong. They're why I wanted the option to go home, until recently."

"You no longer wish to?"

She wasn't sure. "I've worked hard to stay under the radar, Emperor. The reason my parents gave me away has been here, and the last thing I wanted was for him to see me."

"Who?"

"Biological brother," she said simply. "He beat the holy hell out of me when I was a baby. It was the last time he did that convinced my parents to give me up. If they'd kept me, he would have eventually killed me."

Why didn't they give him away instead?

"I'm sure if my father had known, you wouldn't have been placed anywhere near each other."

The odds of distant family members winding up together was slim, simply because so few people were taken. There wasn't enough time to save them all. Out of over a million people in the city, Finn and his team were only able to save 20,000.

"Yeah, well, here we are. Or were. Since he's gone home, I've decided I might as well stay here."

"He's gone home. How do you know?"

"You had the prince bring his sorry ass back for a family reunion, Emperor." She was not happy and didn't care if he knew. "I'd hoped that when he was exiled, it meant permanently. That was the closest I've come to running into him, and I'd like it to be the last time."

Will sat up straighter. "George Denton is your brother."

She nodded.

Oh, are you going to tell her or can I?

"Please tell me the son of a bitch is not being allowed back permanently. If he is, I'm asking you to take me home."

"There is no flexibility in Jax's order of exile other than a compassion visit for Jay's sake. He might be granted one more, but it will be at the hospital. You need not be present."

"Good. Not that he would recognize me, but I'm not convinced I wouldn't rip his head off his neck."

"As one would be tempted, I understand."

She got up again. "I wasn't kidding about smelling myself. Do you know what you need to know, Emperor? And still honoring your word to stay away from the portals? Just long enough for me to shower and change and file my report. After that, go for it. I wouldn't mind tackling another royal today."

You're not telling her? I asked him on the way upstairs.

"Not yet."

You think she's lying?

"No. But I'm not sure what the right thing to do is, Wick. I'd like to consult with Aisha and Aubrey. Perhaps Jax."

Make him feel important. Include him.

"Yes, because being King is not important enough."

Jax was no fool; he knew who was in charge in this household, and it sure as hell wasn't him.

"We're on lockdown," Jax told Red. "No one in or out until the guard gives an all clear."

There was a unit-to-unit search of the buildings surrounding Union Square; they'd located the apartment the gunman had fired from, and there was nothing that pointed to another shooter, but no one was taking a chance. Both the guard and the police were searching, and until they were done, we were staying home.

Red grumbled because he had promised Bree a morning spent at the DeYoung Museum—he counted it as her history lesson for the day, given that he'd taken her out of school for this trip—but the only one affected by a forced day off was Aisha. She had to call and arrange for her classes to be canceled, and since she only had a couple weeks left, she hated having to do that.

"We can play school today!" Hyrum declared. "We have students and we have teachers and we can practice our letters and our numbers!"

"I thought he hated school," Zed grumbled to Jay.

It didn't matter. They were playing school. Aubrey made breakfast, and after that, everyone crowded around the table with tablets ready, and there was paper and pencils for Hyrum and Bree. Aubrey laughed when she realized they were waiting for her, and then said, "All right. Spelling test."

Will and Jax settled into the living room, waiting for Eli. Like Vicat, once the medic left, all he wanted was a shower.

Valerie left. She's not gonna try to go outside, will she?

"She just went downstairs, I think," Will said.

"My mother?" Red asked. "I'd bet dollars to donuts she's unhappy because Hyrum skipped over bible study and went right to school. I'm frankly surprised it was his idea."

What the heck does dollars to donuts mean?

"It's just a saying, Wick." He looked at Red. "We may need reminders in the presence of your mother that you don't understand why we talk to the cat. It occurs to me that if she believes we actually are conversing with him, she may deem it evil."

"A whole lot is going on here that she would put down to the work of the devil. I'd be lying if I didn't admit that I'd like to see the look on her face if you planted a thought into her head, and she realized it."

That's kinda mean.
I kinda like it.

"Still," he went on, "I don't think she'd be terribly surprised."

"What does she make of Aubrey's abilities?" Jax asked.

"She doesn't quite realize the extent of Aubrey's empathic nature," Red said. "When we were young, Aubrey was always able to comfort the other kids, but I'm sure our mother chalked it up to an innate calling to motherhood. Joe is somewhat like her, and Hy—"

We all startled when Hyrum jumped up, his chair skittering backward. He pumped his fists in the air and shouted, "ABCDEFG, I win!"

"I've never gotten used to that," Red said. "Don't feel bad. It started when he was three or four. Little victories mean a lot."

"What'd he win?" Jax called out.

"He can write his alphabet faster than the rest of us," Oz said. "And I think I missed a letter. What the hell? I forgot my P."

Hyrum's hands clamped over his mouth, and he sat down, giggling.

"I honestly hate to say this," Red said quietly, "but he's never had this much fun. After Aubrey left...we were not as good to him as we should have been. She was gone, and he lost his second mother. Bree is the closest thing to a loving sister that he has. As the rest of us grew up, we basically left him behind. Joe makes an effort, but he has a family and limited time."

"I grew up an only child," Jax said. "I have no idea what that's like."

"You forget about all your imaginary siblings," Eli said as he came out of the bathroom. "You left them behind, too. If I leave without grabbing my own clothes, I'm issuing a pre-emptive apology. My shirt is soaking in the bathroom sink, but I don't think those stains will ever come out."

"I'll shove it down the incinerator," Jax said. "You have other shirts."

"Any word on who wanted my brain splattered all over Union Square?" he asked, dropping onto the sofa next to Red. "And how's Vicat? She seemed talkative enough. How badly was she hurt?"

"She's fine," Will said. "And no, the report has not come through. We're still on lockdown."

"Eh, fine. We can assume someone doesn't want me to cast Pacifica's vote."

Red couldn't even promise him it wasn't one of his people. Levi's machination was still in operation, clearly, and there were at least twelve other people who could have issued an order to take him out.

"Twelve is oddly specific," Will said.

"Twelve Apostles," Red said. "The Quorum."

Hyrum's arms shot up again, but this time he didn't jump up. "Twenty times ten, I did it again!"

"Eleven times four," Jay challenged.

"Forty-four and I'll do it some more!"

"Twelve times six," Zed said.

"Seventy-two and it sucks to be you!" He clamped his hands over his mouth and uttered a muffled, "I'm sorry."

Aisha told them to turn the volume down a little and came into the living room. She perched on the arm of Will's chair, waving him off when he started to get up to give her his seat. "He's *really* good with math. Aubrey pulled up one of her advanced student math work pages, and he tore through it in a few minutes. Didn't get a thing wrong."

"Huh." Red leaned forward to see into the dining room. "I don't think Mom has ever stressed anything more than simple addition and subtraction with him. Just enough for him to know how much money he has and how much he's spent."

"Recess!" Hyrum blurted. He ran into the living room, practically jumping at Red. He straddled Red's lap, his hands squeezing his older brother's cheeks together. "I win! Daddy said, 'don't play games like that, Hyrum, you'll never be able to win,' but I did win. I got all my numbers right and I got my letters right."

Red pulled Hyrum's hands away and kissed him on the tip of his nose. "Good job. I'm proud of you. Who taught you math, slugger?"

"Bree," Hyrum whispered. "But don't tell Daddy, because he'll get mad. Daddy said, 'math is for students and men, Hyrum, and you'll never be either.' But Bree said I was smart enough, and she showed me how to learn it." He whispered even lower. "She was only five, Red. She could do times things when she was five."

"No worry there. But I mean it, Hy. I'm very proud of the things you're learning."

"Aubrey is teaching me to read better. Tonight, I'm reading a whole story to Zed. But it's not from the bible so don't tell Mom."

"Mom realizes there are good stories in other books. It's fine."

Oz tapped Hyrum on the back. "Come on. We're going upstairs. There's a great big room up there where we can make noise and not upset the old people."

Red let out an *oof* as Hyrum sprang off his lap.

"I don't know who had more fun," Aubrey said. "Hyrum or the kids. I don't think they were participating simply for his amusement. They actually enjoyed themselves."

Red sighed. "This is the point that Dad would complain that they're spoiling him. Or Mom, if she'd stayed up here. Though she'd mostly be worried that he was getting too excited."

Why can't he get excited? I doubt his head is gonna pop or anything.

"She can't fault us for wanting to keep him occupied." Aubrey bent over and kissed Jax on the cheek. "That lockdown needs to be lifted before lunch, or you're all having bologna sandwiches. I need to go shopping."

"The Queen does her own shopping?" Red asked.

"Unless I can talk one of the kids into it, yes. I also do the laundry and clean the toilets. It's not the life of luxury you might think."

"The guards won't hold me," Will said. "Make a list, I'll go."

Aisha followed her into the kitchen. Red watched them, and then sat forward, suddenly serious. "I have a favor to ask. And not of my brother-in-law. I'm asking the King of Pacifica."

"No, you can't try the crown on."

"Well, now. No. This is more than a favor, really. Consider it a formal request. My brother, David, is cut from the same cloth as our father." He looked to Eli. "No proof, but I won't be the least bit surprised to hear he's behind your attack. A poorly conceived assassination attempt in a guarded venue? That was Levi, and it would be David. If I find proof, I'll hand it over. I ask that you do the same. And if it's him...he has to be extricated from Florida. My only choice, if he's truly trying to overthrow the government and instigate war, is to have him executed."

"And you think we won't."

"You have no death penalty."

"We do regarding attacks on the King," Will said. "The King Emeritus falls under that scope."

Whatever favor Red was going to ask and whatever Jax was going to say was lost when Aisha yelled from the kitchen, "Will, get a mop. My water just broke."

10

He did not get a mop.

He shot out of his chair and darted into the kitchen, where she stood in the middle of a puddle. She looked a bit sheepish and he looked terrified, barking at Jax to call Mass and then call the guard and get the lockdown lifted. He told me to run and get Jay, but I did what everyone else did.

Not much.

Jax disappeared into Aubrey's office nook because the broom closet was in there and she stored her mop with her brooms. Eli and Red stayed in the living room because they didn't want to get in the way and Red knew better than to try to hurry a pregnant woman along. Will was the only anxious person there, and he couldn't grasp why no one was moving.

"We have hours still," Aisha told him. "I haven't even had a contraction. Relax."

"But..." he gestured to the puddle on the floor. "Your water."

"It happens."

Aubrey brushed past Aisha and patted Will on the arm. "Go upstairs and get her some dry clothes, sweetie. Once she's changed and more comfortable, you can call Mass and ask him what he wants you to do."

"And the guard?"

"We have a roof," Jax said as he went to fill a bucket. "Ambulance can land there if it comes to it. Or they'll let Mass and his aides in, and she can have the baby on the balcony with the pigeon gangs watching. It'll be fine."

"But—"

"Bilbo," Aisha said. "Clothes."

"But—"

Eli got up, grabbed a belt loop on the back of Will's pants, and jerked him back. "Go do what your wife told you to, son. And stop worrying. There's plenty of time."

He finally went.

"So, the one with the nerves of steel is going to crumple like a wet towel at your first contraction," he said to Aisha, who had kicked off her shoes and was stepping onto a dry towel that Audrey had tossed down for her. "He's going to be useless for the next few years, isn't he?"

"Timing could be better, but yes, he's going to be useless," Jax said.

"No work talk," Aubrey declared. "You won't say a thing to William about the timing, and you won't draw his attention to anything but this baby."

"Good luck with that." Aisha, feet dry, started for the hallway. She waddled her way across the living room and reached the entry in time to see Hyrum leap off the stairs, three up, his feet slamming onto the tile.

He skipped into the living room and stopped, eyes wide, and whispered loudly to Aisha, "I won't tell. I promise I won't tell." He started to pull his shirt over his head. "You can cover with this. I can get a clean one."

She stopped him before he could get it off. "Sweetie, thank you, but I'm all right. Will went to get me some dry clothes."

He leaned close. "He knows? He's not mad, right?"

"It's not what you think, Hyrum," Red said. "The baby is getting ready to come."

"Oh. Oh! Like when Darlene had Bree, and everything went *whoosh* and then she yelled 'Redmond, this is all your fault!' and then there was Bree?"

"Like that, but maybe not as fast. Bree came sooner than we expected."

"Don't sneeze!" Hyrum called after Aisha. "He might fall out!"

"I don't think that's how it works," Eli said. "Where are the other kids? Aren't they playing anymore?"

"They're coming. I won the race!"

"Today is just your day," Jax said. "You're winning everything."

"That's because I got a head start. I didn't say we were racing until I was at the stairs, and Oz said, 'Hey that's not fair!' but Drew laughed and said, 'You snooze you lose!' so I won."

The noise level shot up uncomfortably, so much that when Will took the clothes to Aisha in the bathroom, he asked if she wanted to go upstairs. Home might be more comfortable, and it would certainly be quieter; on any given day the family together was loud, but with the addition of Hyrum and Bree, it felt like the volume had doubled.

"Unless you want one more shot at wild sex before this baby comes, I'd like to stay here."

"Sex? Now?"

"Last chance, handsome. After this, it'll be a while."

He did not want sex. He wanted to take her to the hospital, where there were doctors and nurses and no chance that Hyrum's warning would come true.

"All right, then," she said as she peeled off her wet clothing. "Could you go ask Aubrey if she has a pad I could have?"

"What?"

"Or Oz."

"What?"

He's gone stupid. I'll go ask Drew. He'll ask Oz. It'll be fine.

Will let me out of the bathroom and I found Drew in the kitchen with Oz, smooching by the refrigerator like no one else could see them. I apologized for the interruption and relayed Aisha's request, and after answering Drew's confused "What for?" with "Drips," she disappeared into their room.

Biology, dude. Study it.

"I know biology, Wick. I just wasn't thinking."

Neither is Will right now. We can mock him a lot and he won't even notice.

We were not, he said, mocking Will. In a few years that would be him, and he was sure he would be terrified out of his mind. It didn't matter that Will had peripherally gone through it when Oz and Zed were born; that was different, that was more like his sister being in labor, and this was his wife.

Once she was in clean clothes and resting on the sofa, Aisha relented and had him call Mass. The faintest of contractions had begun, but the lockdown hadn't been lifted, and she agreed he might want a heads up about that.

The noise level dropped to whispers. Aisha insisted Will put Mass on speaker so she could tell him what she was feeling, and Oz pushed the kids towards her room. They could watch a video or play a game and give Aisha privacy.

"It's still early." Mass sounded far away. "Give it a couple hours, but if they let you out of the house soon, go ahead and check into the hospital."

"I'm barely contracting," Aisha told him.

"But your water broke. I'd prefer you were in the hospital where we can monitor everything."

That only made Will tenser. He called the guard desk to ask how soon they could expect the lockdown to be lifted and complained when he was told it could be two more hours.

"The baby's not coming that soon, Bilbo. Relax."

He did not relax.

He sat next to her on the sofa, legs crossed, foot bouncing so hard and fast that she threatened to rip it from his ankle. Every time she had a contraction, he grabbed his phone to check the time and how long they were, which amused Aubrey until she realized he was checking his phone an awful lot and it hadn't even been an hour.

Quietly, she got up and went into Oz's room. One by one the kids filtered out, except for Oz and Drew, and they went to the kitchen table as if they expected someone to whip up lunch while Aisha was on the sofa, trying to not whimper. When Aubrey came out, she headed for her office, which worried me, so I followed her in and eavesdropped as she called Mass and told him that Aisha's contractions were just minutes apart.

"That baby isn't waiting," she told him. "So, you need to either get over here or send someone."

"Lockdown lifted?" he asked.

"It doesn't matter. She can't go anywhere now, and the guards will let you in if they know what's good for them."

As she hung up, Aisha cried out.

"Here we go, Wick," she said. "You need to stay out of their way, all right? Rhys doesn't need to be born with cat hair up his nose."

Will was kneeling by the sofa, helpless, and she had two of his fingers in her hand, squeezing as hard as she could.

"Bilbo," she breathed hard, "he's not waiting. This is happening."

Don't panic.

"Mass is on his way," Aubrey said. She told Will to help Aisha into Oz and Drew's room and had Jay drag the spare mattress from Zed's room. It would be easier, she thought, if Aisha were closer to the floor than on the bed, and easier for Mass.

"I don't think Mass can get here soon enough," Aisha said through clenched teeth. "I need to push."

Red headed for the stairs. "Hold tight. I'll get Mom."

Aubrey stopped him. "What for?"

He gestured to Aisha. "Mom's delivered a few dozen babies, Aubrey. Including Bree." He headed down the stairs and yelled over his shoulder, "Will, she'll try to toss you out of the room. Fair warning."

"Will not happen."

Valerie Munson stormed up the stairs, far quicker than I would have expected for a seventy-five-year-old woman, and she was tugging on the sleeves of her shirt, pushing them to her elbows as she demanded a bottle of sanitizer so that she could disinfect her hands. She barked orders to Aubrey and Jax, warned the kids to be quiet and respectful, and when she went into the room the nervous tension in the apartment doubled.

"Lots of ladies ask Grandma to be there when their babies are born," Hyrum said, quietly as he was told. "She even knows what to do when they're all turned around and trying to go out the wrong way."

Bree snickered. "She says the babies who are breech are always boys. They never know where they're going."

"We need maps," Hyrum declared. "Maps with pictures."

Aisha cried out, and Jay started to get up. "Jesus. I feel like I need to do something."

"Pray," Hyrum said. "That's what we should do. We should pray for Aisha and Will and your new baby brother." He held his hands out to Bree and Oz, who sat on either side of him. One by one they took hands and bowed their heads. When Oz asked Hyrum to lead the prayer, he lit up and quietly began reciting prayers from his youth.

I couldn't help there. I didn't know the words, and no one was holding my paw. I walked past Jax and Eli and Red, who waited nervously in the living room, and pushed through the cat flap into Oz's room. I wasn't going to get in the way, but I needed to be there. Will was kneeling near Aisha's head and he noticed me come in, but didn't tell me to leave, so I walked the long way around and jumped up onto the window seat where I would be near him.

Valerie glanced at Aubrey and told her to get that filthy cat out of here, but Aisha hissed, "I will bite the person who makes him leave."

"It's a bad idea for a cat to be where a baby is born," Valerie said. "He won't get his first breath, and that cat is carrying germs."

"Good lord, Mom," Aubrey sighed. "He won't steal the baby's breath. That's a tired old wives' tale. The only thing Wick might do is start talking nonstop and drive us each a little batty."

"Wick can sing for all I care," Aisha hissed.

I've never seen you rendered speechless, dude. She's done this before. Relax.

"Here we go," Aisha snorted. "The song of his people."

Will grimaced when she grabbed onto his leg, fingers digging in. He waited until the contraction had passed before he asked, "Is this worse than it was with Jay?"

"Oh, hon, I don't know. I was numb from my boobs down with him. Where is he? Is he all right? I know he's—"

I took that as a request and ran into the dining room to get him. He followed, uncertain, wanting to be there but not wanting to see his mother's pain. Valerie was not happy that he was there—she didn't need to say it, but she wanted the men in the living room, waiting, and would have welcomed Oz and Bree because this was a learning experience for women—but she'd already learned that these people didn't follow the same map that she did.

"Just tell me what to do," Jay said.

She didn't need him to do anything other than be there. He sat with me on the window seat and watched, helplessly, as Will helped lift her up to push. He half held his breath with his hands pressed to his chest when Valerie told her she only needed one or two more good pushes, and on the last one, as Aisha roared with the pain and delight of that final push, his breath hitched and tears spilled over his eyelashes.

"And here he is," Valerie said as she lifted the baby away from Aisha's body. I lost sight of what happened after that, because Aubrey was in the way and I looked more at Will and Jay. They were both crying, but it was manly tears that I wouldn't mock them for later.

Aisha half sat up, using Will as a backrest, and Valerie placed Rhys in her arms. He let out a mighty wail, indignant and cold and angry, announcing to everyone in the house, "Dudes, I'm here, and you're never going to be the same."

I'm guessing.

Jay moved from the window seat to the floor, scooting close to his mother's shoulder, peeking at his new brother. Will kissed the baby's surprisingly hairy head and Jay gently touched his tiny toes; he counted them silently, then did the same with his fingers. I moved to the sofa where I could see them better, risking the wrath of Valerie. Aubrey leaned back just enough for me to give someone a head bonk and she whispered to me, "He's beautiful, isn't he?"

He was eight pounds of screaming, bloody, angry little boy stuffed into a nineteen-inch-long frame and he'd already reduced two men to tears.

Beautiful didn't begin to cover it.

◆◆◆

With the exception of Valerie, who'd delivered him, and Jay—who was right there and no one was telling him no—the first person to hold Rhys was Jax. Will hadn't forgotten that he was the first to hold Oz, before Eli and Donna, and passing that on was important to him. After Rhys had been cleaned up and swaddled, and Aisha was off the floor and in Oz and Drew's bed, Will carefully handed his son to his brother.

I heard the soft click of a camera from the other side of the room; Drew was quietly taking pictures, capturing as many of Rhys's firsts as he could. That was a photo Jay would one day paint on canvas, his dad and uncle both with hands on his baby brother, their foreheads just touching as they gazed down at him.

Mass came— "Well, you didn't seem to need me after all, did you?" — and went after proclaiming Rhys and Aisha both healthy and well enough to stay at home, though he also told Will what to look for and to not hesitate to call or take them right in if he was even a tiny bit concerned. Valerie had delivered more babies than he had and as far as he was concerned, she was the one they wanted on hand.

When Finn and Jo arrived to meet their new grandson, Valerie was the first one Jo went to. She grabbed Aubrey's mother in a tight hug and thanked her repeatedly, and then Finn kissed her on the cheek.

"Babies come out whether we want them to or not," Valerie told Aubrey in an amused whisper. "We wait and catch them, that's all. It just makes the mothers feel better if they think someone else knows what's going on."

She tolerated more affection when Aubrey kissed her. "You know you made all the difference in the world here today, Mom. I don't know what we would have done without you."

"You'd have caught that baby, that's what," Valerie insisted. She nodded toward Will, who was perched at the edge of the bed. "He turned into mush, didn't he? Barely a word. Hard to believe Levi was so frightened of him."

"Was he really?"

"He thought it was hard to trust a man who never ages, especially one whose brute strength is spoken of like a warning behind closed doors. Now Red, he says the Emperor has earned respect among world leaders, but there are still those who are like Levi, and they fear him. That the King of Pacifica has him at his right hand makes other men a bit nervous, I think."

Aubrey pulled her into the hallway. "You've heard a lot over the years. What about the attempt on Eli today? Which of those nervous men would be foolish enough to try to kill the King's father?"

She glanced at Red, who was in the living room with Bree. "The man who never stopped loving Levi," she said. "With God's mercy on my soul and a little bit of proof, I would hand him over if I could. But David, he would be foolish enough to want dead anyone he thinks will get in his way and he'll convince himself it's God's work."

"Why? What does he want?"

"Revenge?" She shrugged. "I don't hear as many things now that Levi is gone. But David wants what he had before the war. Women in their place, suitable men in charge, and Red gone."

"Red knows this?"

"I think he understands that he's making changes that the men in the church's higher ranks disapprove of. That makes him a target. Other men, the ones who raise their families and pay their tithings and never aspire to politics, they love what Red is doing. The sons of my friends, they talk. They want their daughters to have everything their sons do. But they're not the men who count. The Quorum counts, and David wants to sit at the head of their table."

As Jax came out of the room, Aubrey grabbed him by the arm and guided him into the living room. "You three. Go down to the office and talk."

"About?" Red asked.

"David."

"We discussed him earlier," Jax said, gesturing to Red. "There's no proof, not yet. But when the time comes, yes, I'll want to talk to your mother."

Aubrey didn't know what to do.

"We're not worrying the rest of today," Jax said. "From here until morning, everything is about Rhys. Jay and I are going upstairs to get his bassinette and clothes, Oz and Drew are grabbing guards and then going out to get diapers and groceries, and we're spending the rest of today listening to the loudest baby I think I've ever heard."

She didn't want to let Oz and Drew leave. "What if—?"

"They'll have their guards and a few extra. They'll be fine."

She wasn't convinced, but Hyrum came out of Zed's room wearing a clean, tucked-in baby-blue t-shirt, his hair neatly combed, and he came up to Aubrey and said quietly, "I'd like to meet the baby now. Can I meet Rhys? I'll be gentle and quiet, and I won't make him cry."

He held Jax's hand the few steps into the bedroom, and I followed. Will told Hyrum to sit on the sofa, and he brought Rhys to him, carefully setting the baby in Hyrum's arms. He didn't remind Hyrum to be careful, and he didn't ask him to be quiet. He sat next to them and watched, waiting.

Hyrum bent his neck until his face was only a few inches away from the baby's. "Hi, Rhys," he said softly. "I'm Hyrum. You're a big boy. I've never held a new baby who was so big." He looked up at Will. "What's his whole name? Does he have one yet?"

"Rhys Davonte Blackshear. He's named for Aisha's father."

"I like that. It sounds good. If you're mad at him, you can yell the whole thing and he'll know you mean business. And when he's grown up, it sounds like a man's name."

"So does Hyrum," Will offered.

He giggled. "It sounds like an *old* man's name. Can I give him a kiss on his head? I won't kiss his lips and give him germs."

Will nodded, and after Hyrum kissed Rhys, he said softly, "Listen to your daddy, Rhys. He'll tell you important things. Eat your vegetables, say your prayers, and always be nice. But you don't have to eat peas. Peas fit in your pocket and you can flush them later. You're a good boy, Rhys. Everyone says babies are beautiful, but it doesn't matter because if you're good, you're always beautiful." He kissed him again. "I love you, baby Rhys."

Will leaned over and kissed Hyrum at his temple. "Thank you for that, Hyrum. I don't think he'll ever get better advice."

"You should take him now. I don't want to drop him."

"You've never dropped a baby, Hyrum," Valerie said from the doorway. "If ever a man should have been—" She motioned for him to get up. "Come on now. Let's let the new mommy and daddy get to know their baby boy."

"Can we go say a prayer for them?"

"I would love nothing more."

"Can we pray for no peas at dinner, too?"

She was laughing as she closed the door, but I was pretty sure he wouldn't have to eat peas for a very long time.

"All right, Wick," Will said as he got up. "You've been very patient. Come on." He patted the bed, an invitation to jump up. "Meet our boy."

He set Rhys on the bed next to Aisha and undid the swaddling Valerie had bundled him in. Rhys had a towel for a diaper because that was something they thought they still had time to buy, and his protruding belly button was ugly and bloody, though Will assured me it was a stump that would fall off. I sniffed him from head to toe, trying hard to not tickle him with my whiskers, and I resisted the urge to head bonk him.

He had black hair that stuck out in all directions, and his tongue flicked in and out of his mouth. I wanted to see his eyes, but they were closed, and it seemed rude to ask Will to pry one open just so I could see what color they were. He was very pink, pinker than I'd ever seen on a person, but I knew that could change.

This was my boy.

He's acceptable.

"I can't believe it," Will breathed. "He's real. He's here. He's—"

Amazing. Go on. Say it. Drew doesn't own the word.

"Ours," Aisha said. "Everything we ever wanted, Bilbo." She grinned and told him to kiss her, and when he did, she said, "Hi, Daddy" against his lips.

"Hi, Mommy."

All right. I'm leaving you two to get drippy and sweet and vomit-inducing all by yourselves. First one to hurl can blame it on the baby.

11

The next day, after another loud family breakfast during which Hyrum stood and reminded everyone that they needed to be quiet because noise hurts baby ears and if they didn't pipe down, a grownup would get mad and they wouldn't be allowed to play at all for a day or two, Jay took the bassinette back upstairs. He was gone longer than expected, long enough that Will almost sent Drew to make sure everything was all right, and when he came back, he looked worried.

"First," he said, "Dad says congrats on the baby, and he can't wait to meet him. He digs the name and got kind of sniffly about it."

"Second?" Will prompted.

"He wants to see you. He's looked at his life, and when he balances everything out, he'd rather leave it all behind and give George another chance. But, he was all specific in that he won't do anything if it means leaving me behind, and I promised him it wouldn't."

"They didn't actually divorce, did they?" Oz asked.

Jay shook his head. "No, but it's complicated. They'd have to remarry if Dad moves, wouldn't they? If they wanted to be married again, I mean."

"Your father and...George?" Valerie was horrified and looked to Aubrey. "And you're all right with this? With your children being around it?"

"I don't pick and choose other peoples' spouses, Mom. But yes, I'm all right with it. Jay's father is a wonderful man, and if he loves another, who am I to judge?"

"But—"

"Jesus never said a thing about it, Mom," Aubrey said. "I think this is one of those things where kindness is more important than a few verses in the Old Testament, all right?"

Will wasn't about to let a debate begin. "Invite him over," he told Jay. "Upstairs. We'll have coffee, he can meet the baby, and we'll talk."

"I have to get to class—"

"And I'm capable of entertaining your father without you. Your mother will be there, too."

No one wanted to let Valerie launch a moral debate. They cleaned up their breakfast dishes, and there was a lot of kissing of parents with a promise to Hyrum and Bree that they'd be back in a few hours. Drew groaned that he was going to throw up because he had to teach Aisha's class, and then quiet settled in so nicely that I could have taken a nap if not for wanting to keep an eye on Rhys.

I need a raise. The baby has added duties to my day.

I jumped up on Drew's vacated chair and looked over the table at Valerie.

This is killing you, isn't it? You hate this maybe even more than Jax hates me being on the counter.

"I won't lift the order of exile on George," Jax said to Will. "I will allow a few more compassionate visits, but he's not staying."

Will nodded. "James is aware."

"You're all right with it? It means Jay visiting them away from home."

Aisha sighed. "We've talked about it. He's a big boy. It's his decision to make, how often he goes and how long he stays. I'd be upset, but...I want him to have a relationship with his father."

"If things here go to shit, I just might send all the kids," Jax mused.

That was enough to prod Valerie away from the table. She told Hyrum and Bree to clean their dishes, and she would meet them downstairs for prayer and bible study. Red watched her leave, chuckling to himself, and when she was down the stairs, he said, "It's not like she didn't hear that and worse from Dad."

"It's not like she hasn't said that word herself," Bree said.

Hyrum giggled. "One time, she told Daddy to go to hell, but he said, 'Woman, I'm already there.'"

"Hell isn't a bad word, is it?" Bree asked Red. "It's a place."

He explained that he didn't think it was a bad word when used in the context of a literal Hell, but when telling someone to go there, or saying it when you stubbed a toe or made a mistake, it was probably wrong.

"Daddy said, 'If I hear you say that word I'll make you eat soap!'" Hyrum said. "Don't say it. Soap tastes bad."

"I don't get the soap," Bree told him. "I just get Mom's *special* look and that's enough. Or sometimes Daddy frowns and points his finger at me. Maybe I'm just cuter than you."

"I'm handsome. You're beautiful."

"And you're making your grandmother anxious," Red told them. "Go on now, she's waiting for you."

Hyrum wanted to wait for Aubrey, but she thought it would be nice for Valerie to have a morning alone with them. "You did a lot of schooling yesterday. Go make Grandma happy. She'd like time alone with the two of you."

"You just want a shot at holding the baby," Jax teased as he got up. "Will, enjoy the day off. Hell, the week. Dad and I will discuss the vote and call you if we need your input."

"Text first," Will said. "Wake him up, and I'll hurt you."

Red went with Jax, and Aisha handed Rhys over to Aubrey.

"He's not kidding about sending all the kids through the portal if it feels like things are getting dicey," she told them. "He doesn't trust using a safe house again, and no one can touch them if they're sitting in Finn and Jo's apartment two hundred years from now."

Will was on board with the idea. "If it looks like it's getting that bad, you're all going. You, Aisha, all the kids. My parents. Hell, James. I'd want him there for Jay."

"It can't get that bad," Aubrey said, though it sounded more like a wish than truth.

"David Munson has the Quorum in his pocket and his finger on the launch command to nuclear missiles. If he doesn't get the vote he wants, he'll at least threaten." Before Aubrey could get her brain around the idea that her brother was willing to kill them all for land and an ancient idea, he added, "We'll protect your family, Aubrey. Jax has a safe house waiting, the one on Nevada. It's a multiplex and has room enough for all of them."

"It's a big family," she said softly.

"The Munsons are a prolific bunch," he agreed. "Jax knows how many siblings and spouses and their offspring. Some have grandkids. They're accounted for. If they want out of Florida, he can protect them."

You'd send the baby away? He just got here.

"Wick, if it comes to it, I'm sending you, too."

No. You need me.

He bent toward me. "This is our son, Wick. You've claimed him as yours. I need you to be with him and Aisha, all right?"

But I'm your anchor.

"Anything that happens won't last long enough to trigger an issue with time. I need your word, Wick. Where Aisha and Rhys go, you will, too. Protect them."

He had me there.

I married her, too, and I was there when Rhys was made. I'd claimed them.

David Munson couldn't be that stupid.

James Okuda came bearing gifts. He had a teddy bear for Rhys, a storybook for Jay to read to his brother, chocolates for Aisha—because he knew she wouldn't want flowers and wine seemed kind of mean—and a small bottle of extremely good scotch for Will.

I expected him to be more nervous or a little awkward about visiting his ex-wife in her new, very big, very spiffy apartment just one floor up from the King and Queen, but he was so fascinated with Rhys that he forgot where he was. There was a lot of small talk about babies, and then reminiscing about when Jay was born, enough that I started thinking he'd forgotten why he was there.

"Why," he asked as he stared into Rhys's tiny face, "didn't we even think about naming Jay after your father? It's a beautiful name."

"You brought up naming him after you first. And I liked the idea of calling him JJ. And then oops, Jaime."

"Ah, the right baby got the right name," he said. "You were meant to be, weren't you?" He carefully handed the baby back to Aisha. "Jay is thrilled, isn't he? He's already called me four times. Rhys being born at home just about blew his mind."

"Nearly blew mine," Will huffed.

"Do you know if George's baby has been born?" James asked. "I know, you're not exactly friends, but I thought he might be in touch."

"I don't know specifically, but I would assume by now. The baby was due not long after you saw him."

Aisha wanted to know if George having a child made a difference either way for James. It would be a big enough step to leave home to be with him if were just the two of them but adding a baby to the mix made it a massive leap. "You'll have to love that child, James. You can't go and be ambivalent about his existence."

George had loved Jay. Even at his worst, he'd loved James's son. "How could I not? Look at Rhys. Can you imagine anyone not loving this little boy? I love George. I'll love every part of him."

"And the lifestyle changes? The life you currently live will not be possible, James."

He nodded.

"Well, not until he meets people," Aisha snickered. "Sweetie, you have to have a completely open mind about this. Because once you know where he is, if you decide against going, you still can't tell anyone. Not even a hint."

"Unless it's a nudist colony, then I tell all." He shrugged lightly. "I could handle that."

That made Aisha howl. "James, you can't even say the word 'penis.' What makes you think you can be anywhere so open?"

"I'm a bit of a whore," he said simply.

"And for this, you need to be an extremely open-minded whore," Will said. "You don't have to believe anything I tell you, but you have to accept when I say I can prove it."

Start with me. If he can swallow you and me talking, he can swallow anything.

With that, Will got up. He was leaving the room, to the back of the house, and would come back in one minute. During that time, James needed to think of something to tell me, something Will wouldn't ordinarily be able to guess. Aisha was the witness. He left James with his mouth hanging open, wondering what was going on.

"He's not kidding, James. Think of something to tell Wick before he comes back."

"Uh. I don't know. Sixty-two. That's it. Just... sixty-two."

You want it verbatim? I asked Will when he returned.

"Verbatim."

I repeated it word for word, and Will parroted it back. "'Uh. I don't know. Sixty-two. That's it. Just...sixty-two.'" That wasn't quite enough to convince him, because for all he knew Will could hear from the back of the house.

When Jay called him last week he told him the next weekend they have together they should walk across the bridge and go into Sausalito. I don't know what James said but then Jay told him not to be a wuss, it wasn't that far.

He paled a little bit at that.

"How?"

"We're not sure," Will said. "But I've been able to understand him since I was three or four."

"Come on. You expect me to believe that cat is forty years old?"

"He's not," Will said.

"He's probably over one hundred," Aisha said.

The only reason James didn't roll his eyes was because he wanted to be polite. He did huff out an exasperated breath, waiting for them to both laugh, and was confused when they didn't. "All right. Open mind. You're screwing with me, but if this is what it takes, I'll play along."

"James, I had a baby not even twenty-four hours ago," Aisha said. "I'm tired, I hurt, I can't stand upright yet, and I'm not screwing around. This is life here. Will and Wick can converse, Wick is older than all of us, and until you can somehow accept that, it doesn't make sense to take you along any further."

"How does that have anything to do with George?" He sounded a little snippy, but I could hardly blame him.

Tell him the truth. You might as well get it out there.

"What, Wick?" Aisha asked.

"He thinks James is owed the full truth. He might be right."

Before she could agree, or James could ask what the hell was going on, Will put his hand on the back of James's neck. It only took a moment. James's face contorted in confusion—he heard

Will's voice inside his head and couldn't figure out where it was coming from—and then it was fear. His eyes snapped shut as he listened, and when he realized where it came from, he broke away from Will and stood, heading for the door.

"You people are insane," he hissed before bolting down the stairs.

No one's going after him?

"What did you tell him?" she asked.

He'd given James a glimpse of the future. Jay flying in a jetpack. George asking Will to deliver his letter to James. He slipped into the past and let James see him break Aisha's heart on Union Square, gave him a taste of what it felt like to go through a portal, and he left James with the knowledge of how Jay got his surgery, floating in a tank two hundred years from now.

"He'll call Jay," she guessed. "I imagine that will be one high-pitched, shrieking, one-way conversation until Jay manages to get him to calm down."

What if he never believes?

"He will." Will sounded certain. "The moment I take him through the portal, he'll believe."

12

Two days later, he called Jay.

"I was in the art studio with my hands covered in graphite, and my phone buzzed. I ignored it, it stopped, and then ten seconds later it buzzed again. Lather, rinse, repeat until the instructor told me to go wash my damned hands and find out what was so important. I'd be upset, but Dad kind of saved me from one of the worst things I've drawn in the last year or so."

He went outside to call James back and sat on the ground with his back against a tree as he listened to his father go from mildly agitated to a full-blown panic attack. Aisha was right; it was loud, shrill, and Jay thought he sounded like a five-year-old little girl in the middle of a royal temper tantrum.

"I let him wind down, and then told him you hadn't lied. He barked, 'Goddammit, Jay,' and hung up."

"He thought you were going along with a bad joke," Aisha guessed.

"Yeah, and he was pissed about it. I waited five minutes and called him back and told him Will could prove it. He got quiet and admitted Will had said the same thing. Keep an open mind, because he could prove it all. Granted, he said that in the same way he'd say, 'You're all suffering from some mass delusion, and I need to save you, right?' so I'm not sure his mind is as open as he wants it to be."

"It will open when the time comes." Will paced the living room floor with Rhys, trying to coax a burp or whatever else would tone down the crying. "I asked Finn to make an appointment with George. James can spend a few nights, they can talk, and decide where to go from there. He doesn't have to make the leap immediately."

"Angry baby is angry," Jay said, watching tiny fists clutch at Will's shirt. "Is he okay?"

"He's been changed, fed, swaddled, un-swaddled, sung to, bathed, changed again and fed again," Aisha said with a sigh. "Nothing is making him happy, and I am seriously annoyed that it's not fazing Will one bit."

"Will is not fazed," he said, turning to walk in the other direction, "because he knows that Rhys is fine. Consider this lung exercise. And trust me, Oz was worse."

"Was I?" Jay asked.

"You were never a screamer. You just wouldn't sleep through the night. I used to beg you to let me get just three or four hours straight, and you'd smile, and I'm ninety percent sure the cooing answer I got was, 'not on your life, lady.'"

"Maybe he's just upset because he wasn't expecting to have to live life outside the mothership for a couple more weeks." Jay stood and held his hands out. "Can I take him for a little bit?"

Fifteen seconds later, just as Jay got comfortable on the sofa, his arm crooked under Rhys and his hand splayed across his back, there was quiet. Rhys hiccupped once, let out a tiny noise, and stopped crying.

"What the hell?" Aisha laughed. "He just stops for Jay when how long have you been walking with him?"

"Apparently too long."

That's how you get to sleep at night. Toss the baby into Jay's room and run.

The idea either made Rhys very happy or very unwanted because he picked then to cut loose with the real reason he'd been crying. Jay tried to hand him back, but first Will shook his head, and then Aisha did.

"He filled that diaper on your watch," Will said. "Might as well get used to it. You'll be changing a lot of them over the next few years."

"You played me, didn't you?" Jay asked Rhys as he carried him into Will and Aisha's room. "I'll remember this. Wait until they're really old. I'll fob Will off on you when his ginormous man-diaper needs changing."

"Joke's on him." Aisha snuggled up to Will when he sat down. "He'll probably be really old before you, and you'll be changing his instead."

Will frowned. "That's a mental image I did not need."

"Any idea when you're taking James to see

George? Your promise to avoid the portals ended when Rhys was born."

"I also said I was taking a considerable amount of time off. I may not be able to. James might have to wait a bit unless my dad takes him."

"I could be convinced to push back when I return to work. Or I can take him with me. I've allowed students to bring their babies to class, so why not?"

Take turns. He goes to college one day and plans an offense against Florida the next.

"Defense, Wick. We will not be attacking Florida. I hope."

When's the vote? That'll tell you.

"Day after tomorrow. Jax, Red, and I will watch the opening of the Consortium conference in his office. Eli will be the first to vote, and we'll get a better idea of how the members react then."

"If Red is here, how will you know how Florida's Quorum will react?"

It depended on David Munson and how in control of the government Red really was. "General Myers will be in the war room during the initial vote, and he has eyes on Florida's military. If there's troop movement, we'll have a very clear idea. If not, we wait. They may count on whatever lobbying they've done to be effective."

"It doesn't make sense, Will. Why would they have such a knee-jerk reaction to not getting into the Consortium? It doesn't change anything for them."

"Outside pressure. If they're voted in, Russia is happy, and they can take their time moving forward. If they're not, Russia is unhappy, and they'll react accordingly. They want land mass. Russia wants them to have land mass."

"What good does Florida expansion do for Russia?"

"Because they know they can fracture Florida's government. Florida pushes for expansion with Russia's backing, favors are owed, land is traded, and the next push comes. Russia brings its troops in, takes more of Midlam, and ultimately, they'll try to take it all. Florida is just their pawn."

"They have to know Pacifica can stop them."

"Hedging a bet. Stopping them might mean destroying Florida, and they're counting on Jax not having the stones to do that. They have no idea—in the last loop of time, he blew most of Florida off the face of the earth, and this time he'll do it sooner because now he can protect Aubrey's family."

"I'm gonna be freaking drafted, aren't I?" Jay asked as he brought Rhys back. "Man, I still haven't..."

"Haven't...?" Aisha prompted.

"Nothing. But still. They'll start a draft."

Will assured him he wouldn't be drafted. He didn't tell him his asterisk was being shoved through a portal instead, where he would be safe. Instead, he reminded Jay that the draft hadn't been enacted in the last war and that there might not even be another one. Diplomacy and tact might work, and Red was firmly on the side of peace and sanity.

Jay was standing in front of them holding his baby brother. He didn't need to know that Red was likely only a figurehead at this point. Red probably didn't even realize that. But by the end of the first days' voting, he'd at least have a notion. The problem was, so would David Munson.

13

The Consortium, while an off-shoot of the U.N., was not bound by its rules nor its member's wishes. Officially regarded as informal, with none of their decisions legally binding, its stated intent was nonpartisan congress; it was meant as a way for members to discuss and dissect ideas and intent among allies without involving the U.N.

The reality was that deals were struck that greatly influenced the U.N. and the alliances made within could sway relations between the Consortium member countries and those who only had a seat at the U.N. Russia wanted in from the start and had been denied from the outset. They'd never been given a vote. Each request for consideration had been thwarted during the first ten minutes of every meeting held to discuss adding another seat. Centuries of mistrust added up; it would take, Jax thought, a complete dismantling and restructuring of their government before they had the most remote chance of admission.

Florida had petitioned for inclusion following the war. With Red as the new First Minister and the now-public knowledge that he was closely related to Pacifica's Queen, the Quorum felt a new confidence in the possibility. They rested on Red's reputation, and until recently, Jax had been willing to give them Pacifica's vote.

"My father as our representative is what changed things," Jax explained to Red. "He's respected and well-liked, and people will speak with him in more depth that they would most. He understood the nuances of the things they were telling him. And your brother—"

"Spencer is tuned into things not said," Red admitted. "He has a better finger on the pulse of the Quorum than I do, and he has a better sense of the world than the Quorum does. He also has David's confidence, something I admittedly do not."

Jax was perched on the edge of his office desk, waiting for the live feed of the vote to begin. "Spencer was specific in his discussions with my father. He'll actively work to get Florida admitted, but privately he thinks it's a bad idea and suspects the Quorum's intentions. He doesn't believe their ties to the Kremlin ended with Levi's death."

"We've always had a tenuous relationship with Russia. I was aware they'd funded the initial attacks and were prepared to join the fight. I was also made aware after the fact that their President was angry beyond comprehension when Dad abducted Oz and tried to draw you out using her. He'd made it personal. That was a critical flaw."

"The attack itself was a critical flaw," Will said. He was in the comfy chair with Rhys resting on his chest; Aisha needed a nap, so Rhys came with us. "It was not a war Florida could have won, even with their aid. And its end would have meant the destruction of your entire country."

"Hyperbole?" Red asked, hoping.

Jax shook his head. "Eventually I would have had no choice. Once I learned of Russia's involvement, it would have meant taking the drastic measures to end it. And make no mistake, Red. If you lose control of the Quorum and they step in, I won't wait. I will end it."

And to that matter, Will said, it was a good time to consider moving as many of his family members as he could out of Florida. There was a safe haven available; they would be protected. Red argued that as soon as he asked the first sibling to uproot, their hand was tipped.

"Once Eli casts his vote, any move I make is suspicious. I'll have to return to Florida. How do I then move so many people? My brothers and sisters, their families? That won't go unnoticed."

Aubrey had already issued an invitation for a family reunion; siblings, spouses, children, and grandchildren. It came with transportation. She was on record as saying that she missed her family deeply and looked forward to the day when she had them all under one roof for the loudest, and possibly most reverent, reunion possible.

"It's time for the reunion, then," Will said.

"Yes, to the Quorum it will look suspicious," Jax said to Red, "but to the world it won't. Your brother was found and is here recovering. Your mother and daughter are here. As far as the

Quorum knows, you're still in the dark as to their intentions. This reunion will look like a celebration, for no reason other than Hyrum."

"Arguably, it could also be a way to cultivate favor with King Jackson and spur another vote before the end of the year should this one fail," Will pointed out.

"You'll get half of them, perhaps," Red said. "Hyrum...I hate to admit this, but your family has loved him harder and faster than most in his own. And some won't step foot outside of Florida, simply because they were taught to be afraid. They know what's possibly coming, and they're aware they have a safe place to go, but that's not enough. Hyrum *should* be enough, but..."

Will latched onto the idea of Hyrum not being as wanted as he thought he should be. "Why? He's wonderful."

Red became very uncomfortable. "Please understand I in no way share this view, but to my father, Hyrum was defective and a personal insult. He was an embarrassment and a punishment from God for our mother's sins. My youngest siblings grew up with him and are relatively comfortable, the older ones, not as much. They don't trust his ability to keep his—" Red sighed. "They worry about agitating him. They've tended to keep their children from him, and it's safe to say a few of their grandchildren are just now learning he exists."

"And yet, your daughter treats him as if he were her own brother."

"All my daughters do. Make no mistake, Emperor. I see nothing but joy in him and raised my children to treat him as their equal. But that's not the case throughout my family. So don't count on his rescue as being the key to getting them out of Florida. David's family, Elle's...they won't leave. And I can't."

"But you will send your wife and children to this reunion," Jax guessed.

"When I go home, likely tonight, I'm leaving Bree here. If asked, it's because her presence calms Hyrum and she's a help to my mother. But she's also how I can get my wife and daughters to leave. I apologize for the imposition in leaving her here, but—"

"She's not an imposition," Jax said. "Under any circumstance, she's welcome in my home. Hell, even when this is over, if there's any part of you that wants her to stay and get a top-notch education, she's not only welcome, she's wanted."

"Don't tempt me."

"She could be home every weekend," Will pointed out. "Here, she would be assigned guards, attend a very good school, and would have a private shuttle with an escort to get her home by dinner every Friday."

"Seriously, don't tempt me. I can't imagine coming home every evening and her not being there. And my wife? Life would be unpleasant for a while."

"I admit, I was surprised she wasn't with you on this trip," Jax said.

"Grandkids. She watches—" He stopped when the giant wall monitor flashed, signaling the start of the live feed. "Later."

Rhys fussed through the chairman's address of the members, which no one cared about because they already knew the things he was going to say—Florida wanted in, Pacifica would get the first vote, and voting would continue throughout the day, allowing time between blocks of votes so that representatives could consult with their governments—and when he wailed, Jax switched places with Will so he could use the desktop to change Rhys's diaper.

It was not the first time an infant had been changed there and was surely not the last. Will got Rhys cleaned up, handed him to Jax, and excused himself to dispose of the offending diaper and to wash his hands.

The head talking on the giant monitor—I could fit up inside his nostrils a couple times over—was still droning on when he got back. He sat against the edge of the desk the way Jax had, glanced at the baby and realized he wasn't getting his son back anytime soon, and then paid attention, because Eli was about to take the podium.

Eli commanded the room the way he had when he was King. The camera panned the audience, and he had their full attention. The chatter ended abruptly when he stepped up to the microphone, and the only thing the microphone picked up was the sound of his breathing. He waited, building anticipation, and when he spoke, he focused mostly on Spencer Munson, who sat front and center.

"Historically," he began, his voice booming, "Pacifica and Florida have had a tenuous relationship. Offers of aid to Florida have been routinely rebuffed, while blustering bravado has been the response to even small disagreements that the Church of Florida has had with Pacifica. Even with the expanse of Midlam and Texas between them, Florida has often threatened Pacifica with military action, citing their right as the fighting hand of God.

"Nevertheless. We have had, in the last two years, a much friendlier, open, and frankly, comfortable relationship with Florida under its new First Minister, Redmond Munson. He has shown a willingness to accept help where needed, he has taken a stance of humanitarian good over questionable protective secrecy of Florida's charter, and he has implemented a progressive stance in equal rights for all citizens of Florida. He has reached out not only to Pacifica, but to the world, and has demonstrated an interest in developing relationships of good faith with members of this Consortium as well as the United Nations as a whole."

"Here we go," Jax muttered.

"Pacifica is keenly interested in maintaining a positive and open relationship with Florida, engaging in trade agreements, and allowing free travel between our citizens. However—" a low rumble went through the auditorium "—Florida is still experiencing significant growing pains and further gains in human rights, and basic freedoms are needed. Therefore, with the full knowledge of King Jackson, Pacifica's vote to admit Florida to the Consortium is no."

The camera cut to Spencer as Eli stepped away from the podium. He'd expected it; Eli had warned him before and had given him all the reasons why, but he looked into the camera, and it was clear: *We're in trouble, Red. It's hit the fan.*

Their phones rang at the same time. General Myers called Jax to tell him there was troop movement in Florida, a small number moving from bases in central Florida toward an airfield as well as a cluster of missile silos. David Munson called Red to ask him, in language tinged with forced politeness, what the hell was Jax thinking?

Jax told Myers to get a line near the Midlam-Florida border but to sit tight. Red reminded David that the vote was not over; Pacifica only had one vote, and he was heading home on the first shuttle he could get. It was not worth getting upset over, not yet. Spencer was still in New York, still bargaining with other Consortium members, exerting pressure on the ones he knew would bend.

"He knows as well as I do that Pacifica holds the cards here," Red said when he hung up. Before Jax could defend it, Red added, "I know, it's not personal. I wouldn't admit us right now, either."

"What's the plan when you get home?" Jax asked.

"I wish I knew. The Quorum is clearly moving without my input. I can't legally remove them from their positions. If I declare them corrupt and cite divine revelation as a reason for stripping them as apostles, I'm a dead man. I'll die where I stand when I tell them, whether it's in a public venue or the privacy of the church offices."

It didn't matter what he'd grown up believing. He knew now that each member of the Quorum was not called to their position by God Himself; they'd been handpicked and appointed by Levi's father, and then Levi himself. There was not a member of the Quorum that he'd had a say in, and absent the death of one, there wouldn't be.

It was the drawback to an appointment for life.

"I might be able to get ahead of it. If I can determine what they want more—power, land, or even a stronger alliance with Russia—I might be able to pull them back."

"They're already in bed with Russia," Jax said. "Don't let them get comfortable."

Red nodded and got up. "My mother has a portfolio. If the worst happens...ask her for it. Inside there's a directive to keep Bree, Hyrum, and my mother here permanently."

"Neither your mother nor your wife will honor that," Will said.

"Oh, but they will," Red said as he headed for the door. "I'm the head of the Munson family. My word is their law. I may not be able to control my country, but I can control this part of my family. Hyrum and Bree stay. If my mother really wants to leave, let her."

Jax stopped him at the door. "What about the rest of your family?"

"If I can get them on those shuttles for this reunion, keep them as long as you can. Once I'm dead David becomes the family's head, and they may listen to his orders. But I'm begging you, keep Hyrum and Bree here. The directive gives custody specifically to the King and Queen of Pacifica. David won't bother fighting it. He doesn't want Hyrum and Bree is female. Not worth his time. My wife—she'll come. I know she will."

Aubrey won't mind that. If they stayed forever she'd be happy.

"We need to get ahead of Red getting ahead of things," Jax said to Will. "I want to speak with David Munson."

"That shouldn't be difficult."

"As far as he's concerned, Red left here upset. I don't care how, but we blow smoke up his ass, let him believe that the no vote is temporary and given another year, two at the most, we'll call for another one."

"He'll want a reason."

"I'll lay it at his feet. We suspect pressure from Russia. Red refuses to admit it, and as soon as we're convinced there's nothing askew, and they're committed to long-term peace, we'll yield."

"That's neither a lie nor smoke."

Jax nodded. "Yes, but I'm not hinting we're aware of troop movement and the perceived threat of a missile launch. I want it clear without having to say so: anything happens to Red, and everything is off the table. I will send a burn run through Florida so hard and fast, they'll discover the joys of island life."

At food o'clock, I left Jax's office and went to the most likely source of available thumbs. Hyrum and Bree were stretched out on the living room floor reading to each other and Aubrey was at the table with her mother. Interrupting would be rude, so I jumped onto the chair across from Aubrey and set my chin on the table, hoping it was cute enough to attract her attention.

Valerie was in the middle of a story about a nephew Aubrey had never met; he'd recently been elevated to serve as the bishop of a collective of congregations and he was one of the youngest to ever hold the position. Except, of course, for Levi, though she referred to him as "that man." Aubrey was only half listening, distracted by the tablet on the table in front of her.

Her thumbs were going to be utterly useless for a while.

Her focus shifted when Jax came in. He stopped in the living room to see what Hyrum and Bree were reading, and when he turned Valerie got up and went into the kitchen, mumbling about coffee and wanting to know if he wanted something to eat, too. He thanked her and pointed out that he was perfectly capable of getting his own coffee, at which she snorted, "Nonsense."

"How did the conference vote go?" Aubrey asked him as he sat down.

"It went. Where's Red? I thought he'd be in here."

"I thought he was with you."

He's probably packing.

Or maybe he left without saying goodbye. That would be mean, but you never know.

Aubrey tapped a finger against the edge of her computer tablet. "Do you have a few minutes?"

He glanced up as Valerie set the coffee in front of him and thanked her before telling Aubrey he had as many minutes as she needed.

"This," she said, sliding it toward him, "is a request to the school board. I'm seriously considering taking the entire year instead of the semester."

He glanced at it. "A little premature, don't you think? School just started."

Valerie sat back down, as quietly as she could, and she looked nervous.

"Yes, and there's a classroom full of nine and ten-year-old kids who might be more than a little put out that they have a substitute and not the teacher they were promised. But by the end of the semester, *he'll* be their actual teacher, and I'll be the intrusion."

He slid the tablet back to her and realized Valerie was nearly holding her breath, waiting for the fight to begin and for him to impose his wants on her. He sat back in his chair and folded his arms, the corners of his mouth tugging up ever so slightly. Aubrey noticed because she was looking right at him, but Valerie was looking at her daughter and didn't see.

"An entire year's salary. That's a hell of a lot of money to throw away," he said. "Not to mention the expectations of the people. Their Queen works, the same as they do. It's important to them. It makes us real and lets them know we don't consider ourselves special."

"They'll get over it. I want time with my family."

"I'm not sure that much time off would be good for you. Sitting here all day, doing what? Reading? Watching endless drivel in between spots of news? The kids are grown and won't be here for you to care for. You need structure."

How are you keeping a straight face?

"Jackson. I'm not asking your permission. I'm telling you this is what's happening." She scribbled her finger across the screen and tapped on it. "It's done. I'm taking the time."

Then he smiled. "Good for you. Does this mean I get a home cooked lunch every day?"

She raised an eyebrow. "You get breakfast and dinner, same as always. I don't care what you have for lunch. Just...don't eat at the diner every day. Choke down a vegetable every now and then."

"Tsk." He got up and kissed her, and then went to find Red. "My other wives would make lunch for me."

"Your other wives are whipped," she called after him.

"Aubrey," Valerie breathed. Her horror slipped away, and she covered a smile with her hand. "Oh, if I had ever done that?"

"Dad would never have allowed you to work."

"Yes, but if I had? This would have been such a different conversation." She reached across the table and set her hand on Aubrey's. "I am proud of you, daughter. I'm not surprised that you can stand toe to toe with your husband, but I am proud."

Aubrey stretched to kiss her. "Thank you. And you know he was being an intentional jerk, don't you?"

"I'm never sure. Red is like that with Darlene, and I've never gotten used to it. They tease each other all the time. If I'd had even once—"

"You raised Red with respect and he has a sense of humor. Dad was raised with hate and he didn't."

"He was raised to think only of the church."

"Same thing. He thought he *was* the church." She turned at the sound of Bree giggling because Hyrum was slowly pulling the book away from her. "We have to tell him sooner or later."

"No, we have to feed him." Valerie got up. "Lunch first. Let that doctor he's seeing decide when he's ready for the hard things."

"You're all right with that now?" Aubrey followed her into the kitchen, and I followed Aubrey. She didn't seem to see me, so I patted her on the leg and let out a pathetic, tiny meow intended to make her feel sorry for me.

I'm dying down here.

"I don't understand it, but he seems happy and he's still doing his bible studies and prayers. I suppose it can't hurt."

I patted Aubrey's leg again.

Hey. Hungry kitty in desperate need.

"I see you, Wick. Let me get the kids' lunch started, and then I'll feed you."

"Kids," Valerie repeated. "He'll always be one, won't he? Is that my fault? Should I have pushed for more for him?"

"It wouldn't have mattered, Mom." She peeked into the living room to make sure they weren't listening. "Hyrum had brain damage from birth. He's probably exceeded what he would have been if you hadn't been so persistent in keeping him home and at least trying to teach him."

"Would it have been different here?"

Aubrey leaned against the counter and sighed. "In terms of the education available to him, yes, it would have been different. He would have had individual instruction from the outset and would have been integrated into the school system with personal aides. At the very least, he'd be reading reasonably well and would have been taught the skills to live on his own, with social services checking in on him regularly."

"And he wouldn't have had Levi."

"I'd hope not."

Valerie's hand trembled as she brought it to her mouth, her voice watery. "Levi wanted him dead," she said quietly. "He was afraid how it would look when he was standing on the world's stage, having a defective child as a son. He wanted so much and worried that one helpless boy would turn the tide away from him. He was afraid of what that boy could do..."

"Wait. Do you mean he intended to kill Hy? Two years ago?"

Valerie nodded, and the tears fell. "I told him Hyrum had wandered off, and I thought he'd gone to the pond down by Miller's crossing. He waited a full day before he sent someone to look." Her breath hitched. "I left one of his shoes near the water. When he still didn't come home, Levi decided he'd been dragged under by a gator. He forbade me from calling for help, but I knew. Hyrum was well outside Florida by then. And all we told his brothers and sisters was that he was missing. David claimed to have sent men looking for Hyrum, but we know better, don't we?"

Aubrey didn't need to hear anything else. She grabbed her mother into a tight hug and did what she could to soak up some of the pain, and she whispered, "You saved his life, Mom. You know you did."

"But I didn't think it would take so long. I made sure he would get past the border and thought after that he would get lost and confused and would ask someone for help. I nearly beat it into him—find the Queen and warn her. I counted on whoever helped him to contact anyone in Pacifica who might be able to get him to his sister. I never meant for him to walk all that way."

"But he did." Aubrey pulled back, smiling. "Mom, he walked all that way. By himself. Tell me you didn't teach him well."

"By the grace of God," she sniffed.

"God, peanut butter, and you. Take some credit. You deserve it."

Okay, we're ignoring the part where no one told you he'd gone missing and pretended like he was just in the bathroom when you called. Or that this is different than just sending him to tell you Levi wanted to kill Red and Drew. We need Oz.

She might have argued if not for Red and Jax. He came back to tell Bree he was going home for a few days, but she needed to stay and help Grandma and Aunt Aubrey. If everything went as planned, there would be a family reunion by the end of the week, when her cousins and uncles and aunts came to visit.

"Mom will be here, too. Be good, and listen to Jax and Aubrey," he told her. "Daddy loves you. Don't ever forget that."

Bree responded with, "Duh," but Valerie had to turn away.

"He's coming back," she whispered to Aubrey. "Tell me he's coming back."

Aubrey said he would, but no one in that room over 44 years old was certain.

14

Morning had been a bit nipply, but the warms came out in the afternoon, prompting Will to drag Aisha out of the apartment to the bakery at the corner of Union Square. She was finally walking upright, and he'd made sure she got plenty of sleep the night before, so it was time. He grabbed Rhys's baby sling and the diaper bag, told her that they all needed fresh air, and the bakery was a good spot for his first outing.

"He's been out," she grumbled. "Hasn't he?"

He had not. He'd been born downstairs and Mass had come over to do his checkups in the nursery, which meant sunlight had never kissed his brand-new baby skin.

"We're not raising a vampire. Let's go."

Within a few minutes, she agreed, it was time to get out. The weather was perfect, and they had shade from the massive umbrella that pierced the center of their round table. I lounged on the cement on my back while Will went inside to get coffee and donuts, and I listened to people squeal baby things as they walked past. It didn't matter that she was cradling him and no one could really see his face. He was tiny, which meant adorable, and one woman gushed to her partner, "Ooh, I want one."

The warmth on my useless nipples felt so good I didn't really want to move when he came back. I smelled the bacon from where I was and opened my eyes to look at him upside down, but I didn't jump up.

"Decaf tea for you." He placed the cup on the table and then reached into a bag for her donuts. "Extra sweet, and not too hot. I asked for a kid's temperature cup. If it's not warm enough, they'll reheat it for you."

He'd also gotten a kid's lid on it.

Sippy cup already?

"It's to minimize the spill risk," Will said. "We don't want to dribble hot drinks onto the baby. I have a slice of bacon for you, but you have to come over here to get it. I'm not delivering."

Lazy, aren't we?

"Yes, you are. And it's warm, so I'd get it now if I were you." He held up the napkin it was wrapped in so I could see. "Fresh, greasy, bacon."

Warm and greasy.

I got up.

There was no reason to let it cool down and for the napkin to soak up all the tasty lubrication. Fresh bacon slides down easy. While I ate—slowly, to savor the taste—they people-watched and were quieter than usual. I wasn't sure if they were just enjoying being outside or if they were about to fall asleep, but in case it was the latter, as soon as I swallowed my last bite I jumped to the chair closest to Aisha so I could keep an eye on Rhys. The odds of her drifting off and dropping him were slim, but if she did, I could wake one of them before he slipped out of the sling and splattered on the ground.

"Why are you staring at me, Wick?" she asked a few minutes later.

I'm not. I'm staring at Rhys. Making sure he doesn't drop if you fall asleep.

She swore she wouldn't, but that was sweet of me, so it got me a bite of her donut.

"What was the plan, Wick?" Will asked me. "How would you have caught him?"

I wouldn't. I would have turned myself into a landing pad and let him squish my fleshy bits into a furry pile of mush.

I got another bite of donut.

"Just scream if it looks like one of us is about to drift and drop. The way you did when Eli was shot at. That will work."

All right, but that doesn't get me donut bites.

He didn't believe that was why I said I'd do it, but I was spared the debate when Drew arrived. He'd been headed for home but wasn't passing up the chance to see Rhys, and before he sat down he moved another table a little bit so the umbrella from it would shade his little toes.

"We would have moved when the sun hit him," Aisha said lightly. "But thank you."

"No Oz?" Will asked.

She was at Sophia's studying for an anatomy

and physiology exam. "The study images are pretty graphic, and Hyrum is very curious. She thought it might be better to study there rather than risk the wrath of Valerie."

"He has sisters," Will said. "The human body is not a mystery to him."

"But the insides probably are, and she's looking at dissected cadavers."

Aisha grimaced. "Ew." She quickly brightened. "Hey, I had a call from the division head. He sat in on your class this morning and is very pleased with the way you teach. So much so that he wondered what it would take to get you to switch to math instead of engineering and computer science."

"One hundred million billion trillion dollars," Drew said. "I don't know how you do it every day. I feel like I'm re-learning as I'm trying to impart the information. I'm not cut out for it."

"The department head thinks otherwise."

"You don't want to teach." Will dug into the diaper bag and pulled out his computer tablet. "I have something for you. And I don't mean the tablet." He turned it on and slid it across the table. "Two documents forwarded by our lawyer."

Drew squinted as he read. "Award of trademark. Over Ozoo Enterprises?"

"Indeed. That was a given. Flip to the next one."

After reading for a moment, he sputtered, "Hot damn. Patent pending on the nanoglobe. No one else had one."

"Keep reading. He combined files."

"And the nanogel." He looked up. "All right, I've been struck with an extreme case of the stupid. What does this mean, realistically?"

It meant that the manufacturer Will had contracted with could begin production of a basic model of the nanoglobe; machine tooling and dyes had already been struck in anticipation of doing business with the company owned by members of the royal family. And the security of a pending patent on the nanogel meant that they could show more of what they were doing to General Myers. The first systems were intended for Elysium; once they had a solid working model, they could offer it for consideration to Pacifica's government, and with the military on board, it might—and he stressed might—be given consideration over other proposals.

"I didn't know there was anyone else working on it," Drew said.

"There are always others working in it. The government is working on it. Your own father, when he's not playing with mine or tinkering with his exoskeletons, is working on it. The project was abandoned, but hope was not."

He'd struck a deal for the warehouses in the Wastelands, opting for a long-term lease over purchase, reasoning that they wouldn't need to be away from the general population for an extended amount of time. "Property in the city will surely become available over the next few years."

"As long as we're not going to blow up the neighborhood."

"Certainly not our neighborhood. We'll find some other neighborhood to set on fire."

There's a sterling business model. 'Ozoo Enterprises, your first choice in inadvertent explodey-thingies.'

"That should make it easier to hire people," Drew said. "Weed out the weenies."

The hiring needed to begin soon. Will proposed using an agency to field applications and resumes, which would take more time than they wanted. "Initially, Finn has offered a labor exchange. Chemists and engineers, willing to contract for up to three years. That will cut down on the numbers we need to hire."

"What's he want in exchange?"

"To play with the toys."

"He already knows more about this than I do."

"Doesn't matter. He's fascinated by the development. Just don't allow him to guide any of the research or tell you in which direction you need to go."

"The work's no longer really mine," Drew guessed. "My ideas, other peoples' sweat equity."

"To a point. Finish the school year, then you can put as much effort as you want into it."

"Unless I decide to go for a doctorate."

That caught Aisha's attention. Drew was pushing hard to graduate with a Masters, but he'd never mentioned anything beyond that. "That's another couple of years. And nothing you have to jump right into."

"I know. But it's still a lot of time I'd have to take away from work."

Finn's a doctor, did you know that?

"So is my mother," Will said. "Both were deep into their work before that happened. He'd built his time machine and construction on the portal tunnel was under way before he finished."

"Didn't he intend to get into deep space exploration?" Drew asked.

Will nodded. When Finn was young, that was his dream: graduate from college and then enter the program that would send him toward the depths of unexplored space. "I imagine it was the intention of many young men and women. There was a meteor headed for earth and no one had a clear idea of how to deal with it. Escape was an attractive alternative to waiting and seeing what would happen."

"Would Elysium have survived?"

"Not likely."

"Well, there's another project. Figure out a way to make Elysium a self-contained world with propulsion. If the worst happens, at least those people can be saved." He got up. "I promised Hyrum I'd draw pictures with him this afternoon. I think today's theme is David versus Goliath, though he seems to want Goliath to win. I may try to talk him into dinosaurs."

Dragons. Draw a picture of Jeff. And Fluffy.

"Sure. I'll tell him those are Wick's imaginary friends. And then let Aubrey handle all the questions about how I know that."

"I kind of want to be there for that," Will said. He got up and collected their trash. "I guarantee, if Hyrum draws a dragon, he'll add Jesus as its passenger. Valerie's head might explode."

We all wanted to see that.

Except, maybe, for Rhys. All he really wanted was food, and I certainly couldn't fault him for that.

◆◆◆

She was not opposed to the notion of dragons; those were clearly fantasy and because Drew presented Jeff as a friendly dragon who wanted to do good in the world, her head didn't explode. If Drew had opted for dinosaurs, she'd have a problem with that. Dinosaurs chafed against her feelings about evolution and intelligent design, and she wasn't at all happy that the schools in Florida had begun to teach evolution as a theory.

"I don't want that in my son's head. It's fiction."

Bree was in the guest room, reading. She probably knew about dinosaurs and laughed at the tiny, tiny hands of a Tyrannosaurus Rex.

Will surmised that Hyrum could be presented pictures of dinosaurs with the idea that she didn't think they'd ever been real, but she bristled at the notion. He'd hear things. He might not understand that there were people in the world who thought they were real and had existed with Jesus.

Maybe Jesus had a saddle for his dinosaur. You weren't there. You don't know.

"Explain all the dinosaur bones found throughout the centuries, then," Aubrey said.

Valerie waved it off. "Let him pretend with the dragon. That's enough."

You should tell her that some people think dragons are a metaphor for drugs. Then we can all sing Puff the Magic Dragon. Maybe that will explode her head.

I heard Drew snicker from where he was at in the living room, but Will couldn't say anything in front of her. One corner of his mouth tugged up, that was enough.

"How are the reunion plans coming?" Aisha asked Aubrey, sparing Valerie from cranial contortions. "Is everyone coming?"

"Two of my brothers and their families, two of my sisters. Another brother is stuck in New York, but he's sending his wife."

"Joseph," Valerie said, sounding amazed. "Joseph is coming. Can you believe it? He won't even talk on the phone!"

"Technophobe," Aubrey explained. "I've been taking it personally, but his wife thinks he's just afraid of video chats in general. It's too new, too uncomfortable."

But the technophobe had a digital music player. Sure. I bet he's worried that his phone is bugged.

"He wants to meet his sister." Valerie clasped her hands at her chest. "For a long time, I think he believed I had made you up and the older kids were just going along with it."

Hyrum rolled over. "'The Lord was with Joseph and he became a successful man.' Genesis."

"Very good," Valerie said, beaming.

"But his brothers hated him and tried to kill him, and that sucked big fat hairy—"

"Hyrum!"

Drew tried not to laugh, and Aubrey couldn't stop herself. "Well, at least we know he's doing more than memorizing. That takes an understanding of the material. And I promise, I'll speak to Zed about his language."

With a heavy sigh, Valerie waved it off. "He didn't get that from Zed. He got that from Joseph. But it's the first time I've heard him repeat it."

"Joseph isn't as tightly wound as Dad, I take it?"

Valerie dropped her voice so that Hyrum wouldn't hear. "Joseph is agnostic. Can you imagine? I can't repeat the things he's said about Levi, but he thinks that a loving God would never have allowed that man to do the things he did."

"Free will," Will said. "You can have a loving God and still have terrible things happen."

"I thought you were atheist," Valerie said.

He gave a slight nod. "In my youth, I was. The older I get, the more room I've made for the possibility. I'd like to believe there's more after this life, for no reason other than there will never be enough years here to spend with the people I love."

"Your doing?" she asked Aubrey. "You might make a Christian out of him yet."

"I don't proselytize, Mom. He respects my beliefs, and I respect his right to explore his own. And that goes for Jax, too. No poking the bear. He allowed me to raise Oz and Zed with faith, but I don't force it on him."

"Allowed," she snorted. "I don't think he could have stopped you. You're a stronger woman than I am, Aubrey. I would be lying if I said I wasn't looking forward to Joseph and your sisters seeing how much control you have over that man. And he's the King!"

Too bad the other brother isn't coming. You could give him his come-to-Jesus moment and stop the whole Florida Attacks thing.

They started discussing the details of the reunion, which I found boring. It was going to be Oz and Drew's wedding reception all over again, but with far fewer people and no wayward fly to chase, and there was a good chance I wouldn't be invited anyway. I was not a Munson, and I didn't think most of them would be thrilled if I were there.

I left them in the kitchen. Aside from the boring topic at hand, in a minute or two Rhys was going to announce the effectiveness of his digestive system. I plopped down in the middle of Hyrum and Drew's artistic efforts to make sure Drew knew I was there.

We should take Hyrum to the Ferry Building. They have real live fresh dead shrimp bites and there are boats for him to watch. He's been cooped up all day and he never gets to go out for just fun.

"You meow a lot, Wick," Hyrum giggled. "Lazybones never meowed like you."

"Wick is mouthy and he talks a lot. Hey, how about you and I get out of the house for a while?

We can walk down to the water and watch ferries coming in."

"Can we?" He popped up and ran to the dining room. "Will, can Drew take me to see the boats?"

Will looked confused. "Ask your mother, Hyrum. It's not up to me."

Now Hyrum looked confused.

"He defaults to the oldest authoritarian male," Aubrey reminded Will. "He sees you as family, thus being in charge. Mom? Drew will keep a close eye on him."

She nodded. "He can go. Hy, you do what Drew tells you. Go wash your hands, and then you can go."

Will watched him run down the hall. "I understand when he asks Red for permission. I would never presume—"

"If you hadn't been here he would have asked Jax," Valerie explained. "It's just the way it is. And he wouldn't ask any adult male, only the ones he feels are family. He would ask you, Drew, Zed, or Jay."

Drew was pulling my sweatshirt over his head. "I won't give him permission for anything important without asking you or Aubrey first."

"That's right, you're from Midlam."

He nodded. "It's more that you're his mother, and I'm not. But yes, Midlam is traditionally a matriarchal society. Women are the heart and head of the family, as far as I'm concerned."

"You think of Oz as having dominion over you."

"No, I think we're equals. But in a uniform sense, I think women do better at governing, even families. When we have kids, I'm sure I'll look to her for permissions, too."

"Huh."

"Look at the world. Where are we fighting? Butting heads? And where are we negotiating peacefully, with tact and reason? Men fight. Women discuss. Men dig in. Women aren't afraid to ask for opinions."

Aubrey decided to poke at him. "Andrew, are you saying that Jax is less of a leader than he could be?"

"No, I'm saying that he has you, and a strong woman next to you makes all the difference in the world."

"Good boy. Now keep an eye on my baby brother, and don't stuff him with junk. I want him to be able to eat dinner tonight."

That was an order, dude.

You know that means we have to break it.

Fifteen seconds after I warned Drew it would happen because there was more street noise than usual, Hyrum latched onto his hand. That was all he typically needed to feel safe, the hand of someone he trusted to hold onto, and Drew didn't mind. He felt like he was walking his slightly hairier and older little brother down the street, and enough people knew about Hyrum now that they didn't give a second look. Even the tourists knew that Hyrum was the Queen's brother; it wasn't as cute as Hyrum holding hands with the Emperor, but if Prince Andrew wanted to hold hands with him, too, so what?

Maybe you'll start a trend. People should hold hands more often, even if it does make the cat wobble. Everyone seems happier when they're holding hands with someone they like.

We headed for Oz and Drew's favorite spot to ferry-watch. It was a bench on the pier, where there was a full view of the Bay Bridge to the right and Treasure Island in the distance. It wasn't the Ferry Building where the bites of shrimp lived, but he wanted Hyrum to see the boats without being jostled and possibly upset by tourists and ferry passengers.

"Oz loves to come and sit here," Drew told him, though Hyrum was not about to sit down. He was plastered to the railing, bouncing on his toes, and pointing at a blue and gold ferry speeding toward the dock. "Did you know that when she was six years old, she snuck onto a ferry and rode it all by herself? She went to Sausalito." He pointed toward Marin County. "All the way over there. You can't even see it from here."

"All by herself? She was the only passenger on the boat?"

"Well, no. I meant she didn't have a grown up with her. She just marched onto the ferry and went for a ride. She thought she could get a cupcake in Sausalito, but all she got was in trouble."

"When I was six I got to ride my brother's bicycle down the sidewalk. I fell off."

"I never had a bicycle." He leaned close to Hyrum. "Don't tell anyone, but I don't know how to ride one."

"Me either! That's why I fell off! Does Oz have a bicycle? Maybe she could teach us."

She had one, but she'd outgrown it when she was twelve and it had been put into storage. "I think her old bike would be too small. I don't think she got another one because of all the hills in the city and Will drove her to the places she needed to go if they were too far to walk. And Will likes to walk everywhere."

"Oh. I've never gotten to ride one since then. Daddy said, 'That boy will break your bike, and I'm not buying you a new one!' so David wouldn't let me try again. Then it was Spencer's bike and I was too big."

Take him on a bike taxi.

Drew turned and looked toward the Ferry Building. There were always bicycle taxis nearby. Meant mostly for tourists who wanted to avoid the long walk between Pier 39 and the Ferry Building, the bicycle-pulled trailers were a cheap way to have a few minutes of fun.

"Hyrum, we're going to ride on a bicycle," he said, tugging him away from the pier railing. "And we won't even fall off. Come on."

If you run and I bounce, I'm biting you.

They ran anyway. Drew held me steady with one hand, but it was still uncomfortable. When he stopped near the taxi stand, I set my teeth on the edge of his hand, just to make a point. When that didn't bother him, I turned my head and licked his palm.

"Gross, Wick."

"Lazybones used to lick me and Red said that he was tasting me to see if I was ripe yet."

"Did he ever bite you?"

"No." He snorted a laugh through his nose. "He was a nice cat and only bit mice and bugs and one time a gopher. But if I died in the house alone and he couldn't go outside to hunt, he would have eaten me. Red said that, too."

Red was right.

"Do you think Lazybones really would have?"

"Cats gotta eat! I would want him to. I didn't want him to starve. Would you let Wick eat you?"

"If it were the difference between him living and dying, I know I'd want him to."

You'd be dead. It's not like I'd give you a choice.

"Daddy said that was stupid because I need my body in the next life. But Red said that Jesus would fix me if Lazybones ever had to eat me."

"From everything Aubrey has told me about Jesus, I think Red is right. But I don't know a lot about him."

"I can read Bible stories to you," Hyrum offered. "Joseph says that even if you don't believe in it, the stories are interesting. He used to read them to me after Spencer got married and moved."

Dude, you know that would make Aubrey happier than it would Hyrum. And his brother is right, the stories are worth knowing.

Hyrum's excitement grew the closer the next taxi got. He was bouncing on his toes, pulling on Drew's sleeve, squealing for him to look. "It's a red bike! Red's my favorite color!"

As soon as the bike driver let his passengers out and turned around, Hyrum let out a disappointed sigh. He pointed at the sign on the side of the trailer, the list of prices, and said, "I don't have any money, Drew. I lost my wallet."

"It's okay, I do." He tapped his bank card on the optical reader and told Hyrum to hop on and sit still so that the bike wouldn't wobble. "Look at us. On a bike ride and neither of us knows how to ride one ourselves."

"You've got to be kidding me," the driver said as he scooted onto the saddle. "You're the prince, right? And you never had a bike?"

"Sheltered life growing up in Chicago," Drew told him. "Hell, I *just* learned how to drive."

"Ha! Even I can drive a car!" Hyrum blurted. "Red taught me when I was fifteen!"

"Hold on," Bike Boy said. "I'm gonna give you your money's worth. We'll drop off the promenade up there—" he gestured to a parking cutout "—and we'll ride fast to the Hyde Street cable turnaround."

"We get to go fast, Drew?"

Drew leaned forward. "If he yells for you to slow down, do it. He's the Queen's little brother. If I scare the hell out of him, I'll have to hear about it for a long time."

With a laugh, Bike Boy took off. True to his word, once he maneuvered out into the street, he picked up speed, pumping the pedals as hard as he could. Hyrum raised his arms the way kids do on roller coasters and squealed his excitement; if it had been possible to go faster, he would have wanted to, and never hinted that he was afraid.

The ride should have ended at the turnaround, but Bike Boy turned a little early and took us down by the aquatic park, cutting in front of the bleachers to get to Van Ness. He looped around the block and took us in front of Ghirardelli Square, where Drew asked him to stop.

"That was amazing, man, thanks. I think his day is made."

"I can take you all the way back. No charge. This was fun. Not too many customers get into it the way he does."

Drew nodded toward Ghirardelli. "I was ordered by the Queen to not stuff him full of junk. So, yeah. There will be chocolate."

"Was that fun?" he asked Hyrum as they climbed the stairs. "It almost makes me want to learn to ride a bike."

"Can we do it again before I go home?"

"I don't see why not. And maybe Zed will give you a ride on his air bike. That's some *serious* fun. If Jay takes his, we can all go together."

He gave Hyrum a choice between a chocolate bar and an ice cream sundae—either one might wreck his dinner but that was half the point—and it took him several minutes to decide.

"Which is messier?" he finally asked.

"The ice cream, I think."

"Then that's what I want! You won't get mad if I get ice cream on my chin, right?"

"Nope, I won't. You won't make fun of me if I dribble some onto my shirt, right?"

"Probably I will."

Fine, there's nothing for Wick here and the whole Ferry Building thing was my idea, but whatever.

Drew bought them each a sundae with three scoops of vanilla and chocolate ice cream, and we sat outside in the shade. Hyrum said a quick prayer over his sundae and told Drew it had to be quick because otherwise the ice cream would melt and that was wasteful. Jesus was okay with quick when it meant not letting the ice cream melt.

There was plenty of whipped cream, and Hyrum kept offering me tastes of it off his fingertips, even after Drew reminded him that I licked myself and he was sticking fingers with cat spit back into his whipped cream.

"I can't taste it. I don't care."

"Don't give him too much. It might upset his stomach."

"It might upset mine, too, but I don't care. I haven't had ice cream in forever, since Eli let us go that time." He thought about it. "Before that? Maybe for Bree's fourth birthday? She had cake and ice cream and she swiped all the icing off her cake and put it in Red's hair. But he wasn't mad, so she didn't get a spanking. He said, 'Thanks, honey, now I have to wash my hair,' and she said, 'You better wash it while you have it because you don't have much.'"

"Bree's pretty funny, isn't she?" Drew laughed at the image of Red with frosting in his hair. "She calls Oz a lot. It's our favorite time of the week, when she calls on Sunday evening."

Hyrum scooped out the last of his ice cream and set the bowl aside. "I missed two of her birthdays. I missed two of everything she did."

"I know, bud. She's just glad you're okay. All she wants is her uncle. Now you're back, and she's happy about that. That's what matters to her."

"Do you think she's proud of me for finding the Queen?"

"Man, we're *all* proud of you for that. You know, I thought it was a big deal when Will and Zed and I walked about a hundred, hundred fifty miles a couple years ago. That was nothing compared to what you did."

"Why'd you walk so far?"

Careful. He doesn't know.

"We went on a long hike together," Drew said. "We camped out at night under the stars and during the day we walked through Colorado. It's very pretty there."

"I don't think I walked there. I don't remember a lot of pretty places. Just a lot of peanut butter. I don't ever want to eat peanut butter again."

"Can't blame you for that." He grabbed their bowls and got up. "Come on. How about a ride on a cable car to get home?"

Hyrum popped up. "Can I stand and hold onto the pole and wave at people?"

"Maybe. It depends on who gets on it before we do. It's still fun, no matter where you wind up."

Liar.

You only like it when you get to hold the pole.

Luckily, we were the first ones on and Drew headed right for the front seat by the pole. He told Hyrum to hold on tight, and if he got scared, he could sit down.

He did not get scared.

Hyrum laughed the entire way home, waving at every person we passed, and when we got off, he grabbed Drew in a giant hug. "Thank you for taking me out today. I had fun."

"So did I, Hyrum. We have to go for another bike ride soon."

Hyrum grabbed Drew's hand as they crossed the street, but it wasn't from fear. "Can I tell you a secret?"

"You can tell me anything."

"I don't want to go home. I want to stay here. I like it here. Everyone is nice, and Aubrey is teaching me things to help me read and write better, and she lets me read stories about real things that aren't bible stories. At home everyone is grumpy, and Mom only teaches me things for little kids. I don't want to be a little kid forever."

Drew stopped at the corner. "You're not a little kid, Hyrum. You're grown."

"No, I'm not. Will asked me if I wanted to be a man and I didn't know. He said maybe I'm in between, and that's okay. I don't mind being in between. But if I go home, I have to be a little boy again. And everyone is afraid of me."

"Why?"

He whispered, "I do bad things sometimes."

"Look at me, Hyrum." He touched Hyrum's chin with his free hand. "I'm twenty-one. Almost twenty-two. I'm half your age, and I'm a man, even though I still like a lot of the things I did when I was a boy. And I screw up sometimes, too. No matter where you are, here or Florida, you're a man. You're a full-grown man, and don't let anyone tell you that you're not."

"Mom says I'll always be her little boy."

"Well, yeah." Drew dropped his hand away from Hyrum's face and started for home. "Of course she does. I'll always be my mom's little boy, too. Zed will always be Aubrey's little boy. That's just what Moms say. It doesn't mean you're not also a man."

"Is Will Jo's little boy?"

Drew snorted. "Hell, yeah."

"I still don't want to go home."

You stayed here, too, dude. You know how he feels.

"Yeah, I hear you on that. Talk to Aubrey. Maybe she can make it happen."

"She's the Queen, so people have to do what she says. Mom can't make me go home."

"Not necessarily." We stopped just inside the door, and Drew sat on the stairs near the guard desk, patting the step so Hyrum would sit next to him. "Aubrey doesn't like to do that. She knows she could make people do what she wants just because she's the Queen, but she also knows that's kind of mean. If you tell her you want to stay here, she'll talk to your Mom for you. But she can't just tell your Mom you're staying at that's it. She can only tell her that you want to. The only one who can tell your Mom you're staying and that's it is you."

"Jax is the King. He can say I have to stay."

Drew nodded. "He could, but he won't. It's your decision, Hyrum."

Softly, "What about Will?"

"Come on. Why don't you want to make the decision yourself, and tell your mother?"

"Because my mom is a mom and she would have to ask Daddy, and he's going to say, 'Valerie, that boy doesn't know what he wants. Get home.' And then I have to go because he's the Daddy and he makes the rules."

Drew took a deep breath. "All right. Let's say Red wanted to stay here. Would he have to get your father's permission?"

"No. Red is a grown up."

"That's my point. So are you."

"Daddy doesn't think so," Hyrum whispered. "I'm too stupid to be a grown-up."

"You're not stupid. Come on, who won the math game? It wasn't me."

"You know math. You're teaching it for Aisha."

"I'm pretty good at it. But I have to think hard to get the answers. What's sixteen times six?"

"Ninety-six."

"Jonah," Drew got the guard's attention. "What's twenty-three times three?"

He scowled and started counting on his fingers.

"Sixty-nine," Hyrum said.

"Recite Matthew, chapter seven, verse one."

"'Judge not, lest ye be judged.'"

"I have to take your word for it," Drew said. "Because that's something I don't know. You know a lot of things that I don't, Hyrum. You're not stupid. There are just some things you haven't been taught yet."

"Daddy lied?"

Drew got up and held a hand out to Hyrum to help him up. "Man, I hate to say this, but your Dad was always a dickhead. Yeah, he lied. I know you love him, but he sucks, and I hate all the mean things he said to you."

"I don't love him, Drew." Hyrum started up the stairs, slowly. "But don't tell Jesus, because it's a sin and I don't want to make him cry."

15

The Munsons descended in a pack; their shuttles landed on the street in front of the royal house, and they were led up the elevator in groups by the guard; everyone went straight from, "Wow, it's been over thirty-five years, Aubrey, you look spiffy," to "Family reunion, woohoo! Where's the food?"

Still, the hugging took nearly half an hour, and that was after some of them gave up and decided just being there was enough. There was a monogamy to the way they dressed: men in dark slacks and white, button-down shirts with equally white t-shirts underneath, neatly tucked in, with black belts and shiny black shoes to match. The women were all in modest dresses that went past their knees and covered their arms almost to their elbows—Zed snorted, "Gotta hide those porn shoulders," and then Aubrey tapped the back of his head with her hand—and the makeup each wore was restrained and subtle enough that it was hard to tell they'd bothered with it.

Like Valerie, every adult woman had long hair, brushed and tied back, the same way Aubrey favored when she was on her knees cleaning the kitchen floor or scrubbing the royal toilets. The younger women seemed to be allowed any length of hair they chose, and one smaller girl, I thought she was five or six, had her hair in half a dozen little ponytails.

"That's Sarah and Ruth." Hyrum pointed to the women clustered around Aubrey. There had been another massive hug, and they were still touching each other. Aubrey squealed like someone reconnecting with a long lost best friend even though this was the first time meeting her youngest sister; they'd spoken on the phone and on video a lot, so I supposed they felt like they knew each other.

He pointed to men waiting on the fringe. "That's my brother Joseph, and the other one is Bryce. Bryce is Sarah's husband. I like him. He's always nice, but one time he told Daddy to shut the fuck up because his marriage was none of Daddy's business and if he wanted to let her work in the mail room then she damn well was gonna work." Hyrum's eyes went wide, and he clamped his hands over his mouth. Muffled, he said, "Please don't tell anyone."

"You didn't say it. Bryce said it." Zed knocked his shoulder against Hyrum's. "I say it sometimes, too. But Jay, oh man, Jay says it *a lot*."

"Do you get spanked?" Hyrum asked Jay.

"No, just glared at. Aunt Aubrey *really* doesn't like hearing it."

"You need to watch your mouth today," Oz said. "The level of righteous indignation would skyrocket if you let loose, and they wouldn't be wrong. Mom hasn't seen her family in over thirty years, so we're all on our best, all right?"

We were on the top floor of the royal house, using the multi-purpose room for the Munson family reunion. Two of Aubrey's brothers had come, Red and Joseph, and two of her sisters. Red was a surprise; he hadn't expected to make it but realized it would look odd if he didn't go. Her brother, Spencer, was stuck in New York but his wife had come because she wasn't passing up the chance to meet the sister who got away; the fact that Aubrey was a queen was incidental. Everyone brought spouses and kids and grandkids, and ten minutes in Drew gave up trying to remember who was who and which kid went with which parent. He could pick out the adults, but Bree was the only one of the younger kids he was sure about. He'd met Red's adult daughters in Kansas, but he had trouble remembering what name went with which daughter.

"When they're all in one place I can't remember, either," Hyrum told him. "There's too many of us. You don't need to, you just need to have fun."

"Yeah, but stick me in a formal reception, and I can remember the names of all the dignitaries," Drew said. "I should be able to do this."

"In church, if you can't remember someone's name, you just call them 'brother' or 'sister,'" Hyrum said. "Mom says that sounds respectful and then no one's feelings get hurt. We call each other that most of the time anyway. Even at the gas station."

"Still," Drew huffed.

Oz gave him a kiss on the cheek. "Don't try too hard. Just go be nice. They'll understand." She left us and started for the middle of the insanity, where she struck up a conversation with a few of her adult cousins.

Zed agreed, they should mingle. He nudged Jay, and they went to meet Aubrey's brothers, leaving Drew standing alone with Hyrum. I was on his shoulder, unsure if I should even be there. As soon as Valerie spotted me she would surely frown, she might growl, and she would probably tell Drew to take me downstairs. I belonged with Will and Aisha, who were not there because they'd forgotten what sleep was like and both looked like zombies and might want me to babysit long enough for them to nap.

"Who's not here?" Drew asked Hyrum.

"David, but that's okay because he's grumpy and doesn't like people. And Elle isn't here. I don't know why because she liked Aubrey when we were little."

"She was four when Aubrey left home. Maybe she doesn't really remember her."

"She remembers. Aubrey used to sneak candy to us. I bet her husband wouldn't let her come. He's an apostle's son."

I think that's a nice way of saying he's a dick.

"Is he mean?" Drew asked.

Hyrum gave a tiny nod.

"Well, should we go say hello to everyone? You can introduce me to Joseph and your sisters."

"Joe and Red and talking to Jax. We're not allowed to interrupt."

"Wanna bet?" Drew laughed. "It's a party. If they don't want to be interrupted, they can go talk somewhere else. Come on, I've never met Joe. If you like him, I'm going to like him."

Hyrum took Drew's hand and let out an exasperated breath. "They're gonna get mad, Drew. Daddy said, 'Never interrupt men when they're talking.' Men have important things to talk about and we—"

"We're men, Hyrum. We get to join in."

I don't know for sure, but I think Hyrum squeezed Drew's hand a little bit. Whatever the men were talking about couldn't have been all that important, because they stopped blabbing and Joseph lit up, grinning. Hyrum tried to hide behind Drew, peeking around his arm, but Joseph cocked his head a bit and said, "I see you there, Hyrum. Come on now."

Still holding Drew's hand, he stepped forward.

Joseph set his hands on his hips. "I hear you had yourself a little adventure. Gone two years and you never called me? What's that about?"

Voice shaky, Hyrum sputtered, "I didn't know how. I'm sorry."

"I missed my big brother." He held his arms out. "Come on. I want a hug. I'm so happy to see you. I can't believe you were gone so long."

Voice small, Hyrum squeaked, "I had to find the Queen."

"I know. But I didn't know it then, and I was worried. We had people looking for you, but they never even found a trail."

"I bet it was David." Hyrum pulled out of the hug. "He probably didn't look hard."

"You know what? I always knew you were tough. You never give up, do you? I don't know how, but you always push through."

Hyrum stood a bit straighter. "'I can do all this through him who gives me strength.'"

"Which one is that from?"

"Philippians. You don't know?"

"I don't know scripture as well as you. Jesus, how did you survive?" He hugged him again and kissed the top of Hyrum's head. "I swear, I will never doubt you again, Hyrum. 'The name of the Lord is a strong tower; the righteous run into it and are safe.' I should have known you'd be okay. I think that tower was built around you."

"Proverbs."

"I'll take your word for it." Joseph pointed to where his sisters were. "They'd like to see you, too. Expect to be kissed a lot."

"They're not mad at me?"

"They love you and missed you. No one's mad, Hy. You did an important thing and we're all very proud."

With a wide grin. Hyrum skipped over to them.

"The family agnostic speaks of righteousness," Red chuckled.

"He has faith, Red."

"He's also nervous," Drew told them. "I'm not sure why, but getting him to come over here wasn't easy. He thought you'd be mad if he interrupted."

"He's been told too many times to not butt into grown-up business," Joseph explained.

"Yeah, well, that's just it. He *is* grown up. He deserves a place with the adults, but he's so damned sure he'll never be allowed."

Red nodded. "We know. But you need to understand, Andrew, *he* didn't start approaching that conclusion until he got here. He spent forty-one years under our father's thumb, pressed down to his knees. Even though that's gone, it'll take a while for him to get up."

"He doesn't know Levi is gone," Drew hissed. "He's tied up on knots worried about what everyone will tell *Daddy*. And he hasn't said it, but he's terrified Levi will show up and—"

Jax slid his hand across Drew's shoulder. "Step back, son. This isn't the time."

Joseph didn't take offense. Instead, he grinned. "You're protective of him. I like you, Prince Andrew. And you're right, he needs to be told soon. Everyone is so worried about how Hyrum will grieve, no one's thinking about how he might celebrate."

"I don't think he will," Red said.

"Come on, Red. A two-hundred-eighty-pound weight will slide off his shoulders. He'll be relieved."

"He'll also be heartbroken. Don't underestimate him."

"I don't. That's why I think he needs to be told."

Red took a step closer to Joseph. "If he finds out now, he'll make the leap, Joe. Dad's gone, and David is standing there waiting to take his place. It's another layer of fear, and we don't know how he'll react. Just wait."

"Oh, hell, *I'm* not telling him. I'm not half that brave. But Hyrum is."

He turned and left, wading through a sea of kids to meet Oz.

Jax gestured to the smaller kids. "One of them is liable to blurt it out. It doesn't matter how much their parents stressed for them to keep it quiet."

"They only need to keep quiet for a day or two," Red said.

"Then what?" Jax pressed. "We've kept him from most of the news since he's been here, but I can't promise that forever. How betrayed will he feel if he hears it from someone else? I understand not telling him right off the bat, but he's been here long enough, and he's clearly healthy and balanced. It's time, Red."

He wanted Aubrey to make the decision. She was the one who accompanied him to his therapist and who heard the secrets he shared with the doctor and no one else. He thought she knew the most about Hyrum's mental state. Drew huffed lightly, crossing his arms. Later, he would tell Oz that was one of the biggest cop outs he'd heard in a long time. Red wanted to pass it off to

Aubrey because he didn't have the guts to face his baby brother and possibly break his heart.

She didn't argue the point but reminded him they didn't know enough about Hyrum's family life between six and forty-one, and it wasn't up to them.

"They keep worrying about how he'll react. What he'll do. He'll do what everyone else does. He'll cry, but we can deal with that."

"Not up to us, Drew," she told him.

He didn't have the chance to argue with Red and Jax. Will, circles under his eyes and with several days' beard growth, came up the stairs and headed straight for Jax. He had a burp cloth over his shoulder and a onesie sticking out of his back pocket and was not happy to be there.

"Myers," he said simply. "The swarm was released five hours ago, and he's getting on-the-ground live video. Daily life is uninterrupted, but there's activity around five silos, all with trajectories that aim toward central locations in Midlam, Pacifica, and Texas."

"Texas?"

They both looked at Red.

"Lopez sides with Pacifica," Red explained. "The Quorum is likely counting on him noticing the movement before the final Consortium vote."

"Texas votes in the last block," Jax said. "There's nothing they can do if the numbers don't work in Florida's favor before then."

"Their representative can lobby right up to the end on Florida's behalf," Will pointed out. "He could potentially sway the entire final block."

"But Governor Lopez won't blink," Jax argued.

"A year ago, maybe." Red nodded to Zed. "His daughter is in Pacifica now, and it's well known that she's involved with Zed. The presumption is that she wouldn't have moved here if it wasn't serious. Robert doesn't want her in the line of fire no matter where she is. Point one toward San Francisco, one toward Austin, and he pays very close attention."

"Would your Quorum actually fire any of those missiles?" Drew asked. "They'd destroy the land they purportedly want. It would be decades before it would be usable. The nuclear fallout could even impact Florida."

Will ignored how uncomfortable Red suddenly looked. "You're thinking like a pragmatist, Andrew. A scientist. Faith reigns over science in the Church of Florida. God will protect and provide."

"You're freaking kidding me."

Only he didn't say freaking. He also didn't blink at the look Jax shot him.

"The citizens of Florida, yes, most of them believe that," Red said. "If God wills it, they'll be fine. If He doesn't, they won't. They trust their Lord to do what's right for them, and if He calls them to rest early, it's what's meant to be. The truth, however, is that none of the Quorum holds to the same lines we draw for the faithful. They believe the science, they know the consequences, and they'll protect themselves and their families."

"And will let their own citizens die."

"People breed, Andrew," Red said. "They'll risk losing a million faithful citizens to save a hundred souls because they know the survivors will procreate in high numbers."

"And what about you? What do you believe?"

Red gestured to all the people in the room. "From here, they're headed to a safe house in Nevada. I believe," he said evenly, "that I will die on the sword, so to speak, and I pray—literally pray—that the brothers who survive me can leverage the rest of the world against the Quorum and end this."

"You won't die—"

"Yes, I probably will, Drew. I brought my family here to save them, but I have to go back and face David and the apostles. If I can stop them from moving forward with their plans, I will. But all I can do is delay the inevitable. If David takes my place, and he hasn't secured the Consortium vote, he'll launch at least one of those missiles."

"He'll kill a bunch of people because he doesn't get to join what amounts to a boy's club."

Red nodded. "Including his own family. And to that end, I'd like to spend some time with them, eat a ridiculous amount of food, and forget about it for a while."

He went to his wife across the room, grabbed her by the hand, and went to join his sisters and brother.

"There are already shuttles waiting to take the Munsons to the safe house," Will reminded

Jax. "The guard has swept their hotel rooms and the floor has been cut off from foot traffic."

"But?"

"Myers is prepared to pull them out of bed in the middle of the night and move them if he feels a threat is imminent. For now, he feels that the troop movement is procedural and not indicative of immediate intent. He's seen nothing that leads him to believe Russia has people on the ground in Florida who can man those missiles."

"But they could be there within a few hours," Jax guessed.

"One could assume that there are qualified troops nearby."

Jax huffed, amused, when Will stifled a yawn. "When was the last time you slept?"

"I'm fine, Jax."

"For now. I need you rested, just in case." He looked at Drew. "Go get the baby, the diaper bag, and a few bottles. If Aisha argues, tell her it's by royal order and not an option."

"She'll growl at me," Drew said.

"Let her. You," he said to Will, "take a nap."

Will protested; it was loud here, Rhys would be fussy, Aisha would be nervous. "I don't know if she's pumped—"

"Yes, she has. You know she has. Look around you, Will. Every adult in here is well equipped to handle a fussy infant, and Rhys won't be the only baby. Go home, hand the kid over, so that you can get some sleep."

"You just want my son."

"I wouldn't mind spending a couple of hours holding my nephew, even if I will have to let Aubrey have him for a bit."

"But he's so—"

"Little? Young? I know that. We're not going to bat him around like a tennis ball, Will. I promise you, he'll be fine. But if you don't get a few hours of sleep, you won't be."

Drew handed me to Jax.

"If she bites me, I'm blaming you."

Four hours later, the reunion moved to the roof because the grill and the firepit were there. Three of the little ones were yelled at for getting too close to the pit, and that didn't change even after their mothers had been assured it was not real fire. "That's irresponsible," one generic blonde grumbled when Aubrey wasn't looking. "That teaches them to stick their fingers in fire and next time it might be real!"

Hyrum grumbled right back, "They'll only do it once," and then confessed to Drew that he'd stuck his finger in a candle flame when he was eight because David promised him it wouldn't hurt. "It hurt. But I never did it again."

Generic blonde was not happy and reminded Hyrum that he needed to mind his manners.

"Which one is she?" Oz asked when she was out of earshot. "She's not your sister."

"She's Gwen. Her sister is Joseph's wife,

Erma. She doesn't like me and I don't know why she's here."

Drew knew why she was there; Zed probably understood, too, that a few of the women were there because their siblings brought them along, worried about the suddenness of the reunion and the simmering nervousness of their husbands. "Is Erma shy at all?" Oz asked. "Maybe she brought Gwen so she could be sure to have someone to talk to."

"She could talk to me. Sometimes she does but not today."

Drew turned on the lights over the grass while Jax fired up the grill, and people began filtering between the two spaces. Compared to Florida, it was cold here, and everyone wanted to eat inside, but the kids were fascinated by the tent of lights, and while they waited for the burgers to cook, they stretched out on the grass with Oz and Drew and listened to stories about Jeff and Fluffy while Hyrum provided sound effects.

The younger kids howled with laughter; the older ones sat back and paid attention, but they weren't amused by his additions to the stories and a couple of times the boys rolled their eyes.

They think they're better than Hyrum.

Drew reached out and scratched my head to let me know he'd heard me, and he agreed. They were all of eleven or twelve and already put themselves ahead of their uncle.

Everyone says they missed him. Why aren't they hovering? They're barely talking to him.

"I know, Wick, life is hard," Drew said, tickling under my chin. "You'll get a bite of my burger. I know the smells are driving you crazy."

Maybe a little. But I'm sad for him. These are the people who are supposed to love him most.

He had no answer for that.

Five hours after that, after the food was gone and the roof was quiet, Jay arrived. He'd gone into the apartment, but Will and Aisha's bedroom door was closed, and he didn't want to disturb them. "I assumed I wasn't party crashing too early."

Almost everyone had gone off to the hotel, except for Red, who was downstairs in Drew's old apartment. Oz and Drew and Zed were still on the roof, stretched out on the grass.

"You could have been here from the start," Zed told him. "You're family. You were invited."

"Previous plans made quite a while back. I was not changing them."

Drew snorted. "What could be more important than making small talk with people you don't know over burgers and hot dogs and one disturbing dish called 'funeral potatoes' that made Aubrey weirdly excited?"

"New exhibit at the DeYoung," Jay answered. "Then a dinner reservation that I made a few weeks ago."

"And?" Oz prompted.

"And she needed to get home. Her dad is still a dillhole who thinks a nineteen-year-old needs a curfew."

Oz wasn't letting it go. "Dinner at, what, six? Whatcha been doing for the last five hours, Jay?"

Before he could answer, Zed snorted, "Apologizing. And I'm guessing he started that about four hours and forty-five, fifty minutes ago."

"Shut up." Jay stretched out on the grass with them. "Was the reunion fun?"

"Who cares?" Oz sat up. "Spill it."

It took him a while to answer. "I thought I'd feel different. I dunno, more adult or something. But I don't."

"Why, did it suck?" Zed asked. "Oh, god, you really have been apologizing for over four hours."

"Shut up. No, it was awesome. On a scale of one to ten, I'd give it a fifty. I just...I dunno. Did you guys feel different? After?"

"Oddly, hornier," Drew said. "If it helps, I thought the same thing about getting married. I'd finally feel like an adult. Yeah, no. Now I feel like a horny teenager who gets to spend every night with his girl, but no one gets mad or even acts like it's a big deal."

"Good. It's not just me."

"Not just you," Oz agreed. "I thought I'd feel different, too."

"When *do* we finally start feeling like adults?" Zed wondered.

You never do. You'll only ever feel like a kid with grown-up problems.

"Seriously, Wick?" Drew asked.

Seriously. You'll always feel like there's a step you missed, and that you're just pretending until you get to it. Then you'll have babies and wonder when you're going to feel like a real parent. And

you'll have jobs and wonder when you'll feel like a
success. And then there's stuff like stopping a war
and wondering why anyone trusts you to do it, and
what happens if you screw up.

Oz groaned. "Well, my job is gonna suck."

"Wait." Zed lifted his head. "What happened
to the thing with the council? Didn't you have to
give them some formal presentation about your
Wastelands idea?"

"God," Oz groaned again. "I felt like a puppy
standing in the center of a room filled with hungry,
pissed off hawks. In less than five minutes I was
pretty sure they hated the idea, ten minutes in I
wanted to run out of the room, and fifteen minutes
in I wanted my mommy. Or Will."

"No go, then?"

"For now. Once they were done ripping me a
new one, Dad called for a vote. The consensus was
that it's a promising idea and they'd like to see it
come to fruition, but not at the taxpayers' expense.
They're willing to enter a land-lease agreement
with me, but scratching up the money, investors,
architects, everything would be my problem. And
I don't have a damned clue how to go about any
of that."

"What'd Dad say?" Zed asked.

"He said it was a good time to learn about
city planning and running a business. I get the
feeling he expects me to follow through." She
groaned again. "Really, my job is gonna suck. This
is just the start of it."

"If your dad has his way, by the time you

have it you'll be too old to care if you feel grown up," Drew said.

"Sure, unless Florida blows us off the face of the earth next week."

"Really think we're going to war again?" Zed asked. "Last time kinda sucked."

Drew told them what he'd overheard Will and Jax and Red discussing. "Something's happening, in any case. I got the feeling that it doesn't matter how this vote goes. David Munson and the Quorum want to start *something*. If not now, later."

"Will said we can't be drafted," Jay said.

"No, but we can still serve," Drew said. "My brother enlisted just before the last one."

"Still trying to figure out how." Zed sat up. "Prince Carter Van Hoff going into an enlistment office should have made the news. And your parents would have stopped him."

"Carter couldn't have avoided being a news topic. But Hamid Mor could. He went mostly unnoticed until his first assignment, and his commander knew."

"Hamid Mor?" Jay asked.

"Hamid is his middle name. Mor is my mother's surname. She took my dad's as the official royal name, mostly to piss off my grandfather, but he and I both have identification naming us as Mors."

"Don't get any ideas," Oz said. "Carter needed the discipline and he knew it. None of us really do, not like that. Our job is to figure out what Pacifica needs us for the most before we act on anything."

Pacifica needs you to keep being Hyrum's friend. Don't let him become a pawn in it if things get hairy.

"Hyrum is one of our favorite people now," Drew said. "If he needs us to fight for him, we will."

"How'd he do with seeing all his relatives today?" Jay asked.

"He did fine," Drew said. "He spent most of his time with the kids. The adults? They mostly ignored him after they'd gotten hugs and had a chance to tell him how much they missed him."

"Maybe they knew he was more comfortable with the kids."

"He's been gone for two years. They had no idea where he was or if he was alive or dead and couldn't be bothered to tell Aubrey, who *would* have sent people to find him. It would have taken Pacifica *maybe* half a day to hone in on where he was. Come on. If that had been one of us today? We'd have been smothered and had people hanging on us all night. And no one would freaking leave without another crushing hug. They left like this had been any other party."

"Attached much?" Oz teased.

"He doesn't want to go home, Oz. He wants to stay here, with us. He *knew* how that reunion would go. He knows how life will be if he goes back to Florida. Always the little kid, stuck with the little kids, ignored by the older kids, with only his mother for adult company. And she's clinging to the idea of him being her little boy forever."

"What more could he get here?" Zed asked. "Yeah, us, but we've got school and work and relationships to deal with. He's gotten a lot of time with us lately because it's all new, but face it, if he stays, he's still not getting what he's used to with us."

"But he *will* get our attention. Maybe not as much time as we'd like, but we're not shoving him aside because he's just a little kid. We'll make a damned effort to include him as often as we can. We'll still read stories to each other and spread out on the floor and color a couple times a week. But we'll also treat him like a goddamned man and not like...Rhys."

"We're not the only people who have to consider it, Drew," Oz said. "Mostly, it's my mom's life you're talking about. Most of his care would fall to her. And he does need specific care."

"He needs to stay here."

Oz scooted closer to him. "I love you. It's not our call. But I love that you so badly want him to stay."

"I want him to stay, too," Jay said.

Zed nodded. "It's got nothing to do with his brothers and sisters. Straight up, it feels like having another brother, and I'd like him to stay. I don't mind the idea that I'll have to deliberately carve time out for him. I mean, we'd have to switch up for stuff like bedtime stories, but there's four of us. He's never gonna feel in the way. Hell, he'll probably feel like we're fighting for time with him and he'll get annoyed eventually."

"If it were up to us, it'd be easy," Oz said. "I'm not sure anyone is even going to ask what we think and we—"

She stopped when the door clicked.

"It's complicated," Jax said. He stepped across the lawn and leaned against the light pole. "But, if this is the best place for Hyrum, we'll make it work."

"Mom," Oz said.

Jax nodded. "She's taking a sabbatical. I think in the back of her head she knew there was a chance he'd stay, at least for a while. I'd like him to stay long enough to have his therapist on hand once he knows about Levi, and to give him time to deal with that. But it's not our decision. Red and Valerie—"

"It's Hyrum's decision," Drew said.

"Like I said, it's complicated."

"No, it really isn't." Drew got up. "Hyrum is an adult. He lacks experience making adult decisions, and he favors child-like activities, but the *man* walked across the damned continent. A kid couldn't do that, and you know it."

"I know."

"You could make it happen, Jax."

"I could. But at what expense? This isn't just Aubrey's little brother, and it's not a matter of upsetting a few family members. This is also the brother of Florida's First Minister, and his government is falling apart. We don't know what will happen over the next week or two, and if I insert myself into a situation that hasn't yet been raised, the fallout could bite us in the ass."

"Just talk to Hyrum."

"I'm paying attention, Drew. But don't push."

"Someone has to."

"Andrew."

He stomped off, slapping at the door as he stepped inside. Jax didn't watch him go; instead, he focused on Oz, whose mouth hung open for a few seconds.

"Dad—"

"No, I get it. He's connected with Hyrum about as much as Will has. As long as he doesn't snap at me like that in official situations or in public, we're good." He pointed at jay. "You. We have your brother. If Will or Aisha don't come to get him soon, you get to smuggle him back into their room and put him to bed."

One by one, they got up. Zed wanted to know if Hyrum was still awake, and when Jax told him no, he wanted to know who read him his bedtime story. "He sleeps better if someone reads to him."

"He's also capable of falling asleep without one."

"I bet he's still awake," Zed grumbled as he headed inside. "Man, if he asked someone to read to him and they said no..."

Oz scooped me up. "Dad, we're all attached. Just...I'll rein Drew in, but if it comes down to worrying about what happens if Hyrum stays, there's no question. We're all in."

♦♦♦

Jay didn't have to sneak Rhys into Will and Aisha's room to put him to bed. Two minutes after we left the rooftop to raid Aubrey's kitchen, they came down to get him. Aubrey pretended that she wasn't going to hand him over until Aisha said, "My boobs are ninety seconds away from exploding. Hand the kid over, and please tell me he hasn't eaten in a while."

Keep him. I want to see the exploding boobs thing.

"That's a bit mean," Will said to me.

I'm mean because I'm hungry, too. I haven't eaten since breakfast. Burger bites don't count.

"You." Will pointed at Zed. "Feed Wick. He's starving." Then to me, "Why haven't you eaten? You could have told Drew you needed food."

Drew's been busy all day wedging his panties into his butt crack.

"Ah, I see. Still, if it happens again, interrupt his panty-wedging and remind him you need to eat, too." He turned to Jax. "And thank you. I don't think I've slept that long at one time, ever."

"Just returning the favor. How many times did you walk the floor all night with our kids so we could sleep? Besides, he was a hit. Hyrum carted him around for a while and introduced him to most of his nieces and nephews, and he endured a stream of nursery hymns and disturbing stories about whales eating men and a father who was going to sacrifice his son."

"That was adorable," Aubrey said. "They lined all the babies up and sang very softly. And Hyrum didn't let any of the kids hold Rhys. He kept telling them Rhys was too brand new and he didn't want anyone to break him."

"He changed diapers, too," Zed called from the kitchen. "Rhys had a huge blowout and, like, three moms came at him, but Hyrum waved them off and changed that diaper like a champ."

"He's had a lot of experience," Aubrey said. "Our mother watches several of the grandkids a few times a week. She says Hyrum has always been her little helper."

I swallowed the last bite of my food and went back into the living room. Will and Aisha settled onto the sofa while she fed Rhys, and Jax had dropped into his comfy chair. Zed and Jay headed down the hall, probably to see if Hyrum was awake and Oz had already gone into her room. Drew no doubt needed help plucking those panties out of his nethers.

They talked until Aubrey was starting to fade; she went to bed and Aisha finished feeding Rhys and took him upstairs, but before Will got up he told Jax he'd had an idea he wanted to discuss, however briefly.

"It calls David's hand and prevents Eli's prediction of my father's contribution to the war from coming to fruition. We'll need Myers on board with it, but it should work."

Jax sat forward and listened as Will outlined the idea that had come to him as he was falling asleep. They talked until the stillness of sleep had settled over the house, when he finally sat back and said, "That will bring Florida to its knees, Will. The damage could be long-term and expensive as hell to fix."

Will nodded. "We wanted to drag them into the twenty-fifth century. This could do it. Bring them to their knees, and if the timing is right, take Florida. All of it.

16

The second to the last day of voting was a flurry of nonstop lobbying and negotiation. Spencer Munson met with anyone who could give him five minutes of their time. It didn't matter if they'd already cast a vote. Favors could be traded, and he was counting on faith that the Quorum would deliver on the promises they had authorized him to make. Eli was sure they would get every vote they wanted on this day, but the loss of just one vote on the last day would end the proceedings.

"His heart isn't in it," Eli said. He was in the comfy chair in Jax's office, watching the live feed with Red, Will, and Jax. Little was happening; the first vote of the day had not yet been called for, and on screen was a shot of the conference room and some of the Consortium representatives milling about. "He's doing exactly what he's supposed to, but he seems beaten down."

"Damned if he does, damned if he doesn't," Jax said.

"As long as David sees the effort and knows he's doing his job," Red said.

The rest of their family, everyone who had come for the reunion, was on their way to Nevada. They'd spent another day with Aubrey, promising that when everything had settled and they knew what was really going on, there would be other reunions. There was so much more of Pacifica to see; so much more of San Francisco. They said their goodbyes late at night and by dawn were on military shuttles.

Hyrum and Valerie stayed; Bree went with her mother, despite the hard argument she gave in favor of staying: Hyrum needed her. She was a ready excuse to play, and she didn't think anyone else would spend as much time on games with him that she would. There was no convincing her that he had plenty of company on hand to occupy his time. In the end, Red barked, "Enough. You're going with your mother. That's the end of it."

He hated having said it. Those were words Levi would have used to shut a child up, and the sting in her eyes made him want to back down.

"You can explain it to her later," Aubrey told him. "She'll understand."

She might, but she'd still remember how it felt.

He'd wanted her to stay; he still wanted Aubrey and Jax to take custody of her if the worst happened to him. He amended his written order to include Darlene, and he knew Jax could pull them from the safe house and bring them here with little notice. She'd be angry, but she would honor his last wish, and his other daughters could decide for themselves where they wanted to be though he'd made it clear that Florida would not be welcoming to them in his absence.

While we waited in Jax's office, Aubrey took Hyrum to his therapist. He tried to get out of it—Will couldn't come, and he wanted Will there even if there was no donut after—but Aisha volunteered to go in his stead and promised she would bring the baby. "He lit up at that," Will told Jax. "He told me he's going to hold Aisha and Aubrey's hands, but only because he's protecting them and the baby. I didn't ask what he would do if Aisha needs both hands with Rhys."

"Where's his mother in all this?" Eli asked.

"Sitting in the apartment across the hall from yours, praying." Red gave a slight shrug. "I wish she'd go with him. It would do her good to talk to someone about Levi. Someone who's not trained by the church to parrot the same tired, victim-blaming edicts."

"No shrinks in Florida, then?" Eli asked.

"Not yet, not really. If the Lord can't help, no one can."

Aubrey says God gave men the brains to figure this stuff out. If God didn't want doctors to help, then there wouldn't be doctors, and people wouldn't be able to figure all those things out.

"My sister is smart," Red allowed. "And I agree with her. It's dragging the Quorum into the same line of thinking that's problematic."

Eli nodded toward the monitor. On screen, a woman in a black suit who looked five kinds of upset had stepped up to the podium and was waiting for people to take their seats. There were several quiet minutes while she waited, and when she spoke, it was tinny and loud and brought up a collective groan.

"Ladies and gentlemen," she said, "today's vote is delayed. The representative from Sweden has asked to abstain until tomorrow's vote, and Finland's representative is not yet ready."

What's that mean?

"It means someone is caught up in a backroom deal," Will said. "Spencer may be lining up all the votes he needs."

"He would need every vote from here on out," Eli pointed out. "In spite of everything, I almost hope he's done it."

The phone on Jax's desk went off. He gestured for quiet and then touched the screen, turning on the speaker so that we could all hear David Munson demand to speak with Red.

"Well, hello to you, too, David," Jax said. "Dare I ask how you got this number?"

"The Quorum," David snapped. "This is important. I need to speak with Red."

Red shook his head; no, he didn't get the number from the Quorum. As he leaned across the desk, he tried to sound upbeat. "What's up, David? We're watching the Consortium vote from here."

"Figured. You need to get to New York and help Spencer out. He almost has the votes we need. There are a couple of European block country reps that want to deal with you, directly.

Spencer almost has them convinced, but they're not budging until they've had a face to face with you."

Red glanced up at Will, who nodded.

"I can do that. When does he need me there?"

"He's got meetings scheduled at three. Make it to those, and we're in."

"All right. I'll catch the next shuttle out."

"Military or civilian? Spencer can have someone meet you if you're landing on a public pad."

"Hold on." Red made a pretense of looking up flight information. "There's one leaving from San Francisco city center in about forty-five minutes. Civilian, flight eighty-three-fifteen. I'll make sure I'm on it even if I have to bribe the pilot."

He nodded to Jax to hang up and then leaned both hands against the desk, exhaling. "All right. Will, I don't want to know how you pulled that off, but...here we go."

Jay wanted to complain about being yanked out of class—his mouth was open and a few words fell out—but he noticed Will's very slight shake of the head, and he bit back what he had to say. He sat in the chair Will pointed to, trying to see at once everything in Jax's office, from the display case with the crown Jax rarely wore to the makeshift throne, and we waited for Zed to arrive. Oz and Drew had gotten there first but neither asked questions, yielding to the look on Jax's face. He'd tell them soon enough.

Zed was breathing hard and fast when he arrived; he'd left his bike on the sidewalk by the door and bolted up the stairs because his guard would not have interrupted his class without a damned good reason. Between gasps, he asked, "Is Hyrum all right?" and was visibly relieved when Jax said it had nothing to do with him, but to sit down anyway.

"I take that back," Jax said. "I need you all to step up efforts to keep Hyrum away from the news. No broadcast news, nothing on your tablets. He needs to remain as blissfully unaware of world events as possible."

We were standing with our toes pressed up against the proverbial line in the sand. Florida had drawn the line, and Pacifica was about to stomp right on it. How defined the footprints were and how blurred the line became was up to them.

"I also need you to not trust everything you might hear, if you do stumble upon news coverage. Vet it through Will or me if something comes up you're not sure about, but never with Hyrum in earshot."

"Is this about the Consortium vote?" Oz asked.

"Peripherally," Jax answered. "For now, that's the information you need, and I'll expand upon it later."

Jay looked to Will. "I feel like I should ask questions, but I'm not sure what."

"Nothing needed yet." He picked up his phone when it buzzed, and then reached for the remote to the giant monitor. "Briefing begins in a minute," he told Jax.

When Jax nodded, Will turned the monitor on and tuned into the live feed from the Consortium's conference room. "You made sure there's no coverage in the Nevada house?" Jax asked him.

Will nodded. "They only have access to pre-recorded entertainment and religious services. I spoke with Joseph, and he's aware of the situation and will handle any issues that arise if there's a breach. He wishes to be kept informed, regardless."

The low rumble of voices filtering through the monitor speakers became a roar as members took their seats. They were getting information from their phones and from whispers into the earpieces some wore; by the time Spencer Munson stepped up to the podium, staring with red-rimmed eyes at the crowd in front of him, they knew what he was going to announce.

"Until further notice, Florida formally requests the suspension of this vote." His voice was thin, and he took a moment before continuing. "At approximately three o'clock, the shuttle carrying Florida's First Minister, Redmond Munson, was shot down over northeastern Ohio. At this time, there are no known survivors." He took a deep, shaky breath. "First Minister Munson—my brother—served his country and his Lord well and would take comfort in knowing that there were no casualties on the ground. Our Quorum asks for a respectful amount of time before resuming the voting process, while we mourn and investigate who might be behind this."

He looked up, to where he knew one of the cameras was. "I, personally, am calling on the Queen of Pacifica to use whatever influence she has in convincing their government to aid us in this investigation. Aubrey, he was our brother. Jax knows who did this. Just tell us."

"Kudos, Spencer," Jax whispered as he gestured for Will to turn it off.

"All right," Oz said. "Tell us what we need to be prepared for. Aside from shielding Hyrum from this."

"If this all goes sideways, you need to be prepared to evacuate. Even if it doesn't...at some point, I'll want you where you can't be reached. You'll take Hyrum, his mother, Aisha, and Rhys." He glanced at Jay. "And James."

"My dad? Why? Where are we going?"

"It's not where," Oz guessed. "It's when, isn't it?"

"We're not risking another safe house incident," Will said. "They can't get to you two hundred years in the future. My mother will also go, to make sure you have access to everything you need, and to help ease the transition for Valerie and Hyrum. You'd only be there a short time, but—"

"If they blow up San Francisco, we're stuck," Drew said.

"Until I can build a new portal, essentially, yes."

"If you survive." Jay's voice cracked. "That's why you want my dad there. In case you don't."

"I believe you would anchor each other. Hyrum will have Valerie, and Oz will have Drew."

"Mom has Rhys," Jay said.

"Well, that's all wonderful," Zed groaned, though not at all serious. "Everyone has an anchor but me. I'm the expendable one, aren't I? I'm *that guy*. The one they're gonna send five steps ahead to check for land mines and boogeymen."

"It's nice that you understand your purpose in life," Oz said.

"I always knew that I'd be important someday."

"Sophia," Jax said. "She's going with you. In fact, get her over here by tonight. I want everyone in one place."

"Wait. Seriously?"

"Tell me you don't see yourself marrying her someday."

"Yeah, someday. After I graduate and she's got her business going."

"Well, that won't happen if she's here, you're there, and you're stuck."

"Besides," Oz said, "sending her with us saves her life."

"Zara is heading for New York," Will said before Jay could get his brain wrapped around the idea of leaving her behind. "Her father has a job interview, and he's been invited to bring her along. If she calls you this afternoon complaining about it, encourage her to go. New York won't be a target, and she'll be safe there. Convince her of the opportunities. Museums, Broadway."

Jay nodded, glumly.

Will got up. "For the moment, you're going with me to the lab. Zed, you, too."

"For?" Zed asked.

"You're both getting a transponder. And I'm not asking if you want one. You're getting one."

"Um." Jay gestured to the tray on the center island in the lab. "Please tell me that needle isn't how the transponder goes in. That's freaking huge."

Finn picked up the largest needle, the same one he taunted Drew with before he received his transponder. "It only goes in a few inches. Feels like a pinch."

"Dad." Will sighed. "Stop. Especially now."

You could put Jay to sleep the way you did before his surgery.

"You can go first," Jay said to Zed. "Being the prince and all."

"Hey. So are you."

"No, I'm not."

"Yes, you are."

"Am not."

"You are," Will sighed, "and not the point."

"Fine," Jay said, "but you were one first, and you're older, so have at it."

Zed sat on the stool Finn pointed to and frowned. "I'm less than a month older. And I'm barely a prince that matters. It's not like either of us—ow—will ever hold the throne." His hand went to his neck. "That's it?"

"That's it."

Tell him about the headache.

He saved that until after he'd implanted Jay's transponder. As soon as he was done he pointed them toward the kitchen and told them to have a snack—there were brownies—and then to take some pre-emptive pain medication. When they balked because there was a 50-50 chance that Jo had baked the brownies, Will said, "It's as bad as the post-contraceptive implant pain. Eat and then take the meds. Get ahead of it."

They took the meds.

While they ate, Zed called Sophia and asked if they could come over, and then asked her to get Zara to come downstairs for a while.

"We'll take a walk," he told Jay. "Give you two some time to talk. Or...whatever."

"Yeah, Sophia might want 'talk' time with you, you know."

"She's going with us if we go. Zara's headed for New York either way. Spend some time with her, Jaybird. Even if you keep your clothes on."

"What if Sophia's not on board with the idea? You can't force her to hide in the royal house, and you haven't told her about the portals yet."

She would stay at the royal house because her father would expect it. Robert Lopez had asked Jax to keep an eye on and take care of his little girl; Sophia knew that and wasn't about to push back the first time Jax felt like he needed to honor his word. She could stay in the guest room, and he would stay in his room with Hyrum. "My personal chastity valet," he beamed.

"Lots of places to hide in that building," Jay pointed out.

"No hiding," Will called from across the room. "But if you're going to Sophia's, go. Be home by dinner time. Aubrey expects everyone, and that includes Sophia."

"Do you really think you'll need to send the kids ahead?" Finn asked when the door clicked shut. "There's a plan other than that, right?"

"We're sending them, if for no reason other than to get them out of the way," Will said. "And to that end, it would help if you could open one more portal. It worked in the hospital corridor, it will work in the multipurpose room on the eighth floor."

"If we can get a machine up there, sure."

That'll surprise old Oz and Drew thirty years from now. Suddenly, a portal?

"We'll go back and warn them later," Will said. "We'll use it as an excuse for you to go spend some time with Lux."

We have to take shrimp. I promised Lux some real live fresh dead shrimp bites. There's not much shrimp in thirty years.

"Because you ate them all," Will muttered.

Finn was stuck on the idea of getting his giant egg into the house. "We still need to get a machine up there. The hospital was easy. The elevators are huge."

"Dad, we could get a passenger van in there if we had to. There are things in the building you probably never knew about. Including a rather large mechanical lift that comes up through the stage floor."

"Huh. I always wondered why there was a stage at all. It's not like anyone ever held concerts or plays there. The stage is the show."

"And controlled by the military. And that brings me to another thing. I need you to allow General Myers access to the lab. Specifically, the gates. All of them."

"All. Not the one from the bridge, I presume. It's in pieces."

"Just the ones you have in the lab. I'll control them, but Myers's men need to be here."

Finn folded his arms, squinting as he considered it. "Will, everything we've ever sent through those gates arrived inverted or misshapen."

"I am aware. And I can't tell you much more, not yet."

"All right, then. Jax needs my toys, and I can't very well tell my great grandfather no, now, can I? Just promise me you won't blow up the place. I've become rather fond of it."

"Of course, you are. You stole my playground."

"I'll leave it to you in my will," Finn said, grinning. "You just have to outlive me."

"Nothing personal, Dad, but I'm not sure I want that." He crossed over to the kitchen and sat at the table. "Life without Aisha? I can't let my brain go there."

Finn sat with him. "You looked her up, I presume?"

Will nodded. "At Wick's urging. He knew, and rightly so, that if she'd died prematurely, I'd want to know beforehand. To prevent it."

"And?"

"She lived a long, healthy life the last time around. I can only hope that much of the timeline is intact."

"Well, she has you. That might shave a few years off."

"Just for that, I'm taking my playground back. I'll give you a call and let you know when we need to move the machine into the house. It might be late tonight, tomorrow morning at the latest. And bring Mom, just in case."

17

Drew helped Finn assemble the short track from which he would launch his ship. It ran lengthwise down the center of the multipurpose room, two round rails with a launch sling on one end, little arms that stuck up on each side in the center, and a whole lot of nothing on the other end. Jo muttered about how close he was cutting it; this was going to be the hospital all over again, and with his luck this time he really would smash into the wall.

"There's nothing on the other side of that wall," he told her. "Empty space, I think. No one will get hurt."

"*You* might!"

He shrugged.

"That wall is holding up the roof, Finn!"

"Then I suppose I won't plow through it."

"Finn. You can do this without launching from the track."

"Well, I could, but where's the fun in that?"

Will listened to them bicker for a few minutes and then scooped me up. When it was time to move the ship from the stage to the track, he'd come back to help, but while they worked, he needed to be in Jax's office.

Why aren't Zed and Jay helping?

"They're spending the morning with Hyrum. They went to his therapy appointment and are then taking him out to lunch and to see the seals at the pier."

He's going to bark like a seal all afternoon, you know.

"Undoubtedly. I'm sure he'll stop if he's informed that seals eat raw fish, and if he keeps it up, that's his dinner."

Sashimi's a thing, you know. He might like it.

Sophia had gone with them; she enjoyed Hyrum's company and liked to make him blush by calling him 'cutie' and 'stud puppy.' He giggled a lot around her and nervously spewed out bible verses, and when Zed reminded Hyrum that she was *his* girlfriend, his eyes went wide and he sputtered, "I didn't mean anything!"

"I'm just teasing," Zed told him. "You're allowed to flirt."

Hyrum leaned close and whispered loudly, "Are you gonna marry her?"

Zed whispered just as loudly, "Yes, someday, but don't tell her that. I want it to be a surprise."

"Zed," he said, solemnly, "I think you have a to tell a girl before you marry her."

Where's Rhys? I asked Will.

"With Aisha. Why, would you prefer to go spend time with him?"

Was he crying when you left?

"He was."

Then, no. He cries a lot.

"He's a newborn, Wick. It's his only way of communicating."

Yeah, well, I think he's telling you he wants different parents because unless he's asleep, he's screaming.

"Not that you'd exaggerate."

Okay, he doesn't cry when Jay holds him. Maybe it's just you he doesn't like.

"That's fine. His liking me is not a requirement. In twelve years, he's going to hate me, anyway. I can live with it."

Jax and Eli were already in the office. There was a map on the monitor, the same one we'd stared at two years earlier while mulling over Florida's boneyard. Those planes were still sitting there as if the world didn't know about them and wouldn't think to make sure they hadn't moved. The ones in operation, the planes used to bomb Chicago, were scattered throughout the state, and Pacifica knew where each one was this time around.

Florida knew that, too.

What they didn't know, what the Quorum didn't know, was that Jax also knew where the missile silos were. They'd been added to the map, small red circles near their borders and shoreline. The number of silos didn't match up to the number of missiles Red claimed, and Jax studied the map closely, looking for signs of construction in progress.

"It's not possible for them to have built the number of silos he's claimed in just two years," Eli said. "It's not possible for them to have built even one, not with their available resources."

"They had help," Jax said.

"And it went unnoticed?"

"It did not," Will said. He set me on Jax's desk and took the less comfy chair near Eli. "Their official stance regarding the ongoing use of high-powered laser drills in construction was an experiment in building bedrock housing. They claimed to be fabricating multi-use underground facilities using a silo-like structure. Theoretically, it's possible. Old, abandoned silos in the Dakotas were remodeled into dwellings in the early twenty-first century."

It was possible, but not likely.

"Red said the missiles were actually in place?" Eli asked.

"Some." Jax pointed to several different red dots. "Most of the silos are incomplete. But he said there are missiles that will be placed within a month, which means they're nearby."

"But not available to launch."

"Dad, they only need a couple of the ones that are already in place. We just have to figure out which of those silos are active and which are still glorified holes."

"And he couldn't give you that much?"

"He admitted that he might not have sufficient information," Will said. "He told us where he's been informed they are. That doesn't mean the missiles are actually there."

"Range?"

"Even the smallest could reach San Francisco," Jax said. "And the smallest carries a warhead bigger than the one used in World War Two. My concern is that there's something else, something he's never been told about. Levi was the one to cut the deals to make the silos possible. He was confident enough to go to war before they were ready. What aren't we seeing?"

Maybe what you're looking for isn't there.

"What do you mean, Wick?"

They're not stupid. They know you're looking at those silos and scratching your head. Maybe they have something hiding in plain sight.

"It wouldn't be outside the scope of the Quorum to mislead Red about the location of their armament. Or even what it consisted of. Their military doesn't report directly to him."

"All right, cat," Eli said, "Then where should we look?"

Cuba.

Jax twitched while Eli and Will sat forward.

All those little islands. You could hide a lot there.

"Or behind." Will reached for the remote on Jax's desk. "Puerto Rico and the Dominican Republic wouldn't allow Russia access to their land. But they wouldn't block the shipping lanes."

He shifted the map to include Cuba, and beyond it, Jamaica, then added a live stream satellite layer over it all. Jax was already on the phone, telling General Myers to tap into what he had on his office monitor and to zoom in on the water between the two islands. Less than ten seconds later, we were looking at a line of ships lined up neatly off Cuba's southern border.

"Get closer," Jax said into the phone. "I want to see who those belong to."

There was a moment of fuzziness, and then sharp focus on the flag of one of the ships.

"No one is surprised," Jax said to Myers. "War class, made for plasma missiles and retrofitted to small nukes. What are they operating on? No, not the fuel. I want to know what the system that launches those nukes is powered by."

How many are there?

"Armed?" Will answered, softly so that he didn't disturb Jax's call. "Three. Each capable of carrying multiple missiles."

Eli pointed to movement on the ship closest in view. "There's quite a bit of troop activity there. Does that look like day-to-day or preparatory operations to you?"

"Could be either."

Looks like ants scurrying. How can you tell?

As soon as Jax hung up his call with General Myers, the phone rang. He looked at the screen, sighed loudly, and answered as he put the phone on speaker. "David."

"Your majesty." He sounded snotty and not even a tiny bit respectful. "Familial request. I haven't been able to get hold of Joseph, or anyone else who went to your little reunion for that matter. They need to come home. The Quorum is making funeral arrangements for Red, and they'll want to be here."

"They left here yesterday," Jax said. "I believe they planned on making a stop in Salt Lake City on the way, but other than your mother and Hyrum, you can expect them soon."

"The women," David sighed. "I'm not surprised Joe is allowing them to site-see. My mother is still there, then?"

"She is. Hyrum is still recuperating. It seemed reasonable to have them stay for another week or two."

"Yes, well, reason went out the window when you shot my brother's shuttle down. Send them home."

"You know damn well we had nothing to do with that."

"Then who? If you know, tell us." When Jax didn't answer, he groaned, "Come on. I did not have my brother shot out of the sky. We didn't do this. Tell me who."

"Look in your own back pocket, David. But Pacifica is not responsible."

"Watch some news, Jackson. The speculation is out there."

"Well, then I'd be a fool to send your mother and brother home on a Pacifican shuttle. Who knows what might happen?"

"Send them home," he insisted.

"Come and get them, David. You and you alone will be admitted into the royal house. You're welcome to visit and determine for yourself where they're better off."

Before his phone was back on the desktop, he turned to Will. "Are there any more gates available? Even one more?"

Will nodded. "There's a prototype. I can get it working."

"We need it by tonight. We need all of them by tonight."

He got up, and Will and Eli followed.

"What's the plan, son?" Eli asked.

"For starters? Get the kids and get them upstairs. The minute Finn is ready, they're leaving."

It only took half an hour to get everyone upstairs, ready to go. James took the longest, twenty minutes, but he got there as quickly as a military air bike could manage. Aisha called him and before he could get two words out said, "Come now, come alone, and don't bother packing. There's a soldier on a bike waiting downstairs for you."

He had a vague idea what it was about, but she'd given him none of the specifics. While Aubrey stood near her mother and brother, trying to explain what was happening, Aisha took James to the wide windowsill near the stairs and sat with him. Will wanted James to be clear on the fact that he was stepping into the future, and he was going for Jay's sake. There would be no sympathy for his fears. He was there for his son, to give him something to hold onto. James watched as Finn's ship rose up from the stage and was brought to the floor by a dozen soldiers, and then as they disappeared the way they'd come, and the doubts began to fall away.

"Why aren't you nervous?" he asked her.

"I've done this a few times already, James. But don't let my demeanor fool you. Right now, I'm scared to death. I'm taking my newborn two centuries away from his father...my gut is screaming at me to stay here with Will and *help*."

"Rhys needs you more than Will."

"And Jay needs you. This is the possibility of leaving everything behind, James."

He nodded. "I'd do that for my son."

"And George is there."

That took him by surprise. "I knew that, but..."

"But you didn't believe it. I know. When the rest of us come home, if you want, you'll be able to stay with him a while. Bear in mind, he has a newborn now, too, so it'll probably be a whole lot of not sleeping and diapers, but you'd have time to sort through things."

James reached out and touched Rhys's chubby arm. "I don't mind the sound of a baby crying. If I have any regrets, it's that you and I split before we had another. But you," he bent toward the baby, "I think you're probably worth that regret. I can't wait to see you chasing after Jay, yelling at him to stop being grown up and just play. You're going to own him."

"So what's stopping you from having another one of your own? You never needed me for that."

"No, but be honest. I'd be a wreck trying to raise a baby on my own. I'm reliable for a weekend at a time. Maybe two. And before you say it, I know I need to change that if I have any hope of winning George back. I'm trying. Honestly."

Drew and Will maneuvered the ship onto the rails, and they rolled it down the track without power first, checking for any uneven spots. Once it was pushed back to the start, Finn climbed in and powered both the ship and the track. Will held everyone by the elevator, out of the way, but there was no shielding them from the sight of Finn's ship rocketing forward and disappearing.

Zed uttered, "Cool," while Jay used more colorful language, and Sophia sputtered, "What the—?"

Aisha snickered, though she'd never seen a portal opened and was probably just as impressed, and James was too stunned to do much more than blink. Aubrey was the only one who saw the horror in Valerie's eyes, and how tightly she gripped at Hyrum's arm. She took a step back, her hand to her chest, breath hiccupping.

A few seconds later the ship reappeared, coming to a screaming stop at the end of the track, less than an inch from the wall. Jo sighed; Finn knew he could stop it before it got that far, but he thought it was funny and after all those years she knew he was as mature as he was going to get.

"He can do this without the track," she sighed, speaking mostly to Will. "I swear, the next time he opens a portal, when the ship stops we're rolling it across the floor before he has a chance to climb out."

"I wish you'd thought of that sooner," Will said. "But, to be fair, the track was necessary this time. The portal opens into a hallway back home, not this empty room. It needed to be at a measured position." He pointed to Drew, Zed, and Jay, and told them to help Finn shove the track out of the way.

Valerie inched closer to the stairs near the elevator. "No. Whatever you have planned with that...thing...no. You're not involving Hyrum."

"We kind of have to," Oz said. "Both of you."

"Absolutely not."

Oz glanced at Hyrum. "Dad told you what's going on, right? He wouldn't ask this of any of us if it wasn't important."

Valerie tugged Hyrum toward the stairs. "We'll take our chances."

Hyrum's mouth opened; he had something to say, but he wouldn't go against his mother's order, not unless Will barked out one of his own.

Aubrey stopped Oz before she could go after them. "I'll take care of this. You need to get through that portal."

"What if you can't convince her?"

"Then she won't go. We'll find another way to protect them."

Oz twitched toward the portal. "Wait. If you don't go, Dad—"

"He'll understand. The portal is here, sweetheart. I can be up the stairs and through it in two minutes if I need to. If they launch, I'll have plenty of time." She pulled Oz into a hug. "Take care of them."

Oz studied her mother's face. Aubrey wasn't fighting tears, and she wasn't tense. With a promise that she'd keep an eye on the boys, she kissed Aubrey and nudged her toward the stairs. "If you have to bolt through," she called after her, "drag Hyrum."

With the track out of the way, they grouped around Will. "Ideally," he told them, "you'll be there for ten, perhaps fifteen minutes. Regardless, once you're through, head down to the apartment. You'll be far more comfortable there in case of a delay."

"A few minutes for us, how long for you?" Drew asked.

"Two days, I would imagine. Perhaps a bit less." He bent over to look at me. "Change of plans for you. I need you to stay here for a bit."

So Hyrum will have someone he likes to go through the portal with later?

"Something like that."

Oh. You need me to be here to take Aubrey through.

"Sophia," Will said. "Zed explained? And you understand what's going to happen?"

"As much as I can until I see for myself. I'll grab his hand and not let go."

"Good." He pointed at Zed and then Jay. "I don't want you two using the portal alone until you've had sufficient training. When you head through, think *only* 'follow Oz.' That's it. Be very careful of stray thoughts."

"Say it out loud if you have to," Oz said. "Repeat it until you're through. All of you."

"Normal steps," Will reminded them. "Just walk as if you were heading across the room. Don't pause for anything."

"Why would we?" James asked.

"If you're paying attention, as you move through the portal you'll see a flash of pink. It's tempting to stop and see what it is. Don't do that. It's just mist from the refrigerant that keeps the portal tunnel cool and only appears pink because of the lighting."

Will handed Rhys's diaper bag to Jay and pulled him into a tight hug. "I love you, okay? Take care of your brother."

He glanced at his mother. "Both of them, I swear."

Oz lifted the empty bassinette by the handle, and nodded, indicating that she was ready. Will still wasn't, though. He turned to Aisha, who had Rhys strapped to her chest, and reached for her.

"Be careful," she whispered to him.

"Fifteen minutes." He planted kisses on Rhys's head and then gave her a long one. "If I don't—"

"Nope. I'm going to plant myself on that old sofa in Finn's living room so I can feed the little monster, and you'll be there soon enough to annoy me because I won't be done yet and at least one boob will be screaming at me. We are not discussing anything other than that. You'll be there soon, because I have ginormous, milk-engorged breasts, and not enough time to do anything about it."

"You want me to think about your...breasts."

"Yes, I do, handsome."

Jo patted his arm as she brushed past. "They'll be fine, William. I promise. Aisha and Rhys, not her breasts. Though I assume those will survive as well."

He knew that. Whatever happened here, they would be fine. Jo would be there, would make sure they acclimated to his birth When, and she knew how to access all the funds Will had seeded in an array of bank accounts. He'd made sure that they'd live comfortably if they were stuck there.

Even James. Will had arranged to get a fully funded bank card for him, explained to Aisha how to get to it, and Jay knew how to get in touch with George. Their lives would be comfortable; they had the family home, money, and Jo could arrange for identification.

He knew it all, he knew Mass had already gone home and would be there if they needed medical care, but it didn't take the sourness out of the panic that was forming around the edges of his heart. He held his breath as they stepped through and exhaled slowly when the portal seemed to swallow Aisha.

Now you know how Jax felt when you took the kids to the safe house.

"Indeed."

I stretched to see his face. His eyes were red, and he blinked rapidly, trying to push the tears into the back of his head so they could drip into the pit of his stomach, where sorrow lived.

Finn stretched up on his toes and kissed Will on the cheek. "Come on. Let's go get the rest of this over with. I'm not entirely sure what you have planned, but let's get to it. I'm already tired of having soldiers in my lab and the sooner we get this done, the sooner I get rid of them and the sooner our wives can come home."

◆◆◆

Members of the royal guard stood inside the first level of the lab, one near the door that led downstairs, another on the far side of the room. That guard had a clear view of the entry, and, as of midnight, a monitor above the door that gave him a long view of people milling about on Union Square and a sightline to anyone entering the elevator. Finn grumbled as we went past them, and then grumbled again when Will didn't let the door slam behind him.

"Rod oversaw the assembly of the last gate," Finn said as we entered the level where he played with his transporters. "Rather than place them in a line, he moved them into a circle and said if that doesn't work for you, get the military grunts to move them back. But with the extra one, this is really the only way they fit."

There were already twenty people in the room, the grunts Finn hinted annoyance over. Six were government scientists there to help and, by extension, learn a bit about Finn's research, and the rest were soldiers on hand to provide muscle. They annoyed him far less than he wanted Will to think. His shop had never been so clean, and they'd installed a new, state of the art computer for each gate.

"I'm keeping those, by the way," he said. "Consider it my fee for using my equipment."

"Impressive work for so short a time frame," Will said to the Colonel who was there to oversee his men. "Any word on when the power needed will be available?"

"We're running a second line from the bridge," Colonel Ketchum replied. "This isn't the first time that pipe from the solar farm has been useful. Remind me again why we don't hook it into the main power grid?"

Will fanned his fingers out in front of him, sounding out an explosion.

"Good thing there's a relay, then." He stepped out of the way, gesturing to the main computer. "All yours. And it goes without saying, everyone in this room has the appropriate clearance."

Yet you said it anyway.

Will turned the monitor to get a better look, and Finn crowded next to him.

"Repeating myself, but you realize everything we send through still inverts?"

"I'm counting on it, Dad."

"I'm more than a little confused, Dash. This is only set to deliver through the gate on Richard's end. Exactly what are we sending him that requires this much power and this number of gates?"

"We're not sending anything to Richard. We're taking him out of the equation, entirely."

"That's not possible. If you don't send—"

"I know." He pulled a stool from under the keyboard stand and sat down, his arms crossed. "Dad, you won't like it, but we're lighting a fire under your work, so to speak. The truth is that you don't need a gate on the other end. You never needed a gate. What we're doing this afternoon involves a lot of coding, with a lot of correction to your coding, but without removing the hiccup that causes the materials you transport to invert."

Finn let that sink in. "You know where I'm going wrong."

"*You* know where you're going wrong, you just haven't let it bubble up in your brain. You've done it a dozen times before, every time you've sent yourself from one static location to your ship elsewhere. You activated your transponder and transported."

"And wound up in null space," he reminded Will.

"That happened because you poked your other self so hard the transponder broke and the ship couldn't make sense of which Finn needed to be where. But you still wound up inside the ship." He pointed to the upper crossbar on the gate in front of him, the tiny nodule attached to it. "You essentially transport every time you use a portal, although that's more like stepping through a door.

We're doing this similarly to the way we sent you home when you were lost here without your memory. Guided lasers will embed transponders into each unit that we send. The difference is we're using space as a parameter instead of time."

"How long was it going to take me to reach this point without your help?"

"A few years. We can't wait that long, Dad. We need this working by tonight because if we don't have it, time will rear its ugly head and demand a reset. Pacifica was at war for several years in the last loop of time, and we'd like to avoid the same ending."

"All right. Let's get it done, then. Just tell me what you need me to do so we can get our wives and the kids home."

Will nodded.

"You'll see your sons again, Will. Those weren't goodbye kisses. One was simply an 'I love you,' and the other was a 'be good for Mommy' kiss."

"The day you walked me to the portal, when I was seventeen. What kiss was that?"

Finn let loose a tight chuckle. "That was an 'I'm sorry I'm crying so hard that you're leaving here with my snot on your face, and don't you dare die before I see you again' kiss. But I knew I would, Dash, I just hated what was probably going to happen when I did."

Will outlined for Finn the changes they were about to make and reminded him that he needed to focus. No letting his mind wander to other, shinier projects. There were four to five hours of work ahead. With luck and the Colonel's help, they'd be done by dinner.

Finn stared at the computer while Will spoke, hearing everything his son was telling him, but allowing a thread of consideration to weave its way between the words. He wasn't distracted, though it looked like he was letting his mind wander just seconds after Will had asked him to maintain a semblance of focus. He had split his attention into two parts: the one that was listening to Will and the one that reached an epiphany.

"You not only know where I'm going wrong, you're there, aren't you? You've got transporting nailed down. You've got a working model."

"Dad, come on."

"I don't care, Dash. I don't care if you get to it before I do, I just want to know if you have."

"You don't care," Will repeated. "If some lab rat in New England beat you to the punch, you'd care. You know you would."

Finn reached for a nearby stool and pulled it close to Will so they could talk without the Colonel overhearing. "But I already know that no one else figured it out, Will. If they had, by the time I was born it would have been a thriving industry. If anyone in this world, right now, is going to do it, it's you. And if my son beats me to the punch? I'd be proud, not upset. It would be exciting, and I'd want to know about it. I'd want to play with it."

The silence that fell between them as Will deliberated what he wanted to say made the hairs on the tips of my ears twitch. I knew what he had been doing while Drew played with the box of snot and his nanobots; he wasn't merely supervising, standing back while Drew created things and tested them, then tweaked and smoothed out the kinks. Will had spent a lot of time in the office of the workshop, tinkering with the things he was also interested in, building on Finn's work.

He'd created a personal transporter that worked in conjunction with the transponder implanted in his brain. It was no bigger than his thumb, embedded into a wristband that could easily be mistaken for a watch or bracelet, and it didn't require a gate or a portal.

"But it still hinges on the use of transponders, Dad," Will said as he wound down, quietly, wanting to keep the conversation between them. "It also requires small, wireless connectors worn on the shoe and shirt collar."

Finn's eyebrows knotted. "Why?"

"Because without those, your clothes don't transport with you."

Finn barked out a laugh, loud enough that half the soldiers in the lab twitched. "Please tell me you didn't test this on yourself."

"No. I used one of the drones and transported it to points within the workshop. Once this is done—" he gestured to the computer "—I'll continue the testing and eventually hire someone who doesn't mind being the first human test subject."

"I have a dozen adventurous techs who would jump at the chance, Will. Nearly everyone who helped me create the time pod and the portals would volunteer before you could finish explaining it to them." He reached out and grabbed Will's arm. "Swear to me you won't be the first. I'll do it before you. Promise me that, Dash."

Will gave him his word. There would be no personal testing of the toys until he was positive it worked without life-altering hiccups. Once this was done, the threat of war with Florida behind them, Will promised to share his data and employ volunteers. "You'll still be the first to transport without transponders, I'm sure of it, Dad. I have no intention of venturing that far."

"No gates," Finn sighed. "I was sure these were necessary. Maybe make the transponders portable and not embedded? We could—"

Again, Will gestured toward the computer. "Let's get to the task at hand. We have roughly five hours of work ahead. Think about the possibilities later."

At the four-hour mark, Will woke me from a nap. I was stretched out on a desk in the corner, a little too close to the edge for his taste. He touched the top of my head first and then ran his hand down my back. "Wick," he said softly, "wake up."

I opened one eye. *What?*

"Go home. I know you're hungry. And by now Hyrum could use some company."

By myself?

"You've done it a hundred times. Just look for delivery trucks and taxis before you cross the street."

I'm not feeling lucky.

"Wick..." He sighed and went over to one of the guards. A minute and one radioed conversation later, he came back. "Vicat is on the Square. Go to her, she'll carry you across the street and she'll make sure you get inside safely."

Sure, pass me off to the mean lady.

She'll probably punt me across the street, and then you'll feel bad.

She did not punt me. Vicat picked me up very carefully and nuzzled me close, whispering that I was a soft boy and so sweet, and I could count on her to carry me across any street I wanted. In what felt like a bit of a betrayal to Drew, I gave her a head bonk before she set me inside.

He never had to know.

"My foster mother had a cat that was as soft as you. Tiny, too. I don't think he ever weighed more than four pounds. Between you and me, though? He wasn't nearly as smart. Poor thing used to chase his own tail three or four times a day because he saw it out of the corner of his eye and thought something was sneaking up on him."

We all have those moments. Just maybe not that often.

Once inside, she set me on the floor and asked the desk guard if he thought I could find my own way upstairs.

"That cat? Vi, I think that cat not only can find his way around here, he knows all the door lock passcodes and where the bones of the enemies are buried. If you see him on a hover cart, duck. And lock the door."

She laughed and bent over to speak to me. "I'll leave you to go home by yourself. But if you need anything at all, I'll be in the guards' lounge for a few hours. I want food and a nap."

Check the fridge. I think Aubrey left roast in there. And cake. She makes cakes for the guards.

"You know, he probably understands you," the desk guard said.

"Never a doubt. I just wish I understood him in return."

A few hours later, I'd wish the same thing.

18

Hyrum was curled up on the sofa with a pillow pressed to his head, trying to block out the sound of his mother arguing with his sister. Jax was in his comfy chair, arms crossed, and he looked several degrees of pissed off but was trying to stay out of it. I took a moment to decide who needed me the most, and then realized Will was right. Hyrum needed a friend.

I felt tension uncoil in him when I climbed onto his side and began purring, but he left the pillow in place.

"It's the work of the devil," Valerie hissed as I rubbed my face against Hyrum's arm. "If that *thing* did what you say and carried your children to a different time? That can't be anything but a tool of Satan."

"That *thing* is in place to save your life, Mom. To save Hyrum's life. I'll go with you, just let us take you through."

She refused to believe that her son, the one she admitted was more like his father than anyone else, would truly do anything to hurt them. David's mindset was like his father's, but he wasn't violent the way Levi was. The worst he would do to them was nothing more than the way she'd lived the last two years of her life. He'd order her to stay home, caring for Hyrum, watching her grandkids a few days a week, and nothing more. And that, she said, was not a bad life.

"If it's what you want, yes, it's wonderful," Aubrey said. "But it's still not enough for Hyrum."

"He'll be fine. Life without Levi is so much—"

The pillow shifted.

"—calmer, and he'll thrive without his father there. Everyone is happier without Levi around."

"Mom, stop," Aubrey hissed.

"The house feels lighter without him there. Hyrum will sense that as soon as he walks through the door. Levi was evil. God will forgive me for being glad that man is dead."

The pillow fell to the floor.

Aubrey grabbed her mother's arm. "Mom."

Hyrum sat up. I tumbled onto the sofa, and Jax twitched. He saw Hyrum's face, the tears that sprang to his eyes, but the news settled with him before Jax could do anything.

"Daddy's dead?" Hyrum stood up, pressing his hands to his stomach. "My daddy's dead? *Daddy?*"

Valerie spun around, mouth gaping when she realized what she'd said.

He started mumbling, "Daddy's dead," over and over until it became a wail and he went to his knees, crying, "No" in one long moan. Jax was the first to reach him, lifting him from the floor back to the sofa, holding him on his lap. Hyrum buried his face against Jax's shoulder, sobbing, while he grabbed onto Jax's shirt.

He only let go long enough to slap Valerie's hand out of the way when she tried to touch him.

"It's all right," Jax whispered. "I'm sorry. I know it hurts."

Hyrum's breath hiccupped, and he said, "No," one more time.

Aubrey knelt next to them. She rubbed Hyrum's arm, softly, trying to pull the pain away. "Sweetie, I'm sorry. We were waiting for a better time to tell you. We knew it would make you sad—"

"No. No, no, no, I'm not sad."

Jax leaned away a touch, trying to see the colors around Hyrum. When Aubrey looked at him, he nodded: he's telling the truth.

"Then what is it? What's wrong?"

His nose gurgled as he sniffed. "I'm scared."

"He can't hurt you anymore," Jax said.

"No. I'm not good enough yet."

"I don't understand," Aubrey said at the same time Valerie snapped, "That's nonsense."

Hyrum turned to face her, but he stayed on Jax's lap, one hand still holding onto his shirt. "Daddy's a bad man," he explained. "He's going to Hell."

"Oh." Aubrey set her hand on his free one. "Sweetheart, the truth is we don't know where he is. He might be in limbo."

"No." Hyrum shook his head. "He was bad, really bad, and Red said men who are bad like that go straight to Hell."

She wasn't going to argue with him. "All right. But why does that make you scared?"

He started crying again. "Because I'm not good enough. I do bad things and I don't mean to and if I die I'm going to Hell and I'll be with him for *forever* and I don't want to be with him again. I want to be good and go live with Jesus."

Valerie took a step back, covering her mouth with both hands as her eyes filled. Aubrey reached for Hyrum, pulling him off Jax's lap into a tight hug, and they knelt on the floor together. "I promise you, Hy, you're not going to Hell."

"But I'm not *good*. Daddy said, 'Hyrum, I don't know what to make of you. You're a mistake, and God doesn't like that. What you can do is more wrong than I can fathom.' And he always told me to try to be good. He never said I was good yet."

With an exasperated sigh, Aubrey said, "Daddy was an asshole, Hyrum."

The crying stopped. "What?"

She took a deep breath and put her hands on his face. "Daddy lied to you, sweetie. He lied all the time. You've always been good."

"But I'm not." Hyrum's voice tangled around tears and snot. "I do bad things."

"Listen to me. Do you think I would let you sleep in Zed's room if you weren't good? Or let you play with my kids every day? Do you think Will would let you hold Rhys if you weren't good? Daddy was the only one who ever said you weren't, right?"

He shook his head. "Not the only one."

Anger flashed in her eyes. "Who?"

"David." His voice was soft, sharing a secret. "He says Daddy is right. I'm no good and everyone would have been happier if Daddy had gotten it right when he pushed Mom down the stairs. I never should have been born. But Daddy couldn't make me go away before I was born."

At that, Aubrey turned sharply. "What the hell, Mom? What's he talking about?"

"You know he was violent," Valerie said. "Levi pushed me down the stairs before he was born. More than once." She shrugged. "He'd gotten it into his head that I'd caught with another girl, and he wasn't having that."

Aubrey stood up. "What else did he do to you?"

"With Hyrum? What didn't he do?" She refused to spell it out, not in front of him, but she leaned in and whispered to Aubrey, "It's why he is the way he is. This isn't God's doing. It's Levi's."

Hyrum sat on the floor, and I crawled into his lap, purring.

You got Aubrey to say two things off the bad word list, dude. That's kinda awesome.

"See?" Jax said. "Wick thinks you're good, too."

"Am I, Wick?"

Jax reached over his shoulder and rubbed the top of my head. "He's pretty damned smart. He knows things. Wick, show him. If you think Hyrum is a good person, stand up on your back legs and give him a kiss. If not, get off his lap."

I didn't waste time. I stood up and licked Hyrum's chin, and then his nose, and I kept licking until he giggled.

"Wick would never lie," Jax said, gently. "I don't think he can."

Hyrum nodded. His hands went to my back, holding me close but not too tight. "Red says not telling the whole truth is kind of like a lie."

Jax patted the cushion next to him, and Aubrey sat on the sofa with them. "That's called a lie of omission," she said. "Did you need to tell us more?"

He nodded. "I never told anyone because David said not to. But he's like Daddy." He looked at Valerie. "He does too hit. He hit me all the time. David said, 'Dad's right, Hyrum. You're proof of sin. You're all wrong.'"

Thinly, "But David loves you."

"Did he hurt you?" Jax asked. "More than just from hitting?"

"He broke my arm. I didn't fall out of the tree, David broke my arm and said I had to lie about it or Daddy would punish me. He said Daddy loved him best and would be mad if he knew I'd done something to make David hurt me."

"Oh my God," Valerie said under her breath.

"What else?" Aubrey asked.

"I think he broke one of my ribs. It hurt to breathe for a long time. And once, I tried to ride Joseph's skateboard and David caught me and pushed me off and my finger bent all the way back. He said if I told, then Daddy would know I stole the skateboard."

"You asked Joseph first, didn't you?" Valerie sputtered.

"Not the point, Mom!" Aubrey snapped. "I don't care if he *did* steal it. That's not the point."

"Joe *said* I could play with it! You believe me, right? I *tried* to be good."

"I believe you." Aubrey got up and kissed him on the forehead. "You can stop trying so hard, Hyrum. You *are* good."

He sniffed again. "I don't want to go to Hell with Daddy. If I do, he'll punish me all the time and time never goes away there."

"Never again," Aubrey declared. "You're never going to Hell, and as far as I'm concerned, that includes Florida." She looked at Jax. "I don't care how you make it happen. Revoke his travel rights. Declare him a ward of the King. He's not leaving Pacifica."

19

Minutes away from David Munson's expected arrival, Valerie restated her refusal to dabble in the devil's work by going through the portal and Hyrum wouldn't go without her. Jax promised I would go with him, and Drew and the other kids were just on the other side, but he started to cry again, worried that his mother was right and everyone else was lost forever.

"I've been through the portals before," he tried to assure Hyrum. "It doesn't hurt, and you get to come back. You'll be safe there."

He shook his head and muttered, "Better the devil I know than the devil I don't. That's not from the bible. But Red says it a lot. It means—"

"I know what it means, son. But I'd feel better if David didn't have access to you for a while."

Voice soft, scared, Hyrum said, "I won't let him hurt me again. I know how to make him stop." He rubbed the tips of his fingers against his shirt. "I don't want to see him, Jax. He's mean. But I don't want to go where Drew went."

Jax gave up and told Valerie he wanted them to stay in the apartment downstairs until he had spoken to David, and he'd decide from there what to do, whether she should see him or not. We went down the stairs together and waited until they were in the apartment with the door shut, and once we were near the guard desk, Jax told me to stay inside. I could watch out the window if I wanted, but he didn't want me on the street when David's car pulled up.

"Sir, there are photographers at five and seven o'clock," the desk guard said. "One on the sidewalk, one in the street. Neither are local. There's a San Francisco Chronicle camera at one o'clock, just past the steps up the Square."

"And on the rooftops?"

"Guards. Twelve, two, three, eleven, ten, and nine o'clock, as well as directly overhead. Doormen will be on your six."

I jumped onto the desk so I would have a better view.

She's gonna kick him in the nads, I told the guard. *He'll be all, 'Aubrey, it's been so long,' and she'll be 'Jerkface!' and* whomp, *right in the jimmies*.

They waited until the car was parked and the guard standing at the curb had opened the car door to let David out. Once he was on the sidewalk, another guard pulled the house door open so they could step out together. I couldn't see Jax or Aubrey's faces, but when David got out of the car, he was scowling.

The moment he saw her, he softened.

I think she did, too. There was a moment of awkwardness—David didn't know how to greet the King, if he should bow or shake his hand or just say "hey"—but Aubrey ended it by reaching out and pulling her brother into a hug.

She thought he was an asshole, but he was still a brother she hadn't seen for thirty-five years and she loved him.

I glanced at the desk guard. *You know if she had kicked him, it would have made the news.*

While they stood outside and chatted, Jax directing David's driver to a spot down the street, Vicat stuck her head out from the lounge. "I'm still here if you need anything, Wick. There's an old TV marathon playing if you want to watch it. Some guy traveling through time in a box. Seems like your kind of thing."

I stretched my neck forward, so she would follow where my nose was pointing, toward the door.

"Ah. Official business. All right."

The desk guard muttered, "Damn, I'd watch that."

Sucks to have to adult sometimes, doesn't it?

I followed them upstairs; a guard walked ahead, a guard walked behind, and once upstairs they positioned themselves at the entryway so that they could see inside the apartment as well as down the stairs. Another guard went out onto the balcony; as far as I could tell he was there to guard against ninjas, even though we'd never even been threatened by one, but I couldn't figure out why he was out there.

They stayed in the living room, exchanging pleasantries and discussing the reunion David had missed, even though it quickly wore thin with Jax. His jaw set and nostrils flared, just a tiny bit, not even enough for David to notice. I did, and when David sat on the sofa in the same spot where Jax had tried to calm Hyrum not even an hour earlier, I heard a rush of pissed off air shoot from Jax's nose.

I jumped to the coffee table where I could glare at him.

I'll sit here and threaten to bite his face off.
I bet he tastes like mouse.

We needed Will. He was better to have around than three guards. David could see the guards and knew they meant trouble. With Will he wouldn't know and might relax and say what he really thought instead of talking about his kids and their siblings.

Aubrey knew she had siblings and she knew David had kids; that wasn't the conversation she wanted to have. She wanted an explanation for why he treated Hyrum like he was less than the family dog, but she was never quite able to push him toward the subject.

But Red, he was willing to talk about. He was appropriately upset about their older brother's demise; he said all the right things, yet as much as he said losing Red hurt, his eyes remained dry, and he didn't dwell on it longer than it took the appropriate words to fall out of his mouth.

"Are you coming home for the funeral?" David asked Aubrey. "Day after tomorrow. It's been declared a national day of mourning."

"You know I can't," she said.

He was not surprised. "No, I didn't know that. I assumed your husband would give you permission to go home for this. Red was our oldest brother. He deserves to have us all there."

She turned to Jax. "Sweetheart, he thinks I need your permission."

"That'll be the day. You really don't know your own sister, do you?"

"Fine," David huffed. "You do things differently here. That doesn't change anything."

"Yes, it does. Because here, I'm free to say whatever I think, whenever I choose." She leaned forward. "We both know who's responsible for bringing Red's shuttle down, David. I won't step foot in Florida until the guilty are held accountable."

He matched her glare. "Why not? I'm here in Pacifica and presume *you're* the ones responsible."

"You really think I'd have the First Minister of Florida assassinated," Jax said.

"It wouldn't be the first time, would it?"

"Don't even try that, David," Aubrey said. "Dad might have been the gaslighting master, but the odds that you can match him are slim."

David snorted. "Aubrey, anything Dad could do, I can do far better. He worked off mania and ego. I work off faith."

"Faith that allows you to kill your own brother."

"Now what would be the point in that?"

She looked at Jax. "Tell me what you see."

"He believes he can do better than Levi. He's lying when he says he didn't kill Red. Though I have no way of knowing whether he ordered it or simply went along the plans of others."

"I had no reason to kill him," David argued. "Red was sinking fast. He didn't have the support of the Quorum and his own Second Minister wanted him gone. The only thing necessary to remove him from the Prophet's seat is a call of the Quorum. If they each receive a revelation that his time is done, then it's done."

"All of them," Jax stated.

David nodded. "If God were to speak to one about this, he'd speak to all."

"Yeah, well, he's not lying about that," Jax said to Aubrey. "It would have to be unanimous."

"Then he didn't have the entire Quorum in his corner," Aubrey said.

"Red?" David asked. "He had none of them."

"You," she said. "You don't have their full support."

"Nonsense."

Jax decided to cut the crap and go right for it. "You've either got Russia supporting you or they have a gun to your head. Which is it? I'm betting it's the former, but I'm not willing to dismiss the idea that none of this is your choice." When David didn't answer, he went on. "Call it off, David. You're posturing for a war you can't win."

"We don't want war."

Jax's eyes narrowed as he studied the colors flaring around his brother-in-law. "Yes, you really

do. But why? We know what your Quorum wants, but what's in it for you? A seat at their table? A calling to become an apostle? Second Minister?"

"I will not become the Second Minister," he said flatly.

"No, your ambition goes beyond that."

"My ambition is to serve my God."

Jax nodded. "I can see that. But who's your God, David? I don't think it's the usual suspect."

"Oh, come on."

Aubrey let slip a surprised, "Oh," her hand going to her mouth the way Valerie's did when the truth slapped at her. "The Second Minister is already dead, isn't he?"

David stood up. "This is ridiculous. I came here to get my mother and brother. Where are they?"

"They're not going anywhere," Jax said. "Hyrum is here for the duration, and your mother stays with him."

"That should be her call."

"Really." Aubrey got to her feet, too. "She listens to the eldest male in the house, and right now, that's Jax. Failing that, it's his father, Eli. And neither of them will give her permission to leave right now."

"She'll listen to the head of her *family*," David insisted. "And with Red gone, that's me. She's coming home with me, period. She and Hyrum."

"You don't even want Hyrum," Aubrey said. "You'd keep him hidden away like a horrible family secret. Why should he go back to that?"

"You ran away. What do you care? If you gave a damn about him, you would have stayed to protect him."

"From you? You know, if I'd known he needed protecting from you, I might have. I would have endured all the abuse to protect him. Silly me, I assumed his brothers would do that for him, not add to it."

"They're not leaving with you," Jax said. "They're staying here, under my protection."

"As your hostages, you mean."

"Is that a threat?"

The guards near the entry stiffened, ready.

"Take it any way you want it, King Jackson. If they stay here, as far as Florida is concerned, they're hostages of the realm. Prisoners of war."

"Is that a declaration?"

"I'm not in the position to declare anything. I'm just the son and brother of dead First Ministers. I'm here to collect my mother and brother so that they can attend Red's funeral. Nothing else."

"They're not leaving." Jax signaled to the guard. "Escort him out."

"You'll regret this," David said as he headed for the stairs.

"I already do."

Jax turned to comfort Aubrey; they didn't need me, so I followed David down the stairs. He stomped dramatically, as if a temper tantrum would make Jax run after him, saying that he changed his mind and David could have everything he wanted. His footsteps echoed the way Zed's did when he was twelve and hated everyone, which almost always ended with him uttering things off the bad word list, getting him grounded. It never ended with him getting his way.

The stomping was loud enough to attract attention, and when we reached the bottom of the stairs in front of Drew's old apartment, the door cracked open and Hyrum peeked out. David stopped, twitching away from the guard who nudged him to keep going.

"He's my brother. I only want to say hello."

The door opened another inch.

"Hyrum. Thank God. I am so glad to see you. You look—are you okay?"

Hyrum nodded.

"Come on, let me see you. Can you at least walk me down the stairs? There are guards, it's all right."

Geez, dude, no. Hyrum, go back inside.

He stepped out into the hall. "Why'd you come here, David?"

"Honestly? I came to see if you and Mom wanted to go back home for a bit. Just a few days."

Hyrum shook his head. "Nuh. I want to stay here."

"All right." David nodded toward the door. "That's all I needed to hear. Just walk me to the door, okay? I haven't seen you in so long."

"Just the door."

David nodded. "I missed you, you know. When Mom said you were missing, we sent dozens of people out looking for you. You must be pretty fast, to get far enough away that we couldn't find you."

"I had a map," Hyrum said. "I walked."

"That took guts. I admire that." He looked at the guard and then out the door. "I have to leave now, but I'll call, all right? We can talk."

"Mom knows how to call you."

"I know. Ask her to, okay? Now, can I have a hug before I go?"

Hyrum stepped back, but then sighed and said, "Okay."

I didn't hear what David whispered in his ear, but once he was out the door—he turned and waved before heading down the street to where his car had moved—I looked up. Hyrum had tears in his eyes, and the fur on my back started twitching. He pressed up against the glass and watched David walk away, his breath hitching.

Go back upstairs, Hyrum. Please.

I heard him sniff. His nose gurgled, and he dragged his fingers across the door, forehead pressed to the glass.

The guards went into the lounge; David was gone, and no one had given them orders about Hyrum. I peeked in to see what they were doing: raiding the fridge. Vicat was right where she said she'd be, on the sofa watching the TV marathon. One leg was draped over the arm of the sofa; she had shoes on, she was ready to move. I ran over, jumped on the sofa, and started patting at her arm.

"Whatcha need, Wick? A snack?" She looked over the back of the sofa. "Any meat in there for the cat?"

I patted harder. Then hissed.

That got her attention, and she sat up sharply. "What was your assignment?" she asked. "Just now."

"Making sure the Queen's brother didn't pull a fast one," one of them said.

The other guard said around a mouthful of sandwich, "The little brother came out to say goodbye, but I don't think he's gonna miss the bastard."

That got her off the sofa and out the door.

"Hyrum," she snapped at the desk guard. "Where'd he go?"

He gestured to the door. "Said he wanted to take a walk."

"And you let him go?"

"What? He's old enough to be my father. Like I'm going to tell him no?"

She reached across the desk and grabbed him by his shirt. "Get your ass upstairs and get the King. Tell him your sorry little piece of shit brain didn't stop to think that the Queen's baby brother has *never* walked out this door by himself. He *always* has an escort. And then you figure out how to explain how the *cat* is the one who noticed and managed to send someone to help. And find me some freaking backup."

She didn't say freaking.

She reached into her pocket for something and slapped it on the desk. "Track me. You damn well track me."

I didn't even have to ask. She scooped me up and bolted out the door, asking me which way she should turn. I looked down the street in the direction David had left, and she started running. I was pressed against her chest with one hand and felt the rush of her breath across my head; Vicat was fast, almost as fast as Will. She sprinted down Geary toward Grant, and turned at the corner, scanning the fringes of China Town for Hyrum, who was short enough to be lost behind people.

"Market," she huffed. "He'd go toward Market. Bigger crowd closer to the Ferry Building, easier to get lost in."

David was half a block up Market Street, waiting by his car with the door open, and Hyrum was walking toward him. I braced myself, ready to be tossed down so she could go after David, but she skittered to a stop when Hyrum cocked his arm back, fingers splayed, and sent a hot-white ball of electricity right into David's face.

20

The blast wasn't enough to knock David off his feet. He stuttered back a step or two, blood spurting from his burnt nose, painting his hands and shirt in red. It gave Vicat just enough time to drop me and then slam her body into his, preventing him from taking another step toward Hyrum. She had him on the ground and was pummeling her fist into his face when the first guard air bike shot around the corner, and he was a bloody mess by the time the second one screamed up the street. Jax and his guards rounded the corner as she was getting off him.

When Hyrum saw Jax, giant tears began rolling down his cheeks, his breath hiccupping as he gasped for air between sobs. I scrambled up his leg and he grabbed onto me, but he didn't take his eyes off Jax.

"He said he killed Red and if I didn't come, he was going to kill Mom, too."

"Jesus," Jax muttered under his breath. He held out his arms and Hyrum tumbled against him. "Not gonna let that happen, son. I promise."

David had been jerked to his feet, arms braced behind his back. Vicat got an inch away and hissed, "You threatened to kill his *mother?*"

She didn't wait for an answer. She drew her leg back and did what I wanted the Queen to do: kicked him right in the groin, a hard, sharp knee straight up. "That's for Hyrum, motherfucker."

Hyrum tried to cover his mouth with his hand, but he had a cat in it and wound up stifling the surprised giggle with my foot.

"Hyrum's hand, your Majesty," Vicat said. "He got—well, I don't know what he got. It was like he shot electricity from his fingers that morphed into a tight ball of light that smacked right into this asshole's face. I don't know any other way to explain it. A crackle of lightning, then a ball of bright white light."

Jax stepped back and reached for Hyrum's free hand. His fingertips were red and there was a little bit of blood, but it didn't bother him when Jax touched the tip of his red and raw pointy finger. "I need to get you back home, okay?" he said quietly, just to Hyrum. "Aubrey needs to see for herself that you're all right."

"Is Mom okay?"

"She's fine. She's with Aubrey."

"He killed Red, Jax."

"Come on." He kissed Hyrum on the forehead. "Let's go home. We'll talk about it there." Before we left, he turned to Vicat. "He's your arrest. Escort him to the tank. It'll be a while before I can deal with him."

"Yes, sir."

"Ideally, I need him to be able to talk," Jax said. "But if he gives you any crap, it's your call how to handle it."

"She'll kill me!" David screeched after him.

Jax shrugged and kept walking.

◆◆◆

Hyrum was still holding me when he ran to his mother. I was squished between her boobs and tried not to complain about it, but I let out a tiny, involuntary squeak that made her step back. Still, he didn't put me down when Aubrey went to hug him, though she was more aware of my presence and gave me some breathing space.

Jax gave them an abbreviated version of what happened. He made sure Valerie knew David was alive and in custody but didn't tell her how badly he'd been beaten. He let Hyrum tell them the rest, but before he did Jax made sure Hyrum understood that he was to stay in the apartment with Aubrey and Valerie until either he or Will came to tell him it was all right to leave.

"I did the thing, Mom," Hyrum said, sadly. "I'm sorry. I was just so mad, and he said he killed Red, and he was gonna kill you, and—"

"What thing?" Aubrey asked.

"He's a human stun gun," Jax said. He held his hand up, wiggling his fingers. "Shoots it from his fingertips. I didn't see it, but I gather it was quite effective."

"I'm sorry," Hyrum repeated. "Daddy said, 'Hyrum, that comes from evil and I won't have it. Do it again, and I'll cut off your hands.'" He blinked and sent tears over his cheeks. "Please don't cut my hands off."

"Don't believe a word of it," Valerie hissed. "He has such an imagination—"

Aubrey ignored her and slipped her arms around Hyrum. "It's all right, sweetie. Everyone in this family has a special gift. We don't punish them for it, we celebrate it."

"Don't," Valerie said. "Don't make this normal."

Jax sighed hard. "Valerie, here, it's as normal as normal gets. In fact—" he narrowed his eyes as he looked at her "—you *want* us to find it normal. You're terrified we'll harm him for it." He turned to Aubrey. "Her static color is pale yellow. Right now, she has red and blue swirling around her, with a hint of green. She's terrified, hopeful...and jealous."

Eyes wide, she took several steps away from him.

"You're safe here," Jax told Hyrum. "Your mother is safe. I promise. Whatever that thing you can do is, we'll figure it out later."

"I can keep my hands?"

"Well, it's not like I need a spare set. You might as well hold onto them."

Hyrum held his hands out for Aubrey to look at. "I know how to not do it," he said, softly. "I won't hurt anyone, I promise."

She touched the tip of his pointy finger. "Does it hurt?"

"Nuh. It tingles. Are you scared of me now? Everyone else is scared of me."

"No, Hy. I'm not scared. I swear. I'm angry with David but I'm not afraid of you."

"How can you not be afraid of this?" Valerie demanded. "He can hurt people. If he loses control, he could kill someone or set everything they have on fire."

"Has he?" Aubrey asked. "When did it start? I'm guessing twelve or thirteen?" She turned to Hyrum. "Sweetie, when I was twelve I realized that if I set my hand on someone when they were in pain, if their feelings were hurt or they were sad, I started to feel the same thing. And when I let go, they felt better. I kept their pain for a little while, and then let it go. Daddy knew that about me, and it frightened him."

"He was sixteen," Valerie said. "His adolescence came late. He reached out to stop—" her voice cracked "—it just happened."

Hyrum looked down at his feet. "Daddy was going to take Elle under the stairs. I just got so mad. She wasn't being bad. She didn't need to be punished." He looked up, tears on his cheeks. "I didn't mean to. I wanted to hit him, but the thing happened."

"He lit his daddy's hair on fire is what happened," Valerie said.

"Hyrum? Really?" Aubrey couldn't stop the tiny laugh that escaped. "His hair caught on fire?"

He nodded. "Just a little bit. I put it out."

"That man never touched the girls again," Valerie said, suddenly proud. "Sarah doesn't remember..."

"I set his chair on fire, too," Hyrum blurted. "The one in his office. And the tree behind the church. That wasn't lightning. Spencer said it was because he wanted to see me do the thing but we didn't know I could burn down a whole tree. I think Daddy knew because that's when he said he would cut my hands off. Even though I said sorry."

"I may want a demonstration in a few days," Jax said. "And I mean it. Almost every one of us can do something different, just not quite as impressive as that. We'll talk about it, okay?"

Hyrum nodded.

Jax leaned over and kissed Aubrey. "I have to go. I need to check on Will and Finn before I deal with David."

"The cat lady has David," Hyrum said. "She won't let him do anything else."

Jax took me from Hyrum to save me from being caught up in another hug, and we went to the lab to see how Will and Finn were coming along. The desk guard was gone—permanently, I was afraid—and several others followed us across the Square while more lined the street near the door of the royal house. No one wanted to piss off the King now, because he might be in the mood to literally send heads rolling.

Do heads bounce? I bet they bounce.

Will and Finn were watching live shots being streamed from the war room. On one side of the screen was a view of several of Florida's missile silos, and on the other was a long shot of the ships just outside Cuba. "Activity on both fronts," Will said without looking away. "They've clustered near two silos and are ignoring the rest."

"Gates ready?" Jax asked.

"Ready and waiting on General Myers. His men are on their way." Will finally turned away from the monitor and saw me there. "No luck getting Valerie to leave?"

Jax set me down and grabbed a chair near the desk. He sat down and told them everything; David Munson was a bloody sack of bruised meat sitting in the holding tank of the guard armory, Hyrum had tried to blow David's face off, there would be another shake-up in the guard, and he was about to give Florida's Quorum one more chance to back down.

"Hyrum has a gift," Will said, sounding impressed. "That would explain a lot."

"We'll figure it out later. But, David admitted to Hyrum that he was behind Red's death. That's the opening salvo. We'll admit to knowledge of the silos and strongly suggest they back down."

The door opened, and soldiers carrying large white canisters came in. Will told them to set one on the platform of each gate, directly in the center, and then to back up.

"You still haven't told me what you're sending," Finn said.

Will gestured for the soldiers to grab protective goggles. "Each of those canisters contains an electromagnetic explosive that will, in turn, propel millions of armed mosquito drones set to go off at staggered intervals."

"To—?"

"We're wiping out Florida's power grid, its weapons, computers, and any ability they have to launch those missiles."

Finn blinked as he thought about it. "Dash, if you take out their entire grid, that includes hospitals and care facilities. You'll kill—"

"They have been duly warned to be prepared to go onto alternate power sources in anticipation of a solar flare. They're essentially three centuries or more behind us, Dad. They have combustion engines to use as generators once the grid fails. Their health departments have been warned of a possible failure of the power grid as has their government. They know something is coming, but they have no idea the extent of the damage about to be inflicted."

"And to that," Jax said as he got up, "I'm heading for the war room. Keep your comms available. If the Quorum refuses to back the hell off, we'll send them."

"With Red dead and David in custody—?" Finn prodded.

"By the time I get across the street, Spencer Munson will also be in custody," Jax said. "For his own protection. He knows that, but the Quorum doesn't. We'll see. If all they really wanted was that Consortium seat, they'll back off." He pointed to the monitor. "The armament on those ships are aimed quite specifically. Pacifica, Midlam, and I suspect the Quorum isn't aware, also at Florida. If they don't follow through, Russia will end them without hesitation."

"That seems rather harsh," Finn grumbled.

"War tends to be harsh," Will said. "We're trying to stop it before it gets that far."

"Well, we need to get to it. It's late, and I'm hungry."

Half an hour later, every monitor in the lab clicked on, controlled remotely from the war room. Each one displayed a different location in Florida, streamed live, and one broadcast a feed of the ships near Cuba. It startled Finn when they popped on, but Will calmly got up and went over to the main computer and waited for Jax to call.

"What's this mean?" Finn asked.

"It means the Quorum thinks he's bluffing."

Or they want you to blow them up. Maybe this is that thing Aubrey was talking about last time. The thing where everyone worthy gets called up to heaven while the rest of us sit here and suffer.

"The Rapture?" Will guessed. "They believe they need to build a temple in holy land first. Though to be honest, I think they've lost that thread of the story, and you may be right. They may intend for this to be the start of a holy war."

If they think that, nothing is going to stop them.

"Perhaps. My gut tells me this is more about being caught up in the loose ends Levi left, coupled with a desire to roll back the progression Red made."

Will's phone pinged. He didn't put Jax on speaker, but I saw the way his eyes changed; the Quorum didn't budge. They wanted war.

"All right," he sighed when he hung up, "let's get rolling."

Colonel Ketchum nodded, and when he stepped up to his computer and put his goggles on, his people followed. Will initiated everything, from the countdown to starting their programs, to the final 3...2...1 before everyone pressed their big red buttons to start the gates.

There's always a big red button.

The electric noise as the gates powered up cut through my skull. I cringed, and Finn noticed; he put his hand over my head, trying to plug my ears, but it barely helped. I could feel the room humming, a rapid pulse vibrated through the floor, increasing in tempo until one by one the gates shot bright lasers into the canisters, and they each disappeared.

They repeated it five times, sending a total of thirty toddler-sized canisters into Florida and off the coast of Cuba, and we watched on the monitors as they materialized on the other end, turning inside out, and as the drones escaped in massive bright-light explosions.

The darkness crept through Florida in a series of waves. The first set of explosions went off near the heart of the country, in between their largest military base and the headquarters of their church. Will turned to watch the first monitor to his left, a crisp, clear shot from a satellite that had been positioned to give this strike optimal visibility; the canister appeared and immediately turned inside-out, releasing the protected mosquito drones—they were shielded, he told Finn, by virtual Faraday cages, enabling them to maintain power—and the tiny drones rode on the current of the electromagnetic pulse as it spread, miniscule bright lights that pocketed the view like a field of stars.

Lights in homes winked out, street by street, the pulse spreading like spilled ink. Utility poles cracked and fell when the transformers perched near the tops popped open in a shower of sparks, sending cars on the street below into silent, screaming spins, streaks of rubber left spent on the road when their startled drivers tried to brake hard or accelerate their way out of danger.

He turned to the next monitor. The same creeping darkness spread from the center of the screen outward, sending the northern border into quiet night, and we watched the same thing repeatedly unfold, from its West Virginia border in the north to its tip in the Keys. The drones pocketed the murkiness that fell over Florida, the mute screams of people running into the terror of sudden, too-blackened night, searching for answers, darting between the sparks that fell from lines overhead like snowflakes.

Drones swarmed the now-darkened missile silos, spinning in a whirlpool of tiny stars before descending into the abyss, finding holes and cracks that allowed for entry, where they let loose a series of smaller explosions, rendering the weapons and launch systems inoperable.

The cameras looking down from space captured the confusion, men in uniform bearing flashlights and headlamps, scurrying away from the end of days. They ran for bunkers, praying to not feel the heat of fire on their necks nor see shadows from a mushroom cloud, praying to make it to safety before that happened.

The ships were last. Will initiated the final launch himself, a single canister placed on the center deck of the center-most ship. The satellite zoomed in; it felt as though the cannister sat there for a few heartbeats longer than the others, bathed in bright lights from the command deck, inverting in slow motion, petals gently peeling open, though that was probably just me.

When the pulse came, it shot across the ships like a shockwave. This was no slow seepage of ink; this was a starburst, the drones streaking across the sky, and the blackness fell over the ships like a silk sheet being furled across a bed. Light from the drones reflected off the water, and the ships began to list, slightly, and then slowly they parted, drifting one from another, rocked by waves that pushed them toward Cuba's shore.

The drones, spent, winked out and fell into the water.

From start to finish, it took ten minutes.

There was no joy in that room. No cheering when the canisters inverted as hoped and the drones went to work. They each simply took their goggles off and stepped away, waiting for their orders from the Colonel. Will picked up his phone again when it pinged, and he nodded to the Colonel, who then gestured to the door.

"All right, that's it." Will's voice was laced with his breath. "Dad, if you don't mind, head to Aubrey's and wait there. She'll even feed you if you're nice."

Finn stared at the now-darkened monitor. "How many people will die because of that?"

"Honestly? Considerably fewer than would have died without it."

That didn't make him feel any better. He followed us up the stairs and out the lab door, blinking against the brightness outside.

"Night falls in Florida. Still daylight here. It feels like there should have been more."

Will nodded. "It's not over yet. But I understand where you're coming from. All that and it's just...done."

"And the transporter works."

"With the transponders. You still get to figure out how to do it without. And yes, you get to keep the code we wrote today. Go forth and transport, Dad. Get rich and remember me in your will."

"Ha. I need that money. It looks like I might live forever."

♦♦♦

I expected the holding tank to look like it does in cheesy crime-fighting videos with cops that flex their muscles more than their brains: dark, damp, gray cement walls with a single metal chair in the middle of the room and a drain in the floor where spent blood is meant to trickle. This room, the royal guard tank, was almost comfortable. The lighting was bright and there was a table against the back wall with a couple of cushy desk chairs, and in the center of the room, on plush, squishy carpeted floor, was another desk chair with David Munson bound to it.

He did not look comfortable.

His face was smeared with his own blood, his nose and cheeks raw and red with tiny blisters popping up like wayward pimples. His hands were strapped to the arms of the chair, and his feet were shackled together, a guard standing on either side of him, just a few steps behind where he couldn't really see them. Vicat sat in a padded chair near the door. She popped up when Jax, Will, and General Myers came in, but she didn't say anything and never took her eyes off David.

Her shirt was flecked with David Munson's blood, and her knuckles were an angry sort of red.

You're growing on me. We might have to keep you.

"The three amigos," David snorted. "Doesn't matter how long you keep me here. Kill me if you want. Red's gone, and the Quorum will go on without us. We're incidental. They'll still attack."

"Won't happen. Florida's military has been effectively neutered by a mass electromagnetic attack." Jax described what Will had done and the result of so many of their bombs going off at once. "Pacifica's military is already on the ground. Your Quorum has been isolated, the government shut down. It's over."

"We'll fight, Jax. We'll win."

"The problem is that you don't really know what you're fighting against, David. You're a step behind and have been for a long time."

His eyes narrowed. "I doubt it."

"Your Quorum's first mistake? Asking for a deferral on the Consortium vote. Six months ago, we would have voted in your favor, and a majority would have followed. The request set off all kinds of alarms, David. We got curious. Red got curious."

"Red was oblivious—"

Jax nodded to Vicat. She opened the door, and Red came in, followed by Hyrum.

"That wasn't a good idea," Will said to Red.

"Aubrey thought he needed to know that I wasn't really dead. And he has the right to face David." He looked at his brother and added, "Surprise."

"You've got to be kidding me."

"You shot down an empty shuttle piloted remotely, David," Jax said. "Kudos for location, though. I can't tell you how happy I was that it was over unpopulated farmland."

Red turned to Hyrum. "You have a few minutes. Anything you want to say to him, now's the time."

It wasn't David that Hyrum looked to. He looked up at Red. "He's just like Daddy. He never punished me the way Daddy did, but he wanted to be just like Daddy and then he wanted to take Daddy's job. That's why Mom sent me away. Because Daddy said he wanted to kill you and the prince, and after that David was going to kill me because that's what evil does. It destroys the things it doesn't understand."

"I never hurt you," David said. "You were always safe with me, even with that...whatever the hell that is."

"I could ask the King to tell me if you're lying," Red said, "but I won't bother. Hyrum doesn't lie. Whatever he says you did, you did."

"Hyrum doesn't know the truth," David insisted. "I never meant anything malicious. I was trying to help him learn, and God knows he needed discipline. If he ever had hope of being a man, he *needed* that discipline."

Hyrum finally turned to David. "I know I'm never going to be smart like Red or even a man like Red. But you're mean like Daddy."

He slipped his arms around David, resting his forehead against the side of David's head. "I love you and I'm going to ask God to forgive you when I pray tonight. I think God will do that because I forgive you."

"Hy—"

He pulled away, but stayed bent over, his face close to David's. "Even if we forgive you, you've been bad, and you have to be punished. I don't know who has to punish you but it's not me." He touched David's cheek. "I'll tell you a secret, okay?"

David nodded.

"If you bite the pillow, no one will hear you cry."

21

The finer details of the deal were struck privately, over fried chicken and potato salad, with the chatter of everyone under thirty assembling a complicated structure of red, green, and yellow snap-blocks into a castle hidden just beyond a screaming baby in the background. While Hyrum supervised the construction of the colorful castle and Rhys wailed at the futility of existence without a nipple in his mouth, Red effectively handed Florida over to Pacifica.

"The church *must* separate from the government," Jax said to Red. "We'll appoint an interim Prime Minister, and I presume you'll remain at the head of the church. And before anyone asks, no, Floridians will not be given the same compensation that citizens of Midlam received. The circumstances are different. We purchased Midlam. Florida surrendered."

Midlam surrendered, too, but you told Shazia no.

Red hadn't expected anything and was grateful for the consideration Jax extended to him. His Second Minister was dead, found stuffed into the trunk of his car, and most of the Quorum had been taken into custody. Salvaging the church was Red's priority; restructuring of the government was up to Jax.

"Your citizens are now essentially citizens of Pacifica," Will said. "They're free to leave Florida. Free to choose another way of life. How many do you think will take that choice?"

"Too many," Red thought. "There was a buzz of interest when we opened the borders after the war, but few felt free enough to take those steps. Holding Pacifican citizenship will change everything. We'll lose a large segment of our youth. I imagine that unless I can convince them of changes to the church, Florida's average age will increase annually, and our church will begin to falter."

"You'll lose women," Aubrey agreed. "It will take time for Florida society to reach status quo." She reached across the table and set her hand on his. "You'll still be part of the governing process. Invite other religions in, Red. Once the people see they honestly have freedom of faith, that the Church of Florida is opening more than the borders, they might be willing to stay."

"That will be a hard thing for our elders to swallow. Most will understand that freedom of religion also implies freedom from religion. They'll fear seeing their children walk away from it all."

"Some," Jax agreed. "But unless they have the choice, their religion comes at a price they never agreed to pay. And that spreads out into other sectors. Freedom of education, and the right to work. It's not a requirement but give people a choice, and they typically do."

His wife thought so, as well. "She believes that if she gains employment, and I publicly support her, more women will begin to understand that it's not simply talk on the part of the church. Again, this is an area where the youth will lead us, if they stay."

The first public announcement had been met with skepticism. There had been nothing in the news leading up to a conflict between the two countries, and while Florida's power infrastructure had apparently failed, there was no public explanation offered. Pacifica's utilities commission sent hundreds of workers into Florida to facilitate repairs and power had been restored to thirty percent of the country. In another week, most of their citizens would have electricity and natural gas.

Red stood in front of his nation and the world and admitted that there had been a coup; his own brother had orchestrated a takeover of the Church of Florida and, by extension, its government; its Quorum had threatened Pacifica with nuclear war. He didn't address the issue of Russia's involvement, instead focusing on familial trust and his own lack of awareness that allowed David Munson to get as far as he had.

He was apologetic and contrite, confessing that Florida—foolishly and without his consent— engaged in acts of war against Pacifica, and to that end, he had surrendered.

His family left the safe house in Nevada and headed home; Red thought they were invigorated by the work that was to be done and not swayed by the darkness they would return to. "I honestly thought Joseph would be the one to shrug and decide to come to San Francisco. He's the one most excited to jump in and get things done."

"He's not bound by a constructed moral code," Aubrey said. "He sees a need and will address it for the good of the people, not because he's worried about religious absolutes."

"He's still wrong," Valerie said, mostly to herself.

"And I doubt God will hold that against him. What matters is that he does what's right, not what someone standing at a pulpit demands."

Red agreed. "You can do God's work even when you don't believe He exists, Mom. You'll see. He may be the most righteous of your children, save Hyrum. He's the least like Dad and the most like Hy."

Valerie's voice cracked when she said, "Joe is what Hyrum would have been."

From the living room, Hyrum asked, "What'd I do?"

Red turned in his chair to look at him. "We were talking about Joe, slugger. You and he are a lot alike, you know."

"Maybe, but I'm cuter."

"Of course, you are. You're more modest, too. Come in here for a minute."

With an exaggerated sigh, Hyrum set his blocks down and shuffled into the dining room and stood next to Red. He sighed again when Red pointed to the empty chair next to Aubrey and told him to sit down, and one more time when Valerie told him that was enough of his attitude.

"I'm going home tomorrow," Red told him. "I need to know your plans."

Hyrum barely got his mouth open before Valerie sputtered, "He's going home with us! Those are his plans."

His chin tucked to his chest. "Yeah."

"Hy," Drew called from the living room. "Now's the time."

"Stay out of this, Andrew," Valerie hissed.

He was not staying out of it. He peeled himself off the floor and went over to Hyrum, planting a kiss on the top of his head. "You're not a little boy, Hyrum. You get a say in your own life."

Valerie sputtered again, but Red held his hand up to her. "Drew is right, Hyrum. Tell me what *you* want. Not what you think I want, or what Mom wants. What's *your* plan?"

Without looking up, he said, "I want to stay here."

Drew patted him on the shoulder. "Look up. Say it like you mean it."

Jax snorted and leaned back in his chair. "Son, you enjoy the hell out of poking the bear, don't you?"

He looked right at Valerie. "I'm just standing up for him. He knows what he wants. He's known for a while now, but he's afraid of hurting other people."

"No one will be hurt," Red said. "You want to stay here? Tell me why."

He finally looked up. "I'm not lonely here. And Aubrey is teaching me to read better and do math, and no one says I can't do things because I'm not ready or I'm not smart enough. No one is afraid of me and no one tells me to get out of the way."

"I'll keep teaching you," Valerie said.

"But you don't *know*," he said. "Aubrey knows."

Valerie flinched. "I know enough."

"Mom, you left school in fifth grade," Red said. "Aubrey has a master's degree in childhood education. Maybe she can get him up to speed."

"For what?" she snapped. "He'll never need to work—"

"But I *want* to!" Hyrum said. "If I stay here I get to learn things and I get to keep talking to Dr. Cheshire. Drew said maybe we'd learn to ride bikes together. And it's not hot here and there are no gators. And I like Will's baby, and—"

"Enough," she said. "You're coming home with us. That's final."

Every other adult at the table twitched, waiting for Hyrum's reaction. The only one who didn't was Red, and he folded his arms as he considered his little brother. When Hyrum looked down again, his breath hitching as he fought to not cry, he said, "It's not final. It would do him some good, I think. Hyrum can stay."

"He needs me!" Valerie said.

"He spent two years taking care of himself without you, and that was your doing," Red reminded her. "If he thinks this is best, then he stays. It's not your decision." He scooted his chair a little closer to Hyrum. "I think you need this, Hy. There's a lot to learn here, and not just from Aubrey."

"I can learn from Aisha, too. She knows math. And Jay knows art. And Drew knows everything." He looked at Aubrey. "I know I have to grow up. I won't even sleep on Zed's floor anymore. I can sleep by myself."

"Where?" Valerie was still angry, practically spitting. "On the sofa? In the apartment downstairs, alone?"

"He can have the room right next to Zed's," Jax said.

"Your guest room." Valerie glared at him. "He'll always be a *guest*."

"As of now, the room is no longer for guests. It's Hyrum's room. He's family."

"We'll be right down the hall if you need anything at night, sweetie," Aubrey said to Hyrum. "If you stay, you'll have your own room, and your own space."

"Why are you helping him?" Valerie asked. "I understood when David was an issue, but even if you let him live, he'll never see the light of day again. Hyrum will be safe at home, with me."

Will finally jumped in. "He isn't proposing to leave you forever. Truly, he hasn't mentioned leaving you at all. You'd be welcome to stay. The apartment downstairs could be yours."

That made her pause. The idea settled, but then just as quickly, she shook her head. "I have other children who need me. And grandchildren. I can't move here for just one."

"And he can't leave here for just you," Red said.

"Give him until next summer," Will said. "See how he does here. At any time, you can come back, or he can visit you. Your borders are open. You're free to travel."

"Hy?" she said. "If I say yes, will you come visit me?"

He turned to Red. "You won't make me stay there if I do?"

"I promise, none of us will force you to stay. But I think living here for a while will be very good for you. And I'm proud of you for being brave enough to demand it."

"I don't like it," Valerie said.

"And I don't like this part of our family dynamic, but I'll use it. He has my permission to stay. And that's all he needs." He tucked Hyrum under the chin. "I know you'll behave. And even though we all know you're grown now, you'll do what Aubrey and Jax say. Listen to them, slugger. Their word is literally law in Pacifica."

Valerie sat back, defeated, grinding her teeth together. She listened as they asked questions of him, feeling for his expectations, and when there was a moment of quiet she blurted out, "You have better doctors here. You'll fix him, won't you?"

Jax and Aubrey looked confused. It was Will who said, "Fixing implies that there's something wrong, Valerie. Hyrum is not broken."

Drew patted him on the shoulder again. "Come on. Let's go check out your new room. We can figure out how you want to arrange things."

When he was down the hall, Valerie looked at Will and said, "You could fix him, though, couldn't you? Take him wherever that...thing...went to and *fix* him."

Red shook his head. "You're talking decades-old prenatal brain damage, Mom. There's no changing that."

"But *he* could." She nodded to Will. "Couldn't you?"

"Theoretically, there are treatments. His broken bones could be healed as if new. The brain damage could be reversed, but I don't know what that would do to the knowledge he already has, or if it would change his personality."

Aubrey shook her head before he was even finished. "You can't—"

"And I wouldn't. Don't ask me to take him to my birth home and have him treated, Valerie. I won't. He's fine the way he is."

"But you could change that thing he does, the power he spits out, and his life would be so much easier. Especially if he stays here, away from the church."

"Easier does not equate better," Will said.

"And he's God's gift to us," Aubrey said. "We also accept the gifts he has. No one is afraid of that, Mom. There's nothing to fix, nothing worth the risk."

She wanted to object, her mouth was open with another argument poised on her tongue, when Will said flatly, "The risk is that he turns into another Levi."

There was no arguing that.

His footsteps squeaked on the floor just beyond the dining room. "I can really live here?"

He was staying, made official when Jax got up and kissed Hyrum on the cheek and said, "You're now a ward of the King. Red and Will are the official witnesses to my declaration."

"Paperwork?" Red asked.

With a sigh, Jax said, "There's always paperwork. No paper involved, but there's paperwork. Give me ten minutes." He headed into Aubrey's little office. "I'll call the lawyer. It'll be ready to sign before Hyrum goes to bed tonight."

22

A week later, we met George in Will's birth When. He paced the hospital cafeteria floor with an infant strapped to his chest, tiny sock-covered feet kicking at his stomach, and as we got closer I heard him coo, "It's all right, Daddy loves you. It's all right."

Will watched for a moment, amused. "I do that all night," he said. "Apparently, it is not all right, no matter what I do."

George nodded knowingly. "He's been crying pretty much nonstop since he woke up this morning. Tummy ache, I think. If he would just burp."

Put him on the floor. I'll purr on him.

"I'm not sure that's helpful," Will said, but George was willing to try anything. He spread a blanket on the floor by the big window, and gently set the baby down.

I snuggled up, and when I was sure he wouldn't flail too hard, I draped myself over his belly and purred as hard as I could. His crying eased up, then stopped, and George was six kinds of surprised until his baby farted loud enough that it sounded like throwing popcorn into a fire.

"And there we go," Will snorted. "Where's James?"

George rubbed my head and thanked me before he picked the baby back up. "He was afraid if he came, you'd force him home. He's not ready yet." He nodded toward the closest table, and they sat down. "The only thing compelling him back is Jay. He's not sure he'd be a good enough father with two hundred years between them."

"And Jay stayed home because he was afraid he would influence James and make him feel like he had to go home. If it matters, he's been clear on the subject. He'd be happy if you worked everything out, and if James stays."

"How often would we see him?"

"As often as he chooses. He can move through the portals now. I won't stop him from visiting, though I ask you not allow him to stay too long."

"I wouldn't. He has a life there. A girl. James says he's the happiest he's ever been, and I won't take that from him."

Yeah, but do you mean it?

George glanced down at me. "Did he just insult me?"

"He questions your sincerity. Given his experience with you, one can't fault him for that."

"One cannot." He patted the table top and asked me to jump up. "I won't tangle with you again, cat. Who knows what century you'd knock me into?"

I'd introduce you to Fluffy and Jeff.

They made small talk for a few minutes; George wanted to know about Rhys and they talked about sleepless nights, the frustrating joy of it. This didn't feel like two people who hated each other. This was different.

Oh my bast, you're bonding.

Will ignored me.

Are you besties now? I bet you're besties. I'll get Hyrum to make you some of those matching string bracelets.

"This isn't just a visit to see if James is ready to come home," Will finally said. "I'm about to throw a wrench into your life, and I pre-emptively apologize. I brought someone who needed to see you. And you should know up front, she's angry and doesn't know the truth."

Neither did he.

Will met Vicat near the hospital portal; she'd asked for this visit home, but at the last minute wanted to back out. There was nothing left for her in the future and a visit would only stir up bad memories. Leaving it alone was a better idea.

"The truth is there," he said flatly.

"What truth?"

He didn't answer. Instead, he grabbed her by the elbow and dragged her through the portal. Now she was waiting outside the cafeteria, stewing, and Will was confident that she was still there because she really didn't have anywhere else to go.

When he brought her in she stood several feet away, staring at George. Her eyes briefly went to the baby, but she stared until he had to look away. "Will?" he said. "What's up?"

"What was your sister's name?" Will asked as he sat back down.

"Ja—"

"No," she barked. "That name died a long time ago. Speak it, and I'll jam my fist so far down your throat that I'll be able to tie your intestines into a noose. And then I'll use it."

Well, this is fun. You might want to hand the baby to Will.

Will pushed a nearby chair away from the table with his foot and told her to sit down. When she refused, he reminded her that he was her way home, and he was stubbornly patient when he needed to be.

She sat.

"George, this is Vicat. She's a member of the royal guard and was born in this When. She grew up in the city with a foster mother and was told she'd been given up by her birth parents because her older brother had abused her."

Before she could protest, he went on. "Vicat, this is George. He witnessed the death of his two-year-old sister when he was just three. She slipped in the bathtub and hit her head, and his parents led him to believe that he had killed her. The truth, as I have come to learn, is that they were told the likelihood of her surviving without significant damage was minimal unless she received emergent immersive care. They panicked, and signed their parental rights over to Maureen Brower, the mother's sister."

"Wait," Vicat spat, "that's my foster mother."

"Indeed. She capitalized on their ignorance and assumed custody of you because she knew you could be treated and didn't trust them to follow through with it. She had you placed in a surgical tank for three weeks while the damage to your skull and brain were repaired, and then raised you along with her other foster children."

"What the hell," George sputtered.

"You didn't kill anyone," Will said to George. "And Vicat, he never harmed you. His parents were of the sort who would latch onto an excuse to sign away their rights. I truly do not know why. But George has mourned your loss since the day he watched your tiny body taken from your home, and he's blamed himself for decades."

"This is bullshit." She got up, shoving the chair aside. "You can't rewrite my history because it makes him feel better."

"Sit," Will said.

She sat.

"When we were very young, four years old, I ran into him during recess one day. He happened to be thinking about you, and the contact transferred that memory to me."

"What?"

Without asking, something he never did, he placed his hand on her arm and shot the memory into her head. She saw everything from tiny George's point of view; she heard their laughter, his teasing, and felt his horror and his terror when she slipped. She saw the blood on the floor, the thin rivulet that taunted him, and felt the crushing loneliness as he waited for her to come home.

"He is not responsible," Will said when he pulled his hand away.

He braced, expecting her anger and her disbelief. Instead, she leaned back in her chair and asked Will, "What the hell other kind of freaky things can you do?"

"He talks to his cat," George said.

"Everyone talks to Wick."

"No, he *talks* to his cat. He understands Wick."

You think they'd both be asking for DNA, not discussing what weird things you can do.

"Indeed, Wick. I was prepared for a demand for DNA testing. That can be done, here, today, if you choose."

George nodded toward Will. "He's a freak, but he's not a liar."

She shrugged. "We can get around to it. I've known for decades who you are. Now, what the hell. Are our parents still alive?"

"They are, but I've had nothing to do with them. I've never even told them—" He hesitated, but after a kiss on his baby's head, he said, "We had a younger brother, Isaac. He died fifteen, sixteen years ago. I haven't bothered telling them. Hell, we were barely out of our teens when we took the first chance we had to run to another century and never told them we were leaving."

"They sound wonderful," she deadpanned.

George cocked his head a touch. "If this is true...they're sicker than I thought. I was raised to treasure women. To protect them. Before they knew I was gay, my father often told me that the most important thing I needed to understand was that whatever woman was willing to be with me, I needed to cherish her. And they did *this?* Tossed their daughter aside because they didn't think they could handle life if her medical treatment failed?"

Vicat looked at Will. "They didn't know about the tanks?"

Will shrugged. "I only know what's in the official reports, which you now have access to, George. If you have issues getting to them, Finn will help."

George nodded, and after a moment of thought, his eyes flared with anger. "Everything that was wrong between you and me came from a lie. I almost killed you. I damn near *drowned* you, we were what, seven? And for what? Because I thought you would tell the world my secret, and it was all a damned lie."

Vicat was confused, but Will quietly said that George could fill in the details later.

"This is up to you now," he said to Vicat. "You can stay and get to know your brother or go home. But at least you have the truth."

"Stay for a bit," George said. "He's coming back to check on my husband. He can take you home then, if you want."

"I'll want," she said. "My life is back there. I have a damned good job, and I love what I do."

"Exactly what do you do?"

"I annoy the hell out of the Emperor."

"Oh, you and me? We're definitely going to get along."

23

Rhys had barely made a peep when Will slid out of bed. Will wanted to get him before he had a chance to wind up and wake Aisha; she was sound asleep, the first decent sleep she'd had since Aubrey's family reunion, when Jax took the baby hostage. Their ideal, trading nights until she started back to work, flew out the window from the first night; they both woke when he stirred, and they both wanted to be the one to walk the floor or rock him when he was fussy.

She usually won, reminding him that once she went back to work, he would get most of those sleepless nights. She wanted time to bond with her son, but that didn't keep him from staying up with her. They often sat up in bed half the night, talking while she nursed, talking long past the moment when he was full and asleep in her arms.

This night, I was in the bassinette with Rhys, my paws pressed lightly to his head. I was listening, not paying attention to Will until I felt his breath on my ears and he whispered, "What are you doing?"

Listening.

Will slid his hands under Rhys, carefully, and then carried him into the kitchen where he warmed up a bottle. When he settled on the sofa, he said, "All right. What were you listening for?"

Dreams.

"Huh. And does he dream?"

His dreams are different. They're more like feelings. He dreams about faces and what he feels. His brain is busy making new pathways. I can feel them growing when he's sleeping. The places in his brain where he'll learn words are forming.

He wanted to know more but tripped on his own rules. Dreams were private, and he'd cautioned me before about sharing the things I saw in peoples' heads while they slept, but this was his son and he was curious. What the dreams consisted of were less important than knowing how Rhys dreamed; his life experience wasn't grand enough for nocturnal adventures; what could a newborn have playing inside his head?

I decided he should know.

He sees faces hovering over him. Aisha's is the clearest. Then yours and Jay's. Everyone else is still a little fuzzy. He thinks of me as ears and whiskers that tickle.

"He sees all of you, Wick."

Not yet. When I'm close, he sees my ears. When I'm far, I'm fuzzy. His vision isn't perfect yet.

"And he sees Aisha clearly?" The thought made him smile.

Almost. He knows she's his mother. When he thinks about her, he feels happy. She's food and warms and bliss and smiles. And he knows you're his father. He feels safe. He knows your hands and how they feel when you hold him close. He knows your heartbeat.

"And Jay?"

Giggles and kisses. He likes that.

Jay's bedroom door creaked open. He shuffled out in baggy shorts and a wrinkled t-shirt, barely awake, and sat next to Will, close enough that he could touch Rhys's tiny toes.

"I thought I heard him," Jay said around a yawn he couldn't hold back. "I was going to try to sneak him out of your room."

"I appreciate that, but I was still awake."

"When's he moving into the nursery? I'll be able to get him more often when he's next door."

"Perhaps when your mother returns to work. But we don't expect you to get up at night with him, Jay. We'll have a monitor and will hear him."

"Yeah, don't have to but sometimes I want to. He's kind of awesome." He pointed to the bottle. "Can I? I feel like everyone else has gotten to hold him the last few days, but me, not so much."

Will carefully handed Rhys over. "I met George's son today. He's a beautiful little boy named Isaac, after his brother. George seemed perfectly content."

"He was good with me, you know. As long as no one was arguing about what pronouns to use with me or talking about when I should get surgery, he was good. I can see him enjoying being a dad. I used to wonder why he and Dad didn't have one of their own."

"You once told me you thought he was constantly scared."

"Yeah, I think he is."

Will brushed his hand across Rhys's head, fluffing up his thin black hair. "I don't think he is anymore. He's where he needs to be, and no more shadows are chasing him. He has his son, and I daresay he has his husband again."

That made Jay grin. "Really? Good for them." He looked up. "Have you forgiven him? I mean, for everything. I don't really expect it, but I think it would mean something to him."

"I'm not sure forgiveness is the right word, but I don't hold any of it against him. May I ask why?"

"Hyrum, I guess," Jay said. "While we were rearranging his room, he talked a lot about forgiveness. Even forgiving his father. At first, I thought it was just some religious thing, something he was required to do, but he said something that kinda stuck with me. If he couldn't forgive, then everything that was done to him became his burden. If he had to carry that for the rest of his life, he would never be happy."

"Indeed."

"Drew really got him talking. Somehow, we got on the subject of what we all wanted to do when we were done with school, kind of joking about what we wanted to be when we grew up. And Drew asked him, you know, what he wants to be when he's grown up."

"Did he see himself as ever being grown?"

"He doesn't think he'll ever completely get there. But it doesn't matter, because the only thing he wants to be is good. He wants to be sure he's good and goes to Heaven because if he does, he can thank Jesus and God for his mother and his sisters and his brothers, even though he didn't really like David. And he's sorry about that, but that's how it is. Then he got quiet for a little bit and said he wanted to be able to thank God for his Daddy, too, even though he was mean and punished him wrong. Zed asked him why...he said that if he'd had a different father, he might not know that he wanted to be good more than he wanted to be a man."

He handed the empty bottle to Will and moved Rhys so that he could burp him. "I keep chewing on that. I understand when you tell Zed and Drew and me to decide what kind of men we want to be, and just be it, but Hyrum really gets it, and he wants everyone to know. He's like this open book, and he's fine with the whole world reading it." He rubbed his cheek against Rhys's head. "I don't care how many years there are between us, little man. I will always be good to you."

"I've never doubted that about you," Will whispered.

"He's not gonna burp for me." Jay handed him back to Will. "I'll take that personally."

George's baby farted for me.

"All right then. Before he does that, I'm going back to bed."

Will watched him until his door closed, and then he carefully got up. He paced the floor until Rhys let go with a tiny burp—that was good enough—and he took him back into the bedroom for a diaper change and a gentle tummy rub to get him settled. I sat on the foot of the bed and watched: there was nothing else he wanted to be doing, nowhere else he wanted to be. His mouth turned up in a slight smile as he kissed Rhys good night and then slid gently into bed with Aisha. Without waking, she rolled toward him and curled around him, her arm sliding over his chest.

His eyes closed, and I listened.

It was quiet and settled, and sleep was waiting for him.

Will didn't need me for the rest of the night. I made my way downstairs and down the hall, and quietly slipped into Hyrum's room. Toys spilled out of the new blue box in the corner, and picture books were lined neatly on shelves above it. He'd put his dirty clothes in the hamper, legs of his jeans hanging out with one sock left crumpled on the floor. Aubrey had put away the nice white comforter that had been on the guest bed for nearly a decade and replaced it with one Hyrum had picked on his own, a bright red, yellow, and blue checkerboard bedspread. He'd wanted to mix and match his sheets, a bright blue bottom sheet with a neon pink top sheet and pillows to match, and the tasteful, carefully selected artwork that Aubrey had picked out over the years had been stored in favor of posters with cars and bicycles, and one massive picture of Mr. Happy with his trunk raised.

I hopped up on the bed to check on him. The first night he'd spent alone in his new bedroom, he curled up in a ball, not sleeping, too afraid to yell for someone, so I curled up on his pillow and listened as he told me a bedtime story. Most nights I crept in to see how he was, and most of the time he was sleeping flat on his back with a stuffed rabbit clutched to his side, mouth open as he snored gently.

Tonight, he was awake. He giggled when I sniffed his nose, and he rolled onto his back, patting his chest to invite me to sit there. It was nearly four-thirty, and his habit was to wake around five, ingrained from a lifetime of rising before dawn to help Valerie prepare breakfast for the family and to have time for morning prayers before Levi stomped down the stairs.

He waited in bed every morning until he heard Jax shuffle down the hall. Jax had started running a bit later in the morning but still pulled himself out of bed to have a quiet half hour with Hyrum, time when they could talk about home and the things Red reported back.

He missed his family and sometimes cried himself to sleep wanting his mother, but he was resolute in not wanting to go home.

"Is he awake yet?" Hyrum asked me as he tickled my chin. "Today we're going to go have breakfast at the bakery, and then after Aubrey gets up we're going to go see where Drew and Oz and

Zed and Jay go to school! Aubrey says they have teachers who like to teach people my age who didn't get to go to school when they were little. But I hope she still teaches me because I like how she does it."

Aisha teaches at that school. Maybe someday she'll teach you math.

"Drew says if they sign me up for classes I get to walk to school with him and Oz. And we can have lunch together. I'm going to learn about life skills, Wick!"

Will says once you're ready, he and Drew have a job for you. Drew says he needs an assistant. I think you'll be good at that.

He heard Jax at the end of the hall and picked me up as he swung his legs over the side of the bed. Jax greeted him the same way he did every morning, with a grunt and then, "You know you don't have to wait in bed, Hy." He didn't say anything else until he'd made coffee, and then Hyrum got a kiss on the head and a slightly less grumpy, "Good morning. Did you sleep okay?"

Hyrum nodded. "I had a dream about walking to find the Queen. I lost my bag of bread and there was a little store with lots of it, rows and rows, but I couldn't find my money. I tried not to cry but then a man asked if I was okay and I said no, I don't know where my wallet is. And he said, 'are you hungry?' so I said, 'Not yet, but later I will be, and I need lunch before I find the Queen.'"

"What'd he do?" Jax asked.

"He said no one should meet the Queen on an empty stomach and he bought me two bags of bread and some bananas. He said he would buy me peanut butter, too, but I still had some. When I said thank you, he smiled nice and said, 'Go and eat with joy. God approves of what you do.' I wanted to tell him I knew that was in the bible, but I bent over to put the bread in my backpack and when I looked up he was gone. And there was a fresh jar of peanut butter in my bag."

"Hyrum, was that a dream or did it really happen?"

He bit his bottom lip while he thought about it. "I dreamed about it last night but maybe it happened, too. It seemed really real. But I also dreamed that I was lying on a rock talking to Jesus and I was crying because I thought I was gonna die." He grunted. "Jesus sounded a lot like Drew, but he had a beard."

Jax was still thinking about the food. "What happened when you ran out of food? And money?"

"I didn't run out of food until a couple days before Will and Drew and the cat lady found me. There was always bread and peanut butter and sometimes people gave me apples and bananas because they said I looked like I could use some fruit. And one time I found this place with bathrooms and picnic tables, and I sat down for a while because my feet hurt and it wasn't as hot under the trees. A man was there with his wife and kids and saw me, and he came over and said, 'We made more sandwiches than we can eat, would you like to have them? They're ham and cheese.' I almost didn't take them because he was a stranger, but he said he heard the Lord speak, and the Lord told him I was hungry. I ran out of water, though."

"Yet, you found enough dew on plants to drink. How did you know to look?"

He shrugged. "I heard it in my head. 'Hyrum, you need to drink. There's water on those leaves. It won't hurt you.' Mom said that was my common sense kicking in."

"Could be. And you were found just in time. In a place we call the Wastelands. It's rare for anyone to go out there." His fingers tapped on the table, a slow, steady beat that I don't think he was even aware of. "You went to the one building where there was a cool place to sleep, and the one where vegetation was growing. Very little grows in the Wastelands."

"I was lucky."

The drumming stopped. Jax got up and went to get his coffee. "Go on and get dressed, we'll go get some breakfast in a little bit."

Hyrum pushed away from the table and started to turn to the hallway.

"Don't forget your morning prayers, Hy. All right?"

Hyrum headed back to his room and I jumped on the counter. Jax sighed when he spotted me, but he didn't tell me to get down.

"I know," he said. "But he believes. Aubrey believes. It doesn't harm anything to make sure he doesn't give that habit up."

Fine with me. Someone was watching out for him. I get it.

"Just in case, Wick." He tapped his fingers on the table again. "I should go see if he wants help shaving. Hell, see if he even wants to shave. How long has it been?"

A week.

With a tired sigh, Jax pushed himself up and headed for Hyrum's room. When he was done with his morning prayer, Jax would ask him, the same as he did every morning, if he needed help shaving, and Hyrum would answer, the same as he had every morning for a week, "Not today."

ABOUT THE AUTHOR
BECAUSE PEOPLE TOTALLY READ THIS STUFF WHEN THEY'RE DONE READING
THE BOOK

Max Thompson is a writer living in Northern California with The Woman, The Man, and Buddah Pest. He's also a Feline Life Coach for *Mousebreath Magazine*, and writes the hugely popular blog *The Psychokitty Speaks Out*. He's 14 pounds of sleek black and white feline glory, and his favorite snacks are real live fresh dead steak, shrimp, and lots of cheese. He also appreciates that you've read this far, and would give you a cookie if he could.